Delphi League

Delphi in Space
Book Ten

Bob Blanton

Cover by Momir Borocki
momir.borocki@gmail.com \

D1739319

Delphi Publishing

Copyright © 2021 by Robert D. Blanton

Cover by Momir Borocki

momir.borocki@gmail.com

https://www.facebook.com/StarshipSakira/

Table of Contents

1   Where Do They Come From?

"Ma'am, there are Paraxeans in some of these stasis pods," Major Prescott reported. He'd just entered the Fazullan ship they had forced to surrender in the battle for Artemis, Earth's first colony planet. The Fazullan ship had been heading to Artemis for years, and when the Delphineans had contacted them to inform them that the system was occupied, the Fazullans had tried to destroy the colony. It had been two weeks since the battle; they had to wait for the Fazullan starship to decelerate enough that the ship could be boarded. Now that they were finally aboard the ship, they had discovered the unimaginable, their allies, the Paraxeans were being held in stasis chambers.

"Hold on, Major. Admiral?" Captain Fitzgerald prompted Blake.

"Get a doctor over there and wake up a Paraxean or two," Blake ordered. "Call us when they're able to talk."

"Yes, sir," Major Prescott replied.

The ship's doctor was summoned and suited up. They didn't yet know whether the Fazullan ship had pathogens that might be harmful to humans, so they were wearing full spacesuits.

"Paraxeans?" Catie asked her Uncle Blake. "How?"

"Who knows?" Blake replied. "Kind of a long way. But the Paraxeans have three colonies."

"Still hard to believe. Their closest colony is over 300 light-years from Artemis," Liz added.

"Well, we'll know more soon. I'm going to have breakfast while we wait," Blake said.

"Catie, what do you think?" Liz asked. Liz was one of the inner circle of MacKenzie Discoveries, one of the original founders of Delphi City, and Catie's best friend and business partner.

"I don't want to start spinning up theories until we know more. It'd just give me a headache."

"Okay, I'll just make up my own theories and ask you about them," Liz said.

"Go ahead. I'm going to join Uncle Blake for breakfast."

The strategy team reconvened after Major Prescott had awakened two Paraxeans.

"Sir, based on our interview of the Paraxeans, I'm confident that they are from the same colony mission that the Paraxeans at Mangkatar were on."

"I concur," ADI said. ADI was the Digital Intelligence that came with the starship that Marc, Blake's brother and monarch of Delphi, had found years ago.

"That is incredible," Blake said.

"The older Paraxean was actually part of the mission; he was a child at the time, but clearly remembers the name of the ship he was on. It matches the name we have from the Paraxeans," Major Prescott said.

"And the other one?"

"He was born since then. And sir, they're slaves."

"Slaves!"

"What a mess," Blake said. "Anything else?"

"Yes, sir. There are two other alien species in stasis. We haven't brought any of them out."

"Let's wait on that until we have the ship where we want it," Marc said.

"Where do you want it?"

"I'd like to know more first," Marc said. "How did the Paraxeans wind up on that ship?"

"Artemis is over 200 light-years from the system where the Paraxeans were attacked so how could they be the same Paraxeans?" Liz asked.

Catie had brought up a star map and was studying it, oblivious to the continued conversation. After a bit, Marc pinged her. "What are you thinking?" he asked.

"I don't know, I'm looking for a quaternary star system between Artemis and where the Fazullans attacked the Paraxeans. Unfortunately, there seem to be six of them."

"Why a quaternary star system?" Liz asked.

"A natural wormhole, maybe," Catie replied.

"Are you serious?"

"It's the only thing that makes sense. I'm looking at all the star systems between Artemis and the location where the Paraxean colony mission was attacked."

"What do you get when you backtrack the Fazullans' course?" Blake asked.

"It doesn't lead to one of the quaternary systems; besides they're all too far. But it does lead to this system, which is almost in a direct line with that quaternary system. And that system is also approximately in a straight line to the system where the Paraxeans were attacked." The stars she had pointed out formed a very obtuse triangle.

"Can a single wormhole actually extend over 200 light-years?" Liz asked.

"It would only be half of that if the source of the wormhole were in the middle," Catie said.

"You mean they can control it?"

"Seems unlikely, but it might move about on its own. It's the only thing I can think of that makes sense," Catie said. "I need to talk with Dr. McDowell."

"Then get after it," Blake said. "We need to figure this thing out."

"Marc, have you decided what you want to do with the Fazullans and their ship?" Blake asked.

"We need to send them to Earth; we don't have the resources here to figure all this out," Marc answered.

"Do you think that's wise?" Samantha asked. "Foxes and henhouses." Samantha was Marc's wife and Delphi's interstellar ambassador.

"We can send them to Gemini Station in the asteroid belt. That will provide a platform for everyone to work from while they study the ship. It's also close enough so our scientists and the Paraxeans still on Earth can run out there when they need to, but far enough away that Earth won't get too nervous," Marc said.

"Do you think we can trust the Fazullans to fly it there?" Blake asked.

"Leave Major Prescott and his security team on it to make sure. You've seemed to have convinced Captain Lantaq that it is in his best interest to follow your orders."

"Okay. I'll meet them at the fringe with the Roebuck. I think we'll station the Enterprise right next to them until we get everyone off that ship."

"Okay, we'll reconvene in two weeks when it gets there. Then we can do a detailed survey of the ship and figure out what's up with the other aliens," Marc said.

"We should have Major Prescott wake up a few of each so we can get the language thing figured out while they're traveling," Catie suggested.

"Good idea. Do it."

"Dr. McDowell," Catie announced herself as she entered his lab. ". . . Dr. McDowell!"

"Oh, hi, Catie."

"I've got some interesting data I want to review with you."

"Sure."

Catie put the problem up on Dr. McDowell's display. She had taken the gravity estimates for the quad star system and put them into the equation format that they used for the wormholes.

"Interesting," Dr. McDowell said as he studied the equations. "Why do you have this variable cycling?"

"That's what I'm asking about. What would that do?"

Dr. McDowell had pointed to the part of the equation that represented the binary star that made up two of the four stars in the quad star system.

"Well, it would make your wormhole unstable."

"All the time?"

"No, I guess not. Let's see." Dr. McDowell drew a graph to represent the equation. "See the rate of change is slow here, so the wormhole would be stable until here. Then it would collapse, or at least start jumping. When the energy gets to here," he pointed at the next slow-changing section of the graph, "I guess it would open a stable wormhole again. But the vector sum would be different. I would suspect that it would jump to a different star system."

"How many different star systems would it jump to?" Catie asked.

"I think just two . . . no, maybe three. It depends on how stable the other two drives are. How did Ajda make gravity drives so big?"

"They're not gravity drives, they're stars."

"Oh, and this is a binary star?"

"Yes, that equation represents their orbit around each other."

"What about the orbits of the other stars?"

"They're in a thousand-year orbit, so I've ignored that part of the equation."

"Well, we should add it in, it might be important."

"Sure, I'll have ADI send you all the data. I just wanted to confirm that that system would open a natural wormhole."

"It would, or at least that's what the math says. It would be a big one, and could span well over one hundred light-years to the other side."

"That's what I thought," Catie said. "Okay, I'll leave you to work on it. Let me know if you come up with anything interesting."

Dr. McDowell was already playing with the equations, lost in his own thoughts. Catie just shrugged and left.

---

2   Finding Normal

"Hey, Kal, it's been a while," Catie said as she met Kal at Delphi City's Central Park; she'd flown down to the city the day before. Kal and Catie were meeting to practice Aikido, and Kal had wanted to do it in the park.

Kal waved to Morgan and her two assistants, then turned his attention to Catie.

"Sorry I missed your graduation," Kal said as they began circling.

"That's okay, I heard you were out of town."

Catie grabbed Kal's arm and dug her fingernails in.

"Ow! When did you start growing your fingernails long?!"

"Since I turned fourteen, where have you been?"

"Not getting clawed by you. Now stop a minute."

Catie relaxed as Kal walked over still rubbing his forearm where she'd gouged him.

"You should have gone for this pressure point," Kal said pointing to a spot next to Catie's elbow.

"Oh, yeah. I forgot about it."

Kal reached over and pressed his finger on it. "If you'd gotten to it, you could have grabbed my wrist and taken control."

"Ow! Ow! Sorry about clawing you!" Catie hollered as Kal twisted her arm, forcing her to the ground. "And I won't forget that pressure point."

"Good," Kal said, releasing Catie and they started circling again.

"How did it go in Mexico?"

"Pretty good. The team infiltrated the town and were ready when the Mexican army showed up. They rolled up the cartel guys pretty fast," Kal said as he made a move to push Catie over. She countered it and they continued to circle.

"Nobody noticed all the new people in town?" Catie asked as she tried to use the distraction to slide in under Kal's guard.

Kal brushed her aside before answering. "Apparently if they're women and wear scanty clothes, people make assumptions and ignore them."

"That'll teach them. How are you and Sandra doing?"

"No chance," Kal said as Catie made a move. "Sandra and I are doing fine. She's really impressed with the horse park."

"Are you living together?"

"You know we are," Kal said as he countered Catie's move. "You'll have to do better than that."

"Okay, is the sex good?"

Barry walked into the Shack, a well-known barbecue joint in Jacksonville, North Carolina. It was just outside of Camp Lejeune, where Barry had lived before he had gone to Afghanistan and after he'd come home. Barry had arrived early to make sure he got a table, by noon the place would be hopping.

"May I take your order?" the waitress asked, giving Barry a smile. She was cute, Barry figured eighteen to twenty.

"Just some sweet tea for now, I'm meeting someone at noon, and wanted to be sure we had a table."

The waitress frowned, "The boss doesn't abide people just sitting at a table."

Barry laid a twenty on the table. "You just do what you have to so I can stay here and meet my friend."

The waitress picked up the twenty and smiled. "I'll be right back with your tea."

Barry's stomach growled at him. *"That barbecue sure smells good,"* he thought.

Barry sipped his tea and waited; he sure hoped that Raelyn showed up, but he couldn't blame her if she didn't. "Come on!" He kept his eye on the door so he wouldn't miss her.

"There she is," Barry thought as a young woman entered the diner. She was tall and beautiful, or at least to Barry she was. She paused at the

door and looked around the tables. Her eyes passed right over Barry. He waved, and she turned back to him. She gave him a puzzled look but walked over to the table.

"Is that you, Barry?"

"Yep, it sure is," Barry replied.

"But you look different and you've got legs. You said they couldn't give you no artificial legs on account of how you were injured."

Barry slapped his legs, "These babies are real!"

"Real? How?"

"Haven't you heard about Delphi City?"

"I saw something on the news about it, but I didn't believe it."

"Well, it's all true. They grew me new legs and fixed me right up."

"I'll say. You look better than I remember."

"Yep, that's because they fixed my nose. You remember I broke it playing basketball."

"Oh, that must be it."

"Come on, sit down. Do you know what you want to order, or do you want to look at the menu?"

"We always ordered the same thing when we came here. That'll do for today," Raelyn said.

Barry motioned to the waitress. "We'll have a platter of baby back ribs, an order of coleslaw, and some fries."

"And to drink?"

"Sweet tea," Raelyn said.

"Coming right up."

"So, how have you and the kids been?" Barry asked.

"We've been okay. At first, your disability check was coming in and that kept us going. I guess your new legs explains why it quit coming."

"But I sent money," Barry said.

"I figured it was you, I just started seeing deposits from the Bank of New Zealand saying spousal allotment. I wondered what you were doing in New Zealand."

"I was in Delphi City; it used to be part of The Cook Islands, and they're kind of part of New Zealand," Barry explained. "Are you still taking classes at the college?"

"NO! I don't have time for that. I've got a job and I'm raising two kids on my own."

"I'm sorry, but I'm better now. I can give you more money, whatever you need."

"What I needed was my husband, what I got was some jumped-up junkie. So, did they cure you of that when they gave you them new legs?"

"Yes, I'm all good. The doctor fixed all my problems up." Barry clapped his hands making a loud smack. "See, no jumping around now. They took care of that PTSD and the drug thing."

"What are you doing?"

"I'm in the Delphi Marines," Barry said.

"Figures, all you seem to know is how to fight."

"I'm good at it," Barry said. "I'm a staff sergeant now. I'm making good money and I'm in charge of a platoon. We just finished up an op in Mexico."

"You were part of that? Damn, that was on the news. Some serious shit went down."

"Yep, that was my team. We took down a cartel guy in Guatemala last year, then we were in Ukraine, and we just finished up with that cartel thing in Mexico. My boss said he might even make me an officer."

"Now, that I don't believe. If they knew half the stuff you said about them officers, they wouldn't even let you be in the Marines."

Barry laughed. "Get this, the big boss is Kal, you remember him."

"Yeah, we had him over a few times before you shipped out."

"Right, well he's the general in charge of all of Delphi's Marines."

"Really, Kal's an officer; and a *general*?!"

"Here's your food," the waitress said as she set a tray down on their table. "Let me know if you need anything else."

"We will," Barry said. Then he waited until she was out of earshot. "I wanted to talk to you about the kids."

"That's what I figured," Raelyn said.

"I wanted to see you, too," Barry defended himself. "But I haven't seen my kids for almost four years."

"And who's fault is that?"

"I know it's my fault. But, I'm better now."

"I can see that. So how do you want to do it? You can see them with Mama, or with me. I'm not letting you be alone with my kids."

"I understand," Barry said. "With you would be fine. We could go out to the lake and rent a boat. Do some fishing."

"Them kids don't wanna do no fishing. They'll want to play. We can go to the beach."

"The beach is fine. How about the one over at Emerald Isle? That'd be fun."

"Okay. We can meet there on Saturday. Have you talked to your mama yet?"

"No, I wanted to talk to you first. I'll see Mama on Sunday after church."

"You'd better. She finds out you've been in town and didn't come see her, we won't be needing to talk about you seeing the kids."

Barry was waiting in the parking lot at Emerald Isle. Raelyn and he had decided it would be easier on the kids to meet him there instead of having to spend an hour in the car driving with him. He was wearing a Hawaiian shirt, shorts and sandals, and an Atlanta Braves ball cap. There was a nice breeze, but Barry was sweating up a storm.

Finally, he saw Raelyn's car drive up. He waved, and Raelyn drove over and parked next to Barry's rental car.

A boy and a girl got out of the car's back seat and stood next to the car staring at Barry. Raelyn got out. "Devin, Talia, this is your daddy. You remember us talking about him."

Devin was nine and Talia was seven. Barry had checked their birthdays before coming to Jacksonville.

Devin gave Barry a hard look. "Where you been?"

"Devin, it's where have you been?" Raelyn said.

"I've been getting better," Barry said. "I needed to get myself fixed up so I could come back and be your daddy."

"You got legs," Devin said.

"Yep, I got some new legs, and the doctors that gave them to me also fixed up my other problems. I'm all better now."

"Talia, say hi to your daddy." Talia was hiding behind her brother and shook her head.

"That's okay," Barry said. "Why don't we go to the beach and get a good spot on the sand. There'll be plenty of time to say hello."

Barry grabbed the umbrella, two boogie boards, and some mats from the back of the rental car. "Devin, can you carry that cooler?"

Devin hesitated. "Go on, get it," Raelyn told him.

"I got two chairs," Barry said. "I thought we might prefer them to the mats."

"I'll get them. Talia, go get the basket out of the car."

"Let's rest some," Barry told Devin. "You're wearing the old man out." Barry and Devin had been boogie boarding for the past half hour and Barry wanted to get back and spend some time with Talia.

"Come on, let's go again."

"We will, but after I get some rest." Barry grabbed both boards and headed back to where they'd set up their umbrella.

"Devin, come here, let me put some more sunscreen on you," Raelyn said.

Devin stomped over to his mother and Barry plopped himself down next to Talia. "What are you building?"

"A castle."

"What kind of castle?"

"One with a princess."

"Oh, do you like princesses?"

"Yes."

"Guess what, I know a princess."

"You do?"

"Yep, I met Princess Catie of Delphi last year. She was pretty nice."

"Did you really?"

"Sure. Do you want to see a picture?"

"Yes!"

Barry took off his specs that he'd been using as sunglasses and put them on his daughter. "Show pictures of Princess Catie," he ordered his Comm.

"She's pretty," Talia said as the Comm displayed pictures of Catie at her last birthday party when she was dressed up as a princess.

"Yeah, she is. Show Catie in her shipsuit," Barry ordered his Comm.

"What is that she's wearing?"

"They call it a shipsuit. Princess Catie is a pilot, and that's what all the pilots wear."

"She looks like a girl."

"She is. I think she's sixteen right now. I think that picture was taken right before her birthday. The pictures with her in a dress were at her birthday party. I've been told she doesn't like to wear dresses."

"Barry, don't be telling stories," Raelyn scolded.

"I'm not. It might be different now; it's been almost a year. But the story is she spends more time in shipsuits than dresses. And when she's around the city, if she's not wearing a shipsuit, she's wearing jeans or something like that."

15

"Do you really know her?" Raelyn asked.

"I've met her. Show picture of Princess Catie and Sergeant Knox."

"That's you," Talia said.

"Let me see." Raelyn reached for the specs, but Talia pulled away from her.

"Wait," Barry said, reaching into his pocket and pulling out the keys to his rental. "Devin, go to the car and get the blue box out of the trunk." He looked at Raelyn to see if it was okay to send Devin by himself.

"Go on, get it," Raelyn said.

Devin raced to the car and back in two minutes. He was convinced that there were going to be presents of some kind in the box.

"Here, sir," Devin said handing the box to Barry.

"Don't call me sir, I work for a living," Barry said automatically.

Raelyn laughed. "What are you going to say if they make you an officer?"

"I know. If I take that promotion it's really going to mess me up." Barry laughed at the thought.

Devin stood there looking a bit confused. "Don't worry about it," Barry told him. "It's okay with me if you call me Barry, that is if it's okay with your mom."

"It's okay with me."

Barry opened the box and pulled out three sets of specs and Comms. "I brought one of these for each of you." He handed a pair of specs to Raelyn and one to Devin. "Put them on; these Comms you can strap to your arm. They're waterproof. I've got some earwigs for you, but we'll deal with them later."

"Earwigs, Yuk!" Raelyn shuddered at the thought of bugs in her ear.

"They're like earplugs; they let your Comm talk to you when you're not wearing the specs or if you want to be sure nobody else hears. Okay, Raelyn here's your Comm. Press your finger on the glass."

Raelyn pressed her finger to the glass. A second later the Comm beeped. "It's registered to you. I'll help you set up some more stuff, but for now, tell it to show you the picture."

"Show me pictures of Princess Catie and Sergeant Knox. . . . Hey it worked. Wow, these glasses are cool."

"Yes, they will let you adjust the tint, so you can use them as sunglasses. I'll show you how in a minute." Barry turned to Devin and held out another Comm. "Press your finger here." . . . Beep. "Good, it's registered to you. Now you can tell it to show you stuff, or just use them like sunglasses. It'll play music if you want, or even show movies."

"Play Black Panther," Devin ordered his Comm. . . . "Cool!"

"Hey!" Raelyn said.

"Just let him watch a few minutes," Barry said. "You can set rules on it about what it'll show him. I'll show you how."

"Okay," Raelyn said. Then she turned away and whispered something to her Comm.

Barry wondered what she was doing, but decided to ignore it and move on to the process of exchanging specs with his daughter. Talia didn't seem convinced that she should trade in her specs, the ones she had on were working just fine.

"Mama," Barry greeted his mother when she answered the door.

"Barry?! When did you get into town?"

"A couple of days ago. I had to meet with Raelyn and talk about the kids."

"That's good. How come you didn't come early and go to church with me?"

"I didn't want to have to deal with all your friends," Barry lied.

"Well get your butt in here and talk."

Barry followed his mother into the living room and sat down in one of the wing chairs, his mother took the other.

"Where are Eric and Jeremy?"

"Your brothers are out playing with their friends. But you're staying for dinner, they'll be home by then." Barry knew it was an order not an invitation, so he just nodded his head.

"How are you doing?" Barry asked.

"I'm doing just fine. Still working at the market as a cashier. Kelsey and I still go to bingo every Thursday Night."

"That's good."

"Now tell me about what's happening with you."

"I wrote you all about it already."

"Your letters don't say much, they're so short. One would think you didn't know how to write," Mrs. Knox said.

"Mama, I'm good. I told you I'm a staff sergeant now. I have my own team. I'm taking classes, saving as much money as I can, what with needing to send money to Raelyn."

"That's good. You keeping your head on straight?"

"Yes, Mama. The doctors took care of the PTSD, so I'm good."

"What do you do for fun?"

"I train and study," Barry said. "Sometimes I go to a movie or out to a bar with my team."

"No girlfriend?"

"No, Mama. I'm still hoping I can fix things up with Raelyn."

"I don't know why that girl would take another chance on you after you done messed up the last time."

"That was the PTSD," Barry said. "I hope she'll understand."

"We'll see. Right now, my fence needs fixing, why don't you go take care of it?"

"Yes, Mama," Barry said, recognizing another order.

"So why did you want to have dinner without the kids?" Raelyn asked.

"I wanted to talk about something, and I figured we'd do better without having to worry about what the kids hear. Is your mama okay watching them?"

"Sure she is. I work part-time as a bartender so I work nights on those days, she's used to it."

"You seeing someone?"

"I don't have time for no man!"

"Sorry. Just wanted to know."

"So, what do you want to talk about?"

"I wondered if you would be willing to move to Delphi City?"

"Hey, I'm not sure I want you back."

"I know, and you don't have to get back with me to move to Delphi City."

"I've got a job, Mama's here, what would I do in Delphi City?"

"You'd only have to work one job. I have a condo allotment I could give you. That way you'd have a double condo, four bedrooms. You could start taking classes again."

"How do you know I'd get a job?"

"Because everyone gets a job. They're set up to make sure anyone that wants a job has one. And they're growing so fast that it's not a problem."

"What do they do if they have a recession? Kick all the Black folks out of work?"

"Nope, everyone works. Their work contracts say that everyone will have their hours cut back exactly the same for each job class. That way nobody is unemployed. And they're always offering training and education so you can get a better job."

"How's that work?"

"One of my guys' wife just finished up her associate's degree in marketing. She worked as an assembler in one of the factories while she went to school. When she graduated, she interviewed for three jobs, and get this, she got five offers."

"How did she get five offers if she only interviewed for three jobs?"

"Two of the companies said they had another job that she was qualified for, so they made her two offers, she got to choose which one she wanted. And now that she's working, they even let her come in late two days a week so she can take a marketing class at the university. Apparently, some big-shot marketing guy is teaching it."

"But what would Mama do?"

"If she wants, she could come, too. She could open a restaurant. There's nothing there that serves good southern food like your mama's."

"How's she going to open a restaurant? We don't have that kind of money."

"She can borrow it."

"And who's going to loan a forty-five-year-old Black woman money to open a restaurant?"

"The Delphi Credit Union. I've got some money saved that I can chip in. But they'll loan her the rest."

"You're sure confident about that!"

"I know some guys that opened a Jamaican restaurant and they didn't have any money. They borrowed it all from the credit union."

"What about your mama? Maybe she can come and open the restaurant with Mama. They're good friends and your mama's a good cook, too."

"Umm."

"Hey, what's wrong with you? You want us to move there, but it's not good enough for your mama?"

"That's not it. It's just I get along better with my mama over the phone."

Raelyn laughed. "Tough! Are there any other Black people in this city?"

"Sure, lots of Marines are people of color, and they have families, so there'll be plenty of Black people. But Delphi City is really integrated. They mix people up in the various condos. There is the Hillbilly House, but only about half of the people who live there are hillbillies."

"What do you mean by hillbilly?"

"It's actually Appalachia House, they just call it Hillbilly House and call themselves hillbillies. They're the miners from West Virginia. When they first moved to Delphi City, they put them in the same building so they'd be around people they knew. But after that, they mixed in people from other places. There's also a Jamaica House. I think only about half of the people in there are from Jamaica, the rest are from all over."

"What about the important people? The McCormacks are white."

"Sure, but you can't hold that against them. The president of MacKenzie Discoveries is Black."

"Is he really the president, or just some token?"

"He's the president. Kal says that Fred, that's his name, started out as one of the pilots for their private jet. In the beginning, he was going to the board meetings to report on the stuff he was assigned. Whenever someone wanted to give up some work they were doing, Fred volunteered to take it over."

"Just like white people to make the Black man do all the work."

"No, it wasn't like that. The rest of them kind of focused on the new stuff and weren't really thinking about the fact that they were running this big company. Fred cottoned to it right away. He put in for an assistant to help, and Marc, he's the big boss, signed off on it right away. So later Fred asked for another assistant. Kal says that pretty soon he had twenty people working for him. He had them managing other parts of the company so he could review what they were doing once a day and keep everything working. Marc's no fool, he knew what Fred was doing, and last year, he made him the president."

"Anyone else besides this Fred?"

"Well, there's Kal, he's Hawaiian, so he's a person of color. The prime minister is a Syrian. The chief of police is Polynesian, kind of like Kal. I don't keep track of it, I just know that when I go somewhere, I'm treated with respect and I'm just as likely to meet a person of color as a white person."

"Okay, we can go check it out."

"I can't believe they sent a plane for us," Raelyn said.

"Me neither. I just put in the paperwork for you guys to come, and told my boss when we were planning to travel. Then I get this message saying they were coming to pick us up."

"You know Mama's never flown before."

"Yeah, and neither has my mama."

"Why are we meeting the plane at this little airport?" Mrs. Knox, Barry's mama, asked.

"Because it's a private jet. Like those corporate jets you see on TV," Barry explained.

"Is it going to have tiny seats?" Mrs. Knox asked, she was a sizable woman and wasn't looking forward to flying for the first time. "I keep hearing stories about how they keep making the seats on the planes smaller."

"No, Mama, they'll be nice seats."

"My friends will never believe this," Eric Knox said. He was Barry's fifteen-year-old brother.

"Eric, go get your brother. I don't want him wandering around by himself," Mrs. Knox said. Her other son, Jeremy, was wandering over by the baggage claim area.

"Why do I have to watch him?!" Eric whined.

"Because he's your brother, and if you don't, I'm going to smack you upside your head. Pick whichever way you want to do it, but go get him."

Eric shuffled off slowly to get his ten-year-old brother before he got them both into trouble.

"Here comes the plane," Devin said.

"Oh, that can't be it. That's too big," Raelyn said.

"My specs say it is."

"Then you must be right."

The whole group paused what they were doing while they watched the Lynx land and taxi over to their gate. Once it came to a stop, Barry led them out onto the tarmac.

"Wow, that is a nice-looking jet," Eric said.

"Is it all for us?" Talia asked. She was hiding behind her brother again.

"Yes, it is," Barry replied.

The hatch opened and a set of stairs came out of the jet. Then a flight attendant came out. "Hello, my name is Jenny, and I'll be helping you folks out. I assume this is Sergeant Knox and his family."

"That's us."

"Good. We'll be ready to board in a minute, but first, let's get your luggage taken care of." Jenny walked down the ramp followed by a second flight attendant. This one was a young woman. While Jenny had chosen to wear slacks, the other attendant had chosen to wear a knee-length skirt. Eric noticed that she had very nice legs.

"Did they pick a Black girl to make us feel comfortable?" Raelyn asked.

"Hi, Sergeant Knox," the second flight attendant said.

"Hello, C'Anne, when did you start working as a flight attendant?" Barry asked.

"I'm still in training, but Jackie saw this come up, and since I know you, she asked if I wanted to make the run. Of course, I had to."

"C'Anne, this is Raelyn and my family. Everyone this is C'Anne; her father is in my platoon."

"Who's Jackie?" Raelyn asked in a whisper.

"She's head of cabin operations for Peregrine Airlines," Barry whispered back.

"Oh, so you do know some important people."

"I've never met her."

Just then a man came out of the Lynx wearing a pilot's cap. "That's Bill, he'll work with the ground crew here to get your luggage stowed," Jenny said.

As Bill moved down the stairs, Catie was suddenly visible behind him.

"Is that Princess Catie?!" Talia asked.

"I think so," Barry said.

"Talia, hush, don't make a nuisance of yourself," Grandmother Hendricks scolded.

"Yes, ma'am."

"Hey, Barry," Catie said.

"Hi, ..."

"It's Catie in case you don't remember," Catie said.

"Hi, Catie, I'm just surprised to see you."

"Kal told me you were bringing your family, so I volunteered to pick you up in a Lynx. I need the hours, and it's way better than flying commercial," Catie said.

"You can say that again."

"We've got a thirty-minute wait, so I wanted to stretch my legs. You guys can board anytime you want."

"Don't you have to refuel?" Eric asked.

"No," Catie said.

Eric looked confused.

"Oh, I can explain that," C'Anne said. She put her hand on Eric's shoulder and led him toward the back of the plane. "See, these Lynxes have a fusion reactor in them. So even though they carry jet fuel, they don't have to ..."

"Ahem," Bill coughed.

Catie turned and read a message in her HUD. "Barry, you know we don't allow firearms."

"Mama, I told you, you couldn't bring your gun!"

"You don't expect me to go to some strange city and not take my gun. How will I protect myself?!" Mrs. Knox asked.

"It's okay, we'll pull it out when we get to Delphi City," Catie said. "I assume there's only the one."

Grandma Hendricks coughed and raised her hand.

"Mama! I told you!" Raelyn scolded.

"I know, but when Nadine said she was taking hers, I figured you must have misunderstood."

"We'll take care of it in Delphi City," Catie said while Barry just shook his head. "They'll put them in a locker at the range. You can go check them out if you want to do some practice, but there are no guns allowed in Delphi City."

"What about the police?"

"The police don't carry guns either."

"What happens when you have a situation?" Mrs. Knox asked.

"They call us Marines in to deal with bad situations, but those are rare," Barry explained.

"Sounds like they already have that community policing thing figured out," Mrs. Knox said.

"We think so," Catie said.

3   Can We Be Friends?

"Catie, are you going to Gemini Station to survey the Fazullan ship?" Liz asked.

"I'm definitely going for the survey, and I plan on sitting in on the interviews with the Fazullans and the other aliens," Catie said.

"What about the Dutchman?"

"I assume that means you want to go to Gemini as well."

"Yes, but we don't want the Dutchman sitting idle that long, it's already been too long."

"Why don't we send Derek?"

"As captain?"

"Yes."

"He's never been on her."

"But he's commanded the Sakira and the Roebuck. Arlean will be with him, so there's not much risk."

"It's a long run, Artemis with a bunch of colonists, machine equipment; then Paraxea with platinum metals, then back to Artemis with fixtures and some more machine equipment before coming home to Earth."

"It's either that or one of us does the walkthrough and interviews virtually."

"I really want to be there in person," Liz said.

"I do too. I've avoided doing any more of the virtual walkthroughs so I can get the full impact," Catie said. "So?"

"Send Derek."

"I agree. Do you want to tell him since you're the one who hired him?"

"I'll tell him tomorrow."

◆ ◆ ◆

"Catie, what did Dr. McDowell and you decide about your wormhole theory?" Marc asked as he, Blake, Liz, and Catie met to prepare for their interviews with the aliens.

"The math says it's possible," Catie said. "We determined that a quaternary system with the right geometry could generate a wormhole. The measurements we have of the system I picked out indicate it would produce one that would extend to that system next to Artemis, depending on the state of the binary star system in it."

"Does it explain the Fazullans being the ones to attack the Paraxean colony mission?"

"It shows that it is possible. The probe we sent to the star the Fazullans came from on their way to Artemis shows a satellite in a holding pattern where we predicted the wormhole would open. We haven't sent one to where the Paraxeans were attacked, we don't have that many probes available."

"Okay, we'll decide what to do once we talk to the aliens that the Fazullans were holding prisoner."

"Sounds like a plan."

◆ ◆ ◆

"Derek, are you okay with being captain for this run?" Liz asked.

"Hey, if you want to pay me the captain's share, why would I complain?"

"You do have to run the ship. Are you okay with that?"

"The crew will run the ship. I just need to walk around and look important," Derek said. He laughed and gave Liz an idiot smile.

"Okay, I'll mention that to Arlean. I'm sure she'll straighten you out."

Derek laughed again. "I'm sure she will. But seriously, it won't be that different than the Roebuck and I'm sure everyone in the crew knows their job."

"It's going to be a long trip."

"That's okay. I can use a break from carousing at the bars every night. My feet are sore from all the dancing."

"Sounds like you want to hide from someone."

"No, just getting a little antsy being planetside for so long."

"The Dutchman is scheduled to leave in two days. You should go ahead and take over command. That way you can help with the loading. The crew will appreciate the help and you won't look like so much of a freeloader."

"I'll head up today."

"Hi Nikola, hi Ajda," Catie greeted the two women. She and Liz were meeting them at the Delphi airport before catching their ride to Gemini Station. They were going to be part of the survey team that would examine the Fazullan starship. Nikola also planned to join Catie and Liz on the team that would be interviewing the aliens they had awakened from the stasis pods. Major Prescott, the Marine major who had led the team that first entered the ship, had awakened several aliens from each of the three representative groups. During the trip to Gemini Station, ADI and ANDI had been studying the aliens and working with them to learn their language so everyone could communicate.

"Hi, Catie, who else is going with us?" Nikola asked.

"Just us four," Catie said.

Dr. Nikola frowned, "Don't tell me we're taking a Lynx?"

Liz coughed slightly and hid her smile.

"Yes, we wouldn't want to take an Oryx for just four of us. And the Roebuck left three weeks ago to be part of the escort for the Fazullan starship."

Nikola sighed and motioned Catie to lead on. Their Lynx was sitting at Gate Two, so it only took them a few minutes to reach it. Liz quietly followed Nikola and Ajda into the jet.

"How can you be so blasé about having to spend three or four days restricted to your seat, having to use a ladder to get to the bathroom?" Nikola whispered to Liz.

"Two words, Hover Lynx," Liz said.

Nikola looked at her like she was nuts, but Ajda started to laugh. "Think about it, how does a Hover Lynx work?" she whispered.

Nikola stared at them for a minute then reality dawned, "Gravity drives?" Nikola realized that by using gravity drives instead of the space engine, the Lynx could accelerate toward Gemini Station along the axis perpendicular to her floor, giving them a sense of gravity in the orientation that was normal for the Lynx design.

"Of course."

"She could have told us!"

"What's the fun in that?" Catie asked as she turned around to the trio.

"I would get even with you for making me panic, but that's a losing proposition," Nikola said.

"It might be interesting if you tried," Liz said.

"*Go for it,*" ADI urged Nikola over a private channel.

"Major Prescott, please have them align their orbit one hundred thousand kilometers behind Gemini Station," Blake ordered.

"Yes, Admiral. We are aligning orbits now."

"Captain Clements, can you put the Enterprise ten thousand kilometers starboard of the Fazullan ship?"

"That won't be a problem, Admiral."

"Feel free to give shore leave here on Gemini Station once you've set up your port watch," Blake said. "Major Prescott, please have the aliens set a port watch, then bring Captain Lantaq and the aliens we've tagged for interviews to Gemini Station. We'll have a team meet you at the entry port."

"Yes, sir."

Blake turned back to the team assembled in the conference room, "Well, are we ready?"

"As ready as we can be," Nikola said. "Based on my study of the data from Major Prescott, the Fazullans do not have an antimatter reactor."

"Then how do they power that ship?" Blake asked.

"One very big fusion reactor," Nikola said. "We may be able to learn something from it. I had hoped that Dr. Nakahara would come."

"Once we figure out what to do with all the aliens in those stasis pods, we'll be breaking that ship apart. He'll be able to study the reactor when we ship it back to Delphi Station."

"Are we really going to break it apart?" Catie asked.

"Yes! It gives me the willies to see it. I can't help but fear that there is some kind of hidden code or timer that will tell it to blow itself up. I'll feel much better when it is nothing but a collection of parts."

"Does anyone have any last-minute observations or thoughts to share before Captain Lantaq is brought in?" Liz asked.

"We haven't gotten much out of him, just name, rank, and serial number," Blake said. "The same with the three crew members who abandoned the shuttle before Captain Fitzgerald had it destroyed."

"But they obviously value their lives," Catie said. "Captain Lantaq killed Captain Shakaban before he let him destroy their ship, and the three crew abandoned the shuttle instead of trying to evade the missiles."

"True, but they've barely said a word since then."

"I think we have to figure out what he wants for himself and his crew," Catie said. "I'm sure he wasn't thinking that they should be prisoners of war for the rest of their lives."

"Agreed, but do not discount that he might be playing a long game, hoping to learn things from us that would be to his advantage," Blake said.

"What do you make of the fact that for two of the three alien races they only had males?" Nikola asked.

"Not only that but all the Fazullans on the ship were male," Liz added.

"A patriarchal society?"

"That would explain the Fazullans, but what about the slaves?"

"Breeding," Liz suggested.

"What?!" Catie asked.

"They're using the females for breeding. To increase the slave population. They don't need the males for that, so they're expendable, cheap labor."

"What do you mean they don't need the males? ... Oh," Catie gasped. "Then why would there be females with the third race?"

"Not sure," Liz said, not wanting to share her suspicions.

The sentry posted at the door pinged Blake's Comm. "Major Prescott and the prisoner, sir."

"Bring them in," Blake ordered.

Major Prescott entered the conference room, followed by Captain Lantaq who was pinned between two Marines. In person his blue-tinted skin was lighter than Catie remembered, it made him look a bit like a ghost. His black hair had a reddish tint to it.

"He looks like a cross between a Viking and a Klingon," Catie messaged Liz.

"I thought he was a Klingon ghost," Liz messaged back.

"Captain Lantaq, please have a seat," Blake indicated the seat on the other side of the conference table. "Major Prescott, please join us over here. Your Marines can step outside."

"You don't want security in the room with us? . . . sir," Major Prescott asked.

"I think we'll be safe enough," Blake said. Captain Lantaq gave Blake a curious look before taking his seat.

"Captain Lantaq, let me introduce the others who will be assisting me in the interview. This is Commander Farmer and Lieutenant McCormack," Blake said.

Catie and Liz nodded to Captain Lantaq. Nikola and Ajda had both opted out of the interview at the last minute, deciding to spend the time on the alien ship instead of participating in the interviews. Ajda really wanted to look at the powerplant.

"Captain Lantaq, do you need any refreshments, water?" Blake asked, Captain Lantaq's Comm automatically provided the translation via the earwig he was wearing.

"No, I'm fine," Captain Lantaq replied.

Blake waited until he saw Captain Lantaq shift his position before he began. "Our first question is, what do you hope will become of you and your crew?"

Captain Lantaq was clearly surprised by the question. He started to speak, then stopped. It took him a full minute before he responded.

31

"I would hope we will be returned to Fazulla."

"And what kind of reception do you expect if you return?"

"I would hope my government would understand my reluctance to sacrifice the crew for the ego of our captain."

"Do you think that likely?" Blake asked.

"It is a possibility."

"What can you tell us about your homeworld?" Blake asked.

Captain Lantaq's eyes shifted before he answered. "It is a harsh place, but we make a good life there."

"What about your species' homeworld?" Catie asked.

Captain Lantaq smiled. He was a bit surprised that they knew that they were from a colony planet. "I have no knowledge of that."

"Surely they teach you about where you came from?" Catie asked.

"Only that is far away and long ago."

"What if we could return you there?"

"Hmm, I would not know if that would be a good thing or not."

"Why were there only males in your crew?" Blake asked.

"We are not willing to risk the lives of our females. Without them, how would we have more sons?"

"What about your slaves?"

"The same thing. A male slave dies, you lose one slave. A female slave dies, you lose hundreds of slaves."

"Then why did you have females from that one race?" Catie demanded.

"Someone to clean the ship," Captain Lantaq said, but he didn't sound very convincing.

"Why did your captain decide to attack Artemis?" Blake asked.

"He had invested a lot into the mission; returning home empty-handed would have ruined him."

"Financially or reputation?" Liz asked.

"Both."

"Why did you target Artemis?"

"You must know how rich the system is in metals. Those metals are rare in our system. The profits from mining your asteroid belt or the planet for a year would have been enormous."

"How did you reach us?" Catie asked. "We know that all planets close to Artemis are uninhabited."

"By our starship."

"How long were you traveling?"

"I can't say."

"Can't or won't?" Blake asked.

"Both."

"Can you explain the slaves?" Blake asked, wanting to clarify why they kept slaves.

"One of our many sins."

"Why do you keep them?"

"It allows people in power to have more power. They can farm more land without having to employ other Fazullans."

"Doesn't that cause hardship for your people?" Blake asked.

"It does, but when you have power, what do you care?"

"Do you own slaves?"

"Yes, my sire was a powerful man. He owned many slaves. I inherited them when he died."

"You could have freed them," Catie said.

"On Fazulla the only way to free slaves is to kill them."

"Some of them might prefer that!"

"Some slaves have made it known that they prefer death. It is unfortunate when that happens."

◆ ◆ ◆

The next group to be interviewed was the Paraxeans. The first Paraxeans they had awakened had been able to provide limited information, just enough to tell them they were descendants from the original colony mission. When asked to identify one of their leaders,

33

they had toured the stasis chambers until they identified an old man. Major Prescott told them that he suspected that they had actually just identified the oldest Paraxean that they could find.

"This is Cer Hastra," Major Prescott said, introducing the elderly Paraxean as he led him into the interview room.

"Cer Hastra, thank you for agreeing to be interviewed," Blake said as the old man sat down. "I'm Admiral McCormack and this is Lieutenant McCormack and Commander Farmer."

"Hello, Cer Hastra," Catie said. "You might remember Doctor Mangalax, he was the lead doctor on the colony ship."

"I remember him. Is he here?"

"No, he's back with the other colonists. We can make arrangements for you to talk to him if you like."

"I never liked him before and I'm sure he doesn't like me either. But it's good to know the colony ship made it."

"Can you tell us what you remember after the attack on your ship?" Blake asked.

"Sure. I was even awake at the time, one of the few that survived," Cer Hastra said. "We were attacked and the cargo ship was separated from the others. They went on; they had to if they wanted to survive. Somehow the Fazullans managed to slow our ship down and board her. They were really mad when they realized we'd fused all the electronics and that the reactor was fused as well. They were so mad that they started killing the crew. They tortured a bunch of them before they killed them. Don't know why; we couldn't understand each other so no one could answer any questions."

"How did you survive?" Blake asked.

"I was a maintenance guy, kind of the janitor. I hid in an air duct until they got tired of killing everyone."

"I see, please go on."

"One of the officers had jettisoned the cargo. Set explosives on all the important stuff, so it was destroyed even if they'd been able to go back and find it all."

"Clever of him," Liz said.

"We had weeks to prepare. We saw their ships coming months before they hit us; things take a long time in space. That was the protocol we had. The Fazullans only got material out of that ship, no technology. I guess that's why they were so mad. They could tell right away that we had better stuff than they did."

"Then what happened?"

"They put the few of us that were still alive back in stasis chambers. Fortunately, our protocol didn't require destroying them. They must have brought some kind of power source over to keep them running since they would only have been able to keep them running for a few weeks on capacitors and batteries.

"Anyway, when I came out of stasis, they made it clear that I was a slave. Not much different than before, except that they slapped me around a lot. I had to work in a factory taking care of machinery. Eventually, I learned their language. They took all the women away; I learned later that they were using them to breed more slaves."

"That's what we've been told," Catie said.

"Terrible thing to do to people," Cer Hastra said. "Anyway, I worked as a slave for sixty years, then they put me on a ship and stuck me in another stasis chamber. Then I woke up here."

"What else do you know about the Paraxeans back on Fazulla?" Liz asked.

"I know there are a lot of them. The Fazullans really like having slaves to do their work, so they kept breeding more Paraxeans. The captain that captured us got really rich. He's still getting richer, I assume."

"What about the original colonists, like you?"

"There are lots of them. There were still some of them in stasis when I left. They wake one up every few years to interrogate them. I was used as an interpreter once. I guess the Fazullans can't be bothered to learn a slave's language. Stupid really; the interpreter would give the new awakee the lowdown to make sure they didn't reveal anything important. Made it look like we were trying to encourage them to be cooperative."

"What can you tell us about the Aperanjens?"

"You must mean those big, red people. They showed up about halfway through my time there, I guess that'd make it thirty years ago. That Fazullan captain who brought them in thought he was going to be rich. Big worker slaves. He made some money off of the technology, but it wasn't much. Nobody wanted his slaves."

"Why not?" Blake asked.

"They were scared of them. They're as big as a Fazullan and fierce. One slave killed his master and the whole family after they beat him. They don't take kindly to being slaves. The women don't either, and they're almost as strong and fierce as the men."

"How did they react when the Aperanjen killed the Fazullan?"

"Why they killed every slave in that household. But that didn't cow the Aperanjens any. They made it clear they would rather die than be treated like slaves. So nobody would buy them, and it doesn't make any sense to breed slaves you can't sell. That captain started selling them for missions like this, mining in the asteroid belt or on other planets. Then they could keep lots of guards on them."

"What else can you tell us about the Fazullans?"

"They don't treat their women any better than they treat their slaves. The women seemed to be nice; I was never hit by one of them. Some of the men seemed alright, but the bosses were always cruel. They liked to see you cower when they walked into a room. I guess it made them feel like real big men when someone they could kill whenever they wanted to would duck their head when they walked by."

They couldn't get much more out of Cer Hastra, he'd never been allowed to learn anything but the basics about Fazullan technology. Major Prescott had security take him back to a room where Catie made arrangements for him to call some Paraxeans he remembered from the original colony mission.

◆ ◆ ◆

"Our next guests are the Onisiwoens, there were only eight of them on the ship. ADI has just finished deciphering their language with the help of the ones we pulled out of stasis," Major Prescott said. He pronounced Onisiwoen, O-Ne-Si-Wo-In

"Let's bring them in," Blake said.

The door opened and three Onisiwoens were led in by the security guard. They were very humanoid in appearance. They had dark skin with a blue tinge to it which matched their bright blue hair. They were similar in height to the Fazullans, about 175 centimeters tall. But they were smaller, thin, almost frail. When they smiled, they had teeth much like humans, not the canine-like teeth of the Fazullans.

"Please be seated. I hope our translator is adequate. Please let us know if you are confused by something we say," Blake said.

"Thank you, your ADI and ANDI have been very helpful. They seem to have a good command of our language now," the lead Onisiwoen said. "My name is Charlie."

"Charlie, how did you come up with a name like that?" Catie asked.

"Our names are long and complex," Charlie said. "We use diminutives when we talk among friends, I've selected Charlie after hearing your Marines try to say my name a few times. I like the sound of it better than the mangling of my real name."

"And your two companions?" Blake asked.

"This is Leharo, he is my second in command, and this is Juxtor, he is our doctor."

"I'm pleased to meet you," Blake said. "You know Major Prescott; this is Commander Farmer and Lieutenant McCormack. I'm Admiral McCormack."

"Your daughter? I see a resemblance," Charlie said.

"My niece."

"We wish to express our thanks to you for rescuing us."

"We were happy to assist," Blake said. "Can you tell us more about your homeworld and what happened to you?"

"Our homeworld of Onisiwo is just beginning to explore the fringes of our solar system. We were part of a mission to the outer planets in our system."

"How is your system configured?" Catie asked.

"Our system has two inner rocky planets, then an asteroid belt, then three gas giants, and a few exoplanets."

"So, you were a small crew?" Blake asked.

"Yes, there were fourteen of us. I believe that eight of us were on the Fazullan ship."

"That's correct. We do not have any information about the other six members of your crew. Can you tell us about them?"

"They were all women," Charlie said. "We are not sure why the Fazullans would keep the women."

"Can you tell us how you were captured?" Blake asked, ignoring the comment about the women. It was clear that the other two preferred that Charlie be the one doing the talking. Blake didn't know if it was a chain of command thing, or they were just uncomfortable answering questions.

"Our ship was coming to Yiyara, our second gas giant. We were to land on one of her moons and set up an observation post. That is when a Fazullan ship came out from behind one of the other moons and fired upon us. We were on a peaceful mission and did not have any weapons. We surrendered and they boarded our ship. They took us prisoner and put us in those stasis chambers. We do not know what happened after that."

"You said a Fazullan ship, does that mean you know it wasn't the one you were just on?" Catie asked.

"No, I believe it was the same ship."

"Do you think the Fazullans captured your solar system?" Liz asked.

"I do not think so. We didn't see any other vessels and our planet may not be venturing far into space as of yet, but we do have powerful orbital weapons," Charlie said.

"*He's equivocating,*" Catie messaged to the others. "Dr. Juxtor, did you have any problems adapting to the environment in their ship?"

"We did not. Major Prescott placed us in an isolated set of rooms during our trip here. During that time, I and his team were able to determine that exposure to the Fazullan air and environment did not pose a threat to us. We also verified that your air would be safe as well."

Major Prescott nodded his head. "Ma'am, we spent the first two weeks in full exosuits. It wasn't until two days ago that we got out of the suits."

Catie grimaced. "I'm sure that wasn't a pleasant two weeks."

"We train for it, ma'am."

"So you weren't able to identify any technology from your world on the Fazullan ship?" Blake asked.

"That is correct. Major Prescott had us escorted into all the sections; we saw no trace of Onisiwoen technology."

"What would you like us to do with you?" Blake asked.

"We hope that you will return us to Onisiwo."

"Do you think your world is ready to learn about other civilizations out here?" Catie asked.

"We have been confident that there are other races among the stars. During the two years before our expedition, we got some fragments of radio signals that indicated another civilization. I assume they were from Fazullan scout ships."

"Just fragments?" Catie asked.

"Yes, the signals we first picked up were distorted and lasted for three or four months, then we got nothing for about a year, then they came back. We were supposed to try to get a better read on them during our mission."

"And you never detected them before? Were you looking before?" Catie asked.

"We have been searching the skies for signs of extraterrestrial life for over one hundred years. The first signal we received that strongly suggested its existence were the ones we received just before our mission began."

"Back to the discussion of returning you to Onisiwo," Blake said. "Would you be willing to show us which system is yours?"

"We could try," Charlie said.

"I sense some hesitation."

"You did rescue us, but we really don't know that much about you."

"I can understand your caution . . ."

"Is this your home system?" Catie asked as she put a star map up on the display.

Charlie's eyes gave him away as he clearly recognized the surrounding stars. Blake gave Catie a questioning look.

"Antares probe found it, detected signs of civilization, and moved on. But given our assumptions about how the Fazullans got there, plus the timing of the signals, this is the system that the data points to."

"Yes, that is our system," Charlie said. "If you can tell me the timing of this star map, then I can probably determine the date. That would tell us how long ago the Fazullans captured us."

"This map is six months old," Catie said.

Charlie gasped, then shook his head. He studied the map with his two colleagues for a few minutes; after some back-and-forth discussion among them, they reached a conclusion.

"I believe this shows that our mission was captured four years ago," Charlie said. "But it is hard to imagine so short a timeline."

"Any reason not to tell them?" Catie messaged Marc, Blake, and Liz.

"Go ahead," Marc said.

"Charlie, we believe that the Fazullans reached your system via a wormhole that opened at the fringe of your solar system."

Charlie was shaking his head. "What do you mean a wormhole? That is a hole left in the soil by a small creature. I am confused."

"Sorry, the translation of wormhole is correct."

"Sorry about that," ADI messaged.

"Our translation program didn't have the other meaning we have for the term. We also use that term to describe a dimensional tunnel in space-time. It connects two points that are light-years apart."

"But the gravitation distortion would tear the universe apart."

Catie nodded her head. "If the connection were made in the same dimension, it would create a problem. But the wormholes seem to absorb the mass at the entry completely before that mass can start exiting the other end. So the dimensional transition isolates the two ends."

"Okay, I think I understand," Charlie said. "Please go on."

"Once they reached your solar system, it would only have taken a few weeks for them to reach the gas giant where they attacked you, then the same amount of time to return to the wormhole. We suspect that their end of the wormhole is around half a light-year from their homeworld. We also believe that the wormhole moves every few months among three systems. That would mean that it would only be the time between their leaving your system and reaching Artemis that we have to account for."

"And how were you able to send a probe to our system to make that star map?"

"We've discovered how to create an artificial wormhole," Catie said. "We've been looking for habitable planets with our probes. One of them was directed into the quadrant of the galactic arm where your planet is. As I said, it detected signs of civilization, so it logged the data and avoided the system."

"This is too much; I need time to think," Charlie said. His two colleagues signaled their emphatic agreement.

After a break for lunch, they met the next group of aliens. They called themselves Aperanjens. They were even shorter than the Fazullans, built like fire hydrants. Catie thought they could probably lift one of the taxis they had on Delphi City.

"Thank you for joining us," Blake said as the three aliens were shown into the conference room. "I'm Admiral Blake McCormack; you know Major Prescott; joining us are Commander Farmer and Lieutenant McCormack."

"We are glad to meet you. Please call me Bear, this is Rhino, and she is Wolf," Bear said pointing to his two companions. "We selected names from your language to make communication easier."

"We appreciate that, however the translation program on our Comms wouldn't have trouble with your true names."

"We know, but this makes it easier for us. We have good hearing and can tell when you're using a different name that then gets translated, and the sound of you trying to pronounce our names is very harsh to our ears."

"Then, Bear, can you tell us how you came to be prisoners of the Fazullans?" Blake asked.

"I can tell you," Rhino said. "I have been in stasis since we were captured. Wolf and Bear were just children back then."

"Then please tell us what you know."

"Our colony ship was attacked and captured by the Fazullans. We didn't expect to encounter anyone on our journey to the new planet, so we had no defensive forces with us."

"Can you help us understand where and when this occurred?"

"We can give you an idea of where by using star charts, but we've been in stasis since the attack, so we have no idea of how long ago it was. In fact, most of our people were in stasis during the attack."

"I'll bring up a star chart, tell me if we're close," Catie said.

"Those stars do not look familiar," Rhino said after everyone spent time examining the star map.

"How about these stars?" Catie asked after switching to another map.

"Those do not look familiar," Rhino said.

"Damn."

"Catie, what's the matter?" Marc asked.

"I think the wormhole may have jumped since then. That will make it difficult to find their homeworld. Rhino, can you describe the star system you were passing at the time of the attack?"

"What is a wormhole and how did you know they would be passing a star system at the time of the attack?" Bear demanded.

"It's related to how the Fazullans were able to reach you," Catie explained. "They could only have attacked you within a few million kilometers of a star system."

"Will you explain that to us?" Wolf asked.

Catie repeated her explanation of wormholes and paused to let them ponder it.

"Does that mean you could take us back to our homeworld?" Wolf asked.

"If we can figure out where it is," Blake said. "Is that what you would prefer?"

"We have discussed what we want, and we all agree that we would prefer to finish the colony mission, but that is not possible."

"Can you tell us which star system you were planning to colonize?" Catie asked, "Or were you just looking for one?"

"No, we had a specific system we were traveling to. It is about four light-years spinward of the place we were attacked," Wolf said.

"So we can continue to try to figure out where that was, or we can find another system for you. Was there a specific reason you had selected the system?"

"It was close to our homeworld, twenty light-years, and it appeared to be compatible."

"Would you be interested in another system?"

"If we could find one that was compatible."

"We have a few possibilities. We have Solar Explorer probes that are mapping the various inhabitable planets in this arm of the galaxy. Several of them are high-gravity worlds. That is, assuming your definition of habitable is similar to ours."

"So does that mean you are already planning to colonize those planets?"

"No, we put them on our maybe list. Their gravity is about fifty percent higher than our standard gravity, so we wouldn't be very comfortable there."

"Is this your standard gravity?" Bear asked, indicating the gravity that they were experiencing on Gemini Station. "It is much lighter than ours."

"Yes," Blake said.

"That explains why you're so tall," Rhino said.

"Probably. Now you said you wanted to continue your colony mission."

"Yes, but how could we?"

"We might be able to provide the necessary aid," Blake said.

"We would prefer to do that if it is possible. It has been at least one hundred years since we left our homeworld. It would be awkward to go back, even for those of us that have been in stasis. Things would be too different, our skills obsolete. But on a colony world, that would not matter."

"Based on your statement, we would predict that your homeworld is fifteen to twenty light-years from where you were attacked," Catie said.

"Approximately. You have probably already mapped our homeworld," Rhino said, shaking his head. "We have to trust you because you're obviously far more capable than we are."

"Not as much as you might think," Blake said. "We have a close relationship with one of the other alien species that were on the ship with you. The Paraxeans."

"If they are so advanced, then how were they captured?!" Wolf demanded.

"They were ambushed. They had two military vessels with them, but the Fazullans had a well-planned attack. It occurred over seventy years ago; before we met each other."

"The Paraxean slaves told us they believed the Fazullans had only captured a part of their colony mission, they always wondered what happened to the others," Wolf said.

"They were able to save their colony ship. They tried to continue their mission, but their colony ship had suffered too much damage and they were diverted to Earth, our home planet. We've helped them start a colony, but most of them are still in stasis waiting for their colony world to build enough infrastructure to accommodate the rest of them."

"That must be a major project; we're happy to hear that you're willing to invest so much to help them."

"How many people were on your ship?" Catie asked.

"Twenty-six thousand," Rhino said.

"Oh my," Catie said. "There are only about four thousand of you on the Fazullan ship."

"We know. The rest of our people are slaves on the Fazullan home planet," Wolf said.

"We noticed that your species was the only one that included females on the ship, can you explain that?"

"It is not important," Wolf said. "I think we need to focus on moving forward."

After another hour of questions, Major Prescott escorted the Aperanjens out. Catie immediately brought up a star map of the Fazullan system while Blake's eyes turned to his HUD.

"Hey, you two. What are you thinking?" Liz said as she stood there with her hands on her hips looking between Blake and Catie. "Come on, share!"

"Marc, have you been following along?" Blake asked.

"Yes. You guys seemed to have it covered so I just watched," Marc answered.

"I think we have an opportunity to add another colony to our collection. That would give us more bargaining power when we meet the other races out here."

"What about the Onisiwoens?!" Liz demanded. "Their world could be under attack from the Fazullans right now!"

"The probe didn't detect any signs of a war when it flew by," Catie said.

"But who knows what defenses they really have. Charlie was obviously trying to make them sound tougher than they probably are."

"We could redirect an explorer back to their system," Catie suggested. "It will take a few weeks."

"I agree," Marc said. "Get one to Onisiwo as fast as you can. Blake, how should we deal with getting intel on the Fazullans?"

"Catie, is their wormhole still open over by Artemis?" Blake asked.

"No, the probe we sent didn't detect a wormhole."

"When do you think it will open again?"

"I'm not sure. Our simulations indicate the wormhole will cycle among three different systems over a thirteen- or fourteen-month period."

"Three systems?" Liz said, "My count has them at four. Onisiwo, Aperanje, here by Artemis, and where they attacked the Paraxeans."

"I know. I was trying to figure that out when you started asking questions," Catie said. "My guess is that the whole wormhole network shifted sometime in the last seventy years. We'll have to reevaluate the math to figure out what systems it was cycling through back then."

"Did your simulation tell you that would happen?" Blake asked.

"Dr. McDowell is developing a more complete model. Our current model doesn't predict a fourth system where the Aperanjens were attacked, so something changed since then."

"Ahem," Marc coughed. "Why don't we send a probe to the Onisiwo system now and give everyone time to figure out our next move. We'll review it at the board meeting on Monday."

"Okay."

4   Board Meeting – August 1st

"I call this meeting to order," Marc said. "Any urgent issues to deal with?"

"I don't know if you call it urgent, but I think you need to talk to Prime Minister Nazeri about the quantum relays," Kal said.

"Why?"

"Because at her last cabinet meeting she mentioned that she'd just had a chat with you."

"Oh, I guess that would raise some questions if someone had been paying attention."

"Good thing the only scientist there was Nikola."

"I'll have a chat with her," Marc said. "While you're up, anything else?"

"One of my Marines has a bit of an issue," Kal said.

"Oh, what would that be?"

"He wants to buy his condo."

"Hmm, we haven't been allowing anyone to buy property in Delphi City."

"And according to him, or more likely his mama, that's a problem. How are people supposed to build wealth if they cannot buy real estate? That's the single greatest source of family wealth."

"He would do better to invest his money in the stock market," Marc said. "But if he wants to buy the condo, I don't know. Fred, what do you think?"

"It's a big psychological thing, especially for people of color. I don't see why we don't let people buy them; you still have the community CC&Rs to enforce neighborly behavior."

"How would we set the value?" Marc asked.

"Same way you came up with the rent. Take that and just translate to value."

"And home loans?"

"We have the credit union."

"Okay, put Zane on it," Marc said.

"I think that members of the security forces should be able to get a 100% loan," Blake said.

"Why not? They're probably our most stable residents. Fred, are you going to handle it, or do you want me to appoint someone else?"

"I'll give it to our real-estate person. She's been dealing with all the condo assignments and rent collections. This is just an extension of that, it'll be like a promotion. She deserves one, she's doing a great job."

"We'll need to make sure everyone pays association dues to cover maintenance," Catie said.

"Oh, and what would you know about maintenance in condo buildings?" Blake asked, alluding to the supposed incident where Catie got even with her friend, Sophia, by using the maintenance system to make her shower spray green food coloring on her.

"I learned about it in a class," Catie said, then stuck her tongue out at Blake.

"Sure, sure, we all believe you."

"Moving on!" Marc interrupted the spat. "Catie, what's the status of the new frigates?"

"I've gone over the design with Uncle Blake, Captain Clark, and Ajda. Everyone agrees that taking the Scout design and giving it three flight bays instead of one and shrinking the cargo bay is the best choice. It should always be close to a carrier or a planet, so it doesn't need to handle much cargo. We also had to add a mechanical system to manage environmental; the hydroponics system takes up too much space, and we needed that space for capacitors."

"Are you adding another layer to the hull?" Marc asked.

"Yes, Uncle Blake wants it to be able to take a plasma cannon blast for thirty seconds, so we added a second hull layer with superconductors."

"Good, how long before we have one built?"

"Two months for the first one," Catie said.

"That long?"

"Hey, we have to build out the cabins and everything; do you want us to have Captain Payne bring some of yours back?"

"No, we'll need them to get the new colonists settled. But what's up with that? I thought he was in command of the Roebuck."

"We rotated the crews," Blake explained. "They'd been out for over a year. As soon as they hit the beach, Liz was poaching them."

"Hmm, . . . Should we do something about that?"

"You're putting me on the spot," Blake said tugging at his collar and looking uncomfortable.

"Well?"

"No, it's good for morale. Our people like knowing they have options for civilian jobs. It keeps them on their toes. They like to be asked even if they don't take the job; like a badge of honor."

"Hah!" Catie said.

"Sorry about that," Marc laughed. "I guess we can stand the two-month wait for the frigate. What's the status of getting a probe to the Onisiwo system?"

"It's on its way. It'll be another four weeks before it gets there."

"That long?"

"Space is a big place."

"How are we doing with new colonists?" Marc asked.

"We're set up to handle about twenty thousand right now," Blake said.

"Isn't that using up a lot of space on Delphi Station?"

"No, we're keeping them down here in the city."

"Where?"

"Some smart ex-Marine mentioned how they used to set up a forward base. So as part of their training, we bring them in, put them on a bare quad, and have them build a condo building. We house them in tents while the building goes up. Since we build the condo units separately and insert them in the frame, it only takes them six weeks to get the building up."

"What are you going to do with the next group?"

"Same thing. After twelve weeks, we'll ship the first group to you and release their condo to the real estate group. This will have us adding an extra condo building every six weeks, and it's great training for the colonists."

"How do the construction guys feel about it?"

"We pay them more to deal with the rubes, so they're okay. There's still lots of work, so nobody is losing out."

"Send us the details on how you're managing it. We'll try to do something similar on this side," Marc said. "Now let's talk about our new friends."

"Yes, what are we going to do with them?" Catie asked.

"We'll leave the Paraxeans in stasis. We'll go ahead and send the ones we've awakened to Delphi Station; they can stay with the Paraxean colonists there until we can send them to Mangkatar. It's the Aperanjens that we need to decide how to handle."

"Well, Gemini is too small for all of them," Liz said.

"I'm glad you noticed that. I'm thinking about Delphi Station," Marc said. "If we spin Section Two faster so we have 1.4 Gs in ring six, then ring two would be about 1G."

"We already have people moving into ring six," Liz said.

"I know, but not many, right?"

"Right."

"So, let's move them. Then we can bring the Aperanjens out of stasis and get them ready to start a colony. They'll need a lot more help than the Paraxeans since they don't have anything from their original colony mission."

"You're going to wake them all up?!" Blake asked.

"Why not. There are only four thousand. They need to coordinate with each other and start training. There are bound to be skill gaps, and who knows how they'll react to our tools and systems," Marc said.

"Sounds like fun," Catie said.

"I'm glad you think so. I want you and Liz to coordinate it."

Liz kicked Catie under the table.

"He was going to make us do it anyway," Catie hissed.

"I was, but I feel much better about it now that you volunteered."
Marc gave them a grin.

"Sam, when is the baby due?" Catie asked.

"Five weeks."

"And you're still going to meetings?" Liz asked.

"Women are tougher than men."

Marc sighed, "I think we're done here."

"Hey, Catie. I was reading the shareholder report Fred handed out and
I couldn't help but notice he's now a major shareholder," Liz said.

"Yeah, he owns 3 percent," Catie said.

"Who sold him the shares?"

"I did."

"After his platinum metal scheme?"

"Actually, later than that. When Daddy made him president, we
talked. It made sense that the president should be a major shareholder.
And I wanted to replenish my cash after we started StarMerchants, so I
sold him 2½ percent. Daddy would have, but he doesn't want to give
up control."

"Why, among the three of you he would still have control."

"We would have control. Daddy likes to be able to make a call without
having to get a vote."

"And they say he's not a tyrant."

"Sometimes he is, but he's usually nice about it."

5 Town Hall Meeting

"Whose idea was this?" Chief Nawal asked as she and Prime Minister Nazeri watched the hall fill.

"A town hall meeting is a traditional way to present the state of the city."

"But Delphi is a nation."

"Composed of one city and one space station," the prime minister said. "What's the problem? Are you getting nervous?"

"Yes, it's starting to look like a press conference with five hundred reporters."

The prime minister smiled. "I'm sure the questions will be entertaining. I just saw Sophia Michaels sit down in the back."

"Now that we've assembled, I'd like to introduce our Prime Minister, Fatiha Nazeri," James Buckman, the president of the Delphi Senate announced.

"Good afternoon," Prime Minister Nazeri said to open her speech. "Thank you for joining us for our first State of the Nation address. We selected today because it marks the third year of the founding of Delphi City. Our President, His Excellency Marc, has decreed that henceforth, the eighth of August will be known as Founders' Day.

"His Excellency Marc is unable to attend today's celebration and State of the Nation speech since as most of you know, he elected to lead Earth's first colony mission to Artemis. There he and his First Lady, Samantha, are working to ensure that Delphi and Earth achieve their rightful place as a leader among the spacefaring civilizations in our galaxy.

"Prince Blake and Princess Catherine are also engaged in discussion with envoys from other spacefaring civilizations to establish relationships between them and Delphi. They hope that before the end of the year they will be able to join us and announce treaties between these civilizations and Earth.

"Now to the state of our nation. I am happy to report that Delphi Nation is healthy and growing. Last month we surpassed a population of one hundred fifty thousand. I and many of our early immigrants came to Delphi City as refugees. I'm happy to say that although we continue to take in refugees, the majority of our growth is coming from normal immigration. People are coming to Delphi because it is the land of freedom and opportunity. We are one of the most diverse and richest nations on Earth. And that richness is due to the innovation of our citizens. Today, over twenty percent of our GDP is generated by new businesses formed within the last year. And let me assure you that that is a major accomplishment for a small nation that is home to the richest corporation in the world. MacKenzie Discoveries continues to be our largest employer, but thirty-five percent of our jobs are now in businesses that are outside of the MacKenzie Discoveries umbrella.

"The Nation is running a surplus of fifty million on a three hundred-million-dollar budget. We have a reserve of over one billion dollars. And as of this year, we have introduced a new currency called the Aurora. Your handouts will provide all the numbers for the budget in New Zealand Dollars, U.S. Dollars, and Auroras.

"The University of Delphi is thriving, attracting students and professors from other countries. When the academic year opens at the end of this month, each academic chair at Delphi University will be held by a resident of Delphi City, and sixty percent of the professors will also be residents of Delphi City.

"And our military academy has begun its second year. It will continue to produce the officers we need to lead our nation's armed forces both here at home as well as in the stars. These future leaders will ensure the safety and prosperity of Earth and all of her colonies."

"And in summary, I wish to invite everyone to celebrate our nation's record of safety, diversity, prosperity, and opportunity. I will now take questions."

Reporter: "Why did the budget jump so much this year?"

"This year, the government was responsible for the expense of all health care. Last year, MacKenzie Discoveries covered their employees, which as I said earlier comprise most of the workforce here in Delphi."

Reporter: "A follow-up. Why should the nation pick up the cost of health care for the richest corporation in the world?"

"We determined that it was fairer to our citizens and other companies if everyone had access to the same health care. MacKenzie Discoveries increased their tax payment to the nation to cover the cost. But now the health care we offer to all of our citizens is identical."

Second Reporter: "So someone that is unemployed or who chooses not to work gets the same coverage as someone who works?"

"First, we have almost zero unemployment. Almost all of it can be attributed to new arrivals or people changing jobs. We are committed to finding a job for everyone. Second, we don't think that something as critical to your well-being as health care should be dependent on your job. By offering everyone quality health care, we ensure a healthy population and a strong workforce for everyone."

Second Reporter: "Why isn't college education free?"

"All preschool, primary, and secondary education is free. We felt it is important that a university education be earned. A university is not a place to go just to experience life, but primarily a place where you go to gather the tools for a better life. Any student is able to enter the University of Delphi, earn their degree, and leave the university debt-free. All we ask of those who can't or don't wish to pay tuition is that they contribute fifteen hours a week in labor. Most of our students get jobs working for the very same companies that will hire them when they graduate."

Third Reporter: "But how do the students have money to spend?"

"All of the students have access to free housing which includes a free meal plan. Of those who work, fifty percent of their wages go to the school and they get the other fifty percent to provide spending money for sundry items."

Parent: "What do you have to say about the fact that my children are mostly taught by a computer?"

"Delphi City's educators have spent thousands of hours studying the best way to educate our students. They've found that computer-based teaching that adapts to each student's needs and allows the teacher to be a mentor produces the best results. Allowing teachers to spend time with the students that need individualized help the most while allowing other students to accelerate at their own pace works the best. Advanced students and teacher aides provide additional mentoring and assistance, making sure that any students that need additional help, get it. They have found it is more rewarding for the students as well as the teachers."

A middle-aged woman approached the microphone. She looked around furtively before she finally sat down. "What do you say about the reports that your colony mission is a hoax? That it's really a cover so you can get slave labor for your mining operations in the asteroid belt?"

Chief Nawal patted Prime Minister Nazeri on the arm, letting her know that she would take this one. "Mrs. Lewinsky, we sent you a message from your son."

"I'm sure it was a fake. You have enough technology to fake a video, I'm sure he's dead by now," Mrs. Lewinsky said.

"Your son is perfectly healthy. If what you're claiming were true, don't you think we would have abducted you and sent you to the mines before now? You've been here for two weeks making this claim," the chief replied.

"I . . . I think you're afraid of the news media. I've already talked to them."

"And we can fake the video from your son, but we couldn't fake one from you saying you'd decided to go join him? I really wish you would go to our clinic so we could help you."

"No way am I letting you people experiment on me!"

"I wish you would get some help," Chief Nawal said as one of the attendants helped Mrs. Lewinsky up.

Another civilian approached the mike. "What do you say to the reports that you, Chief Nawal, are wanted for multiple murders in Lebanon. That you immigrated here just before the police caught you." She was apparently emboldened by Mrs. Lewinsky and decided it was time for another conspiracy theory.

"I've always wanted to do this," Chief Nawal whispered to the prime minister. "Ma'am, what is your name?"

"Phyllis McCoog."

"Just a minute, please. ... "

"Your information is ready," ADI told the chief.

"Ma'am, what I say to your accusation is that it is easy to come up with a conspiracy theory about anyone. Have you ever heard the term six degrees of separation?"

"No!"

"Well, it's a theory that claims that you can connect any two people through fewer than six other people. Here I'll give you an example. In the few minutes since you gave me your name, I've connected you to six homicides.

"First, the murder of Janet Carter, she was dating your ex-boyfriend from high school. It was rumored that she stole him from you and you vowed to get even. She was killed five miles from where you lived at the time.

"Second, the murder of Jonathan Liesmann. He is the nephew of the man who owned the hardware store that sold the furnace to your great uncle. The furnace had a defect and your great uncle was killed by carbon monoxide poisoning. Your penchant for getting even is well known."

"That is absurd!" Mrs. McCoog yelled.

"Please let me finish. Third, the murder of Cicely Monroe. She was runner up to the queen of the state fair in 2012, a competition that you entered. You did not make it past the regionals. She was killed forty miles south of where you lived at that time. You were not at work on that day or the day after.

"Fourth, the murder of Jamal Richards. He was a caretaker in the home where your second-grade teacher's mother was living. There was suspicion that her mother died of neglect. Mr. Richards was killed in a suspicious car accident two weeks later. It is well known how much you adored your second-grade teacher.

"Fifth, the murder of . . ." The chief stopped speaking as Mrs. McCoog stormed out of the room.

Another civilian approached the mic. "I don't have a conspiracy theory to offer, but I do have a serious concern. I'd like to understand our prison system. I heard that that murderer, Ms. Randall, was seen walking around town free. By the way, my name is Harry Conrad."

"I can understand your concern. Let me assure you that Ms. Randall wasn't wandering around free. But she does travel to and from her job without an escort. We deem that she is unlikely to be a danger to the community. We have a tracker installed in her body that is impossible to remove without surgery. She also has a neural neutralizer installed that will immobilize her should a constable issue a command via their Comm. She is tracked as she goes to and from work and closely monitored via the security cameras along the way."

"Why do you let her go to work like that?"

Prime Minister Nazeri leaned forward and tapped the chief's arm indicating she would answer the question. "We in the Delphi Government feel that we should be spending our money on our law-abiding citizens, and minimizing what we spend on criminals. Therefore, we require prisoners to pay for their stay in our prison. Ms. Randall was allowed to find a job; I believe she is an assembler in one of our manufacturing plants. Right now, nobody trusts her enough to give her a job with more responsibility. She pays for the cost of her cell, her food, and the cost of the guards that are needed to manage the prison. She is the only one in the prison at this time. We do not think we should waste money on unnecessary security."

"What would you do if you had someone more dangerous than her?"

"We are making arrangements to have the prison expanded so that we can create employment for that type of prisoner within the prison walls. But that creates expenses that we wish to avoid if possible. Ms. Randall is not allowed to make any detours on her trip to her job. She cannot stop to get a coffee or do any shopping. It's straight there and straight back."

◆ ◆ ◆

"Wow, can you believe those conspiracy nutjobs?" Catie asked as the town hall meeting broke up. She and Liz had been watching the broadcast of the meeting on Delphi Station.

"Yes, and I love Chief Nawal's answers. She must have been waiting to use that one about six degrees of separation. I wonder how she got all the information so quickly."

"Ahem," ADI interrupted. "I gave the chief ten murders that could be connected to Mrs. McCoog."

"I should have known. How many can you connect to me?" Liz asked.

"Four hundred sixty-four."

"What!"

"The war," Catie said. "It's easy to arrange for someone to get killed when you're their commanding officer."

"What about besides the war?"

"Both wars?" ADI asked, including the war with the Paraxeans.

"Forget I asked," Liz said, not wanting to see if ADI would connect her to the death of the three men who'd raped her in Iraq.

"Hey, Barry, how are things going?" Catie asked when she met him at Bettie's Burgers.

"Pretty good, especially now that we got to buy our condos," Barry said. "I got a loan for the full value."

"I heard. Smart move telling Kal. We didn't think about how important it was to be able to own the condos."

"That's because you owned all of them," Barry said. He made it sound like a joke.

"Probably, but it could be that we were just stupid."

"Yep, my pappy always said, 'assume it's stupidity before you think it's malice.' Those words kept me out of a lot of fights. Helped me make some friends too."

"That's a good saying, I should probably remember it," Catie said. "You wanted to ask me something?"

"Yeah. Kenyon told me you helped him start his restaurant. Raelyn's mama and mine are wanting to open a restaurant that cooks real southern food."

"I could help. But you just need to go and talk to the credit union. I'm sure they'll loan you the money."

"Kenyon said that, but he suggested I get a referral from you if you were willing."

"Of course, I'm willing. If your mama can cook as well as you can load Russian tanks into an Oryx, then she'll be a success."

"Mama can cook better than that." Barry smiled as he remembered loading up those Russian tanks. "Those Russians sure were confused when we told them we wanted their tanks. Whatever happened to them?"

"The Russians?"

"Yeah, I know what happened to the tanks."

"We kept them in Ukraine in a prison camp until after the war. About half of them decided to stay in Ukraine."

"Probably didn't want to have to answer questions about how they lost those tanks. Too bad the Russians figured it out."

"Yeah. It sounded kind of fun. I wish I could have been there."

"Hey, it was your idea, a pretty good one too. But as I recall, you were captain of the Sakira during that time."

"I guess I wouldn't have traded that," Catie said. "Anyway, how are your kids doing?"

"They're settling in. It didn't take no time before Raelyn decided she wanted to stay."

"Are you two doing okay?"

"I think so, but it'll take time. I was a real ass back then with the PTSD."

"Well, you're a great guy now. Is there anything else I can do for you?"

"Tell me if I should take Kal up on being an officer."

"I'm not sure I can help there."

"What do you think about me as an officer?"

"You're a great sergeant. As an officer, you just need better table manners," Catie said.

"I'll remember you said that. But what else?"

"Are you taking classes?"

"Yes, Kal gave me a list of classes to start taking as soon as I joined up."

"How do you like them?"

"They're okay."

"So you don't hate them."

"Naw. Sometimes they're boring but not always."

"Then you'd probably do okay as an officer. It's being willing to do that kind of work that makes the difference. All that planning and logistics. As a sergeant, your plans deal with more immediate needs. Having to read a bunch of charts and schedule things a few years out kind of makes the difference."

"Anything else?"

"You'd make more money."

"I figured that. Officers always make more than enlisted."

"That's not true," Catie said. "I'm sure you're making more than an ensign."

"Really?"

"Let's check." Catie brought up the pay tables in her HUD. "See, you're making more than an ensign unless they have over eight years of service. And unless they're ex-enlisted, an ensign with eight years of service needs to find another career."

"I'd say. How much more would I make?"

"One thousand a month."

"Auroras?!"

"No, U.S. dollars. I figured you were better calibrated to dollars than auroras."

"So what about after I get promoted to second lieutenant?"

"You pick up another thousand," Catie said.

"That's about the same as if I make gunnery sergeant."

"Looks that way. Delphi forces holds enlisted pay at about seventy percent of officer's two grades below, so an E3 makes 70% of an O1. It starts to diverge once you reach the E7 and O5. If you go for it, with your years in service, you'll be making more money than most of the officers you're working with."

"Hey, I could win some good bets with that. Guys always forget about that years-of-service thing, especially hot-shot officers."

"Right. Anything else I can do for you?"

"Could you take my kids and brothers up to Delphi Station for a tour?"

"Sure!"

"Could you wear a crown for my daughter? She's really impressed with you being a princess."

"Not a chance!"

6   Jump Gates

"Hi, Uncle Blake," Catie said as Blake entered her condo. She'd buzzed him in when his Comm registered with the door.

"Hi. How's it coming?"

"You mean the jump points?"

"Yes," Blake said as he slid down to the floor next to Catie, who was sprawled out on her stomach, leaning on her elbows as she worked on whatever her HUD was projecting. Blake leaned against the wall.

"I should have known you'd be by after I asked you a question about them."

"Why's that?"

"Sheik Dahmani told me that if you let the camel's nose into your tent, you will wake up sleeping with him."

"How's that apply here?"

"He said it applies in business as well as camping. He was telling me why he was so secretive about his businesses. As soon as anyone knows your business, they decide they should be involved."

"I see, so you're saying I'm a camel?"

"If the nose fits."

"Okay, you're right, I want to be involved in these jump points. There are some strategic considerations I want to make sure you're considering and I think it'll be easier if we go over them first."

"Sure, what are you thinking about?"

"First, explain again how they work?" Blake asked.

"Well, basically when you open a wormhole, it is opened along the vector you're targeting at the distance you set. When it opens, it jumps to the closest and lowest gravity spot in the area; it will bend around other gravity wells a little, but it really wants to go in a straight line. The lowest gravity spot is usually defined by the surrounding stars and the system's planets. But if there is a jump probe in the system and it has a wormhole open or it is creating a zero-gravity point, then the wormhole jumps there. If you then open another wormhole into that system, they'll merge. It works best to target the wormhole to the system that has one open. Basically, they cascade from one end to the other. If you move the control to the system without a wormhole and open one from there to the system that has one open, you can continue the cascade and have the most control."

"How big does the wormhole have to be for this to work?"

"Our tests showed that they could be as small as you want. So we could make the probes smaller, but then they wouldn't be able to open a wormhole big enough for them to go through. I haven't decided which is best."

"So we can spend more and make the probes mobile, or we can save money and resources, but then we'd have to send a probe that can open a wormhole to their system if we want to move them. We wouldn't be able to have them just jump to a neighboring system," Blake mused.

"Right, but why would we want to do that anyway? Once they're in place, why would we want to move them?"

"What if someone showed up in the system? We might want to jump the probe to another system to protect it."

"Sure, that would be easy, but wouldn't we see the ship coming for months if not years?"

"Based on what we know, maybe. Starships are pretty small compared to the volume of space that they'd be in while they were approaching the planet. Besides, there might be some cloaking technology that we don't know about."

"I guess if you want to be cautious, then having them able to jump makes sense; you never know when Klingons might show up."

"Very funny. Now, what about the destination point?"

"You mean where you actually want to jump to?"

"Yes."

"Well, once the wormhole is established, the starting point can power it up to whatever size its jumpdrives can manage."

"So your StarMerchant could open up a wormhole big enough to come through."

"Right."

"But what if we want to send the Victory to one of these systems?"

"That would work fine. You'd have to power the wormhole from the end with our jump ships to send her there or to retrieve her."

"Would the same thing would be true if we allowed the Paraxeans to use the jump points?"

"Yes, there would have to be something with a big enough jumpdrive to open a wormhole for their starship, or we would have to open one for them. If there were jump ships in their system, then they could go anywhere and not have to worry about what kind of jump point was on the other end and they would be able to tell exactly where the wormhole was."

"And if we didn't want them to know about the jump ships?"

"They already know about the jump ships."

"Not really, they know we have a jumpdrive. They really don't know exactly how we plan to use it to move the asteroid. And on Paraxea, they only know that the Dutchman has a jumpdrive."

"So why keep it a secret?"

"I'm not the only camel in the galaxy," Blake said.

"But you're probably the cutest."

"Handsomest, not cutest. Now, the Dutchman would need a probe to be in the Paraxean system to open a wormhole from Earth or Artemis."

"Right."

"How long would it take to open the wormhole if the probe jumped in from Paraxea Proxima?"

"Since you only have to establish the connection, it probably could do it right away. It would need six to eight hours of recharge to jump back. But why would we do that?"

"So the probe wouldn't be available for observation or stealing."

"But then you wouldn't know about the system before you jumped. You'd have to send a small probe through to validate that your path was clear."

"Yeah, but we could leave a small satellite in the system to tell us that, and we'd probably want one there to keep track of what was going on anyway."

"That would mean another quantum relay," Catie said.

"Sure, but just one extra at each jump terminus." Blake mused for a minute stroking his chin. "How far out can you open a wormhole to another system?"

"I assume you mean how far away from the star," Catie said. "Sixty AUs is about the minimum from a star the size of Sol and you have to be at least fifty-five AUs out to even be able to open one. The distance is proportional to the mass of the star."

"What if you just want to initiate a wormhole from that end, but are going to power it from the other?"

"That depends; you can open a wormhole while you're out in deep space, you just can't power it enough to jump very far. But if you were powering from the other end, you could jump from anywhere."

"So as long as you're powering the wormhole from one end, you could make a jump from anywhere?" Blake asked.

"From any system close by, or through any cascade of wormholes."

"Okay, let's start with probes being able to jump themselves," Blake said. "I'll think about the jump ships, but for now I assume we won't be allowing other starships to use the wormholes."

"Okay. Does that mean I can get back to work?"

Blake mussed Catie's hair. "What do you mean, we've been working."

"It felt more like an interrogation," Catie said.

"Collaboration," Blake said as he stood up. "Do you want to have dinner with Jackie and me?"

"Where?"

"You assume we're not cooking?"

"I've tasted your cooking and Jackie has better taste, and I know she doesn't like to cook."

"Giorgio's."

"Then sure."

"Yvette!" Miranda called out to get Yvette's attention. "Over here."

Yvette immediately turned and headed to the table where Miranda was sitting with a man she didn't recognize. A very nice-looking man. She was meeting Miranda and friends at Daphne's, a Greek restaurant in Delphi City.

Miranda made the introductions, "Yvette LeClair, Freddy Montgomery, Freddy, Yvette."

Freddy raised up and took Yvette's hand. "I'm pleased to meet you."

"*Enchanté*," Yvette purred.

"Down, girl, he's gay," Miranda said.

"Pooh, what a waste."

"I can assure you that there are many men who do not agree with you," Freddy said.

"But it is for me. I'm just back from my Academy cruise. You cannot date while on the ship, and where do we make port? Nice! Where my mother meets the ship and commands all of my time. Six weeks without a man, and Miranda invites me to lunch with a gay one. *Merde*."

Freddy laughed. "I can see why you would be disappointed. But can we still be friends?"

"But of course. Are you in flight school with Miranda?"

"Yes."

"Then you must have very good taste in men and have many to choose from with all those fighter pilots."

"Down Girl," Miranda said.

Yvette opened a menu, "She is no fun."

"I know. All work and no play," Freddy said.

Liz spotted the trio as soon as she entered the restaurant. She was almost to the table when Miranda spotted her and waved. Liz waved back as she made her way over.

"Hi, Miranda," Liz said.

"Hello, Liz; you know Yvette, and this is Freddy."

"Freddy, Yvette," Liz said as she nodded to them and sat down.

"Hello, Liz," Freddy said in a very inviting tone. "I hear wonderful things about you from Miranda."

Liz smiled. "You have? That's nice of her. I hope some of them are true," she added.

"They were so nice, they must be true."

"Sure."

Miranda looked at Liz, "I thought Alex would be with you," she said.

"We had meetings on different sides of the city," Liz said. "She should be here soon."

"Good. I promised Freddy that I'd introduce him to Alex," Miranda said.

Liz looked at Miranda with curiosity.

"He's looking for a job. He's planning on joining the reserves after graduation and plans to find a civilian job while he does his service."

"You do know that you have to serve on active duty for two years before you join the reserves?" Liz asked.

"Yes, but they will let you work that around a job schedule. Two ten-hour days on the weekend and then four hours each evening during the week," Freddy said. "So I should be able to do that and hold down a job."

"As long as it doesn't require too much overtime or travel," Liz said.

"Overtime I can handle; travel would be tough."

"What's your degree in?" Liz asked.

"I have a master's in marketing," Freddy said.

"Nice. Well, Alex might know of something. She's usually tuned in to the job situation here in Delphi City."

"Here she comes." Yvette stood up and waved Catie toward their table.

"Hello, Alex," Miranda said. "I mentioned I was bringing Freddy to see you. Freddy, Alex MacGregor."

Freddy half stood and extended his hand to Catie. "Delighted to meet you," he purred.

"Hi," Catie said as she slid into the booth next to Liz. "Hi, Yvette, how was your cruise?"

"Lonely."

"You mean boring?" Catie asked.

"Yes, that too."

"Are you rethinking which branch you want to go into?"

"I don't like long cruises, but all the job classifications that would keep me in port are boring."

"Why do you want to be in port?" Liz asked.

"Yvette has trouble with all that discipline you have to maintain when on a ship or space station," Miranda explained.

"Oh, you should apply to be in the intelligence service," Catie said. "They're always playing mind games. You'd like that."

"The intelligence service? I've never heard of it."

Catie laughed. "That's because it's a secret service."

"Hmm."

"Does that mean you'd be interested?"

"Possibly."

"Mention it to Lieutenant Farnsworth," Catie said.

"You mean that boring guy who teaches the history of armed conflict?" Yvette asked.

"Yep. He fades into the woodwork, doesn't he?"

"You're kidding us?" Miranda asked.

"No. But don't go spreading it around. He's just looking for candidates, not spying on the students."

"Maybe I should talk to him," Freddy said.

"Freddy, you do not fade into the woodwork," Miranda said.

Liz leaned over to Catie, "Alex, do you think Freddy would fit in with Marcie? She was saying she needed someone like him on the staff," she said.

"I guess. Are you sure he's what she's looking for?"

"Pretty sure. He's got a master's in marketing."

"But?"

"But what?" Freddy asked. "You do realize I'm sitting right here?"

"Sorry, it's a bit awkward," Catie said.

"It can't be as awkward as sitting here like a side of beef while you two talk about me."

"Well, Marcie is looking for someone who's tuned into the gay scene," Catie said.

"I'm definitely tuned into the gay scene," Freddy said. Then he turned to Liz, "Hey, how did you know I was gay? Did Miranda signal you?"

"Nope," Liz said.

"Then how? Do I have a stamp on my forehead saying gay?"

"No, but, you're attractive and Yvette is ignoring you. You're sitting too close to Miranda unless you're her boyfriend, and since she didn't elbow you when you flirted with me, I assumed you must be gay."

"And how did Alex know I was gay?"

"I didn't," Catie said.

"Our Alex doesn't notice when guys flirt," Yvette said. "She has her head in the clouds thinking about more important things."

Catie gulped and looked offended, giving Yvette a glare.

"It's true," Yvette defended herself.

"Here, let me send you Marcie's contact information. I've sent her a message telling her to expect your call," Catie said.

"You have?" Freddy asked.

"Our Alex has implants so she can type on her Comm by just thinking, they call them a tailboard," Miranda said. "It made it hard to keep up with her at the Academy."

"Please tell me more?" Freddy asked.

"About the implants?" Miranda asked.

"Yes."

"You can get them at the clinic," Catie said. "But you need to be able to get back to the clinic for follow up appointments for the next few weeks. Then you have to be able to dedicate time to practice with them. Also they're a military secret!" Catie glared a Miranda.

"He's in the military."

"I've had mine done recently," Liz said. "You should wait until you're finished with flight school. But Yvette, you could get yours done now."

"I have an appointment tomorrow," Yvette said.

"Miranda, are you still on the Foxes?" Catie asked.

"Yes. I love those jets. And thanks for the heads-up about the simulator. It's been great. I do one to two hours of training on it every day on my own time."

"Good."

"Freddy, which plane are you training on?" Catie asked.

"The Oryx."

"Hmm, are there that many military flights for the Oryx?" Liz asked.

"They're doing more. Mainly for fast crew rotations. They use the Oryx to ferry personnel between Delphi City and Guatemala, and to rotate crews for the surface fleet and Delphi Station."

"Ah, that should make it easy for you to work a civilian job at the same time," Liz said.

"If you're training on the Oryx, how do you and Miranda know each other?" Catie asked.

"Oh, they're making me learn to fly the Fox before they let me learn to fly the Oryx," Freddy said.

"Why's that?"

"Because when one of those crazy Fox pilots pulls a 20G turn and their brains pop out of their ears, they want to be able to recover the Fox, scrape them off the canopy, and put an Oryx pilot in their place. Someone who knows better than to pull a 20G turn," Freddy said.

"Freddy doesn't like dog fights," Miranda said.

Catie laughed. "Oh, that's my favorite part."

"You can keep it," Freddy said.

"What are you and Liz up to for the next few weeks?" Miranda asked Catie and Liz.

"We'll be around," Catie said. "I'm working on a project for MacKenzies so I'll be on Delphi Station quite a bit, but I can come down on the weekends."

"Do you want to go to the new jazz club with us?"

"The one at the Four Seasons?"

"Yes."

"Am I invited?" Liz asked.

"Sure, the more the merrier. Freddy will be there with us."

"I'm her protection," Freddy said.

"Her protection?" Catie asked.

"I chase off any guy that gives her too much unwanted attention."

"How do you do that?" Liz asked.

"I just say and do to them whatever they're saying and doing to Miranda. It gets very awkward," Freddy said with a laugh.

"He's a kick. Why don't we go Friday?" Miranda suggested.

"We're on Delphi Station for a few days. Could we do Saturday?" Liz asked.

"Saturday it is."

"We'll be there," Catie said. "Hey, did any of you go to the town hall meeting?"

"I didn't get back from my cruise until the day after," Yvette said.

"We were doing flight ops," Miranda said. "Was it interesting?"

"The questions at the end were pretty entertaining," Catie said. "You should watch that part of the video. Someone accused Chief Nawal of being a murderer."

"Did she slap him down?"

"It was a her, and the Chief just explained to the woman that she could be connected to several murders and went through the list."

"Oh, nice. So six degrees?" Miranda asked.

"Yep, the chief only had to give three or four examples before the woman got mad and left."

"That must have been hilarious," Yvette said. "Do you want to take a golf lesson with us?"

"I love golf," Freddy said. "I'd be happy to take a lesson with you guys."

"I was asking Alex; I don't think it's the kind of lesson you'd be interested in," Yvette said.

"Maybe it is. Maybe that's why he hasn't asked you out," Miranda said.

"No!"

"Maybe!"

"No!"

"Take Freddy and find out," Miranda said.

"What?" Freddy asked.

"She's been trying to get the golf pro to ask her out," Miranda said. "Two lessons and no bite."

"Oh, he sounds like my kind of guy," Freddy said.

"You mean the golf pro over at the Four Seasons?" Liz asked.

"Yes."

"Oh, he's gay."

"How do you know?"

"A friend told me that was one of the reasons the club hired him. No angry husbands," Liz said.

Catie started laughing, quickly joined by Miranda while Yvette pouted and looked hurt.

"What a waste of time!" Yvette said.

"Well at least you got some help with your game," Freddy said.

"Yvette has a six handicap," Miranda got out between laughs.

◆ ◆ ◆

Bling! Bling! "Out of the way!"

Marc turned to see two bicycles barreling down on him as he was walking across the road. He hopped back to allow them to pass. The second bike stopped.

"Hello, Governor," Katya said.

"Why, hello, Katya. How's business?"

"Booming. It sure is a good thing we got exclusive rights to these trailers. The big boys are real jealous."

"That's good to hear. Aren't you in a hurry like her?" Marc asked, pointing to the first bike that was still barreling down the road.

"Naw, she's got the beer. They won't be in as big a hurry for the steaks and stuff, it's for a picnic."

"You're delivering to a picnic, why the rush then?"

"It's one of those spur-of-the-moment picnics. They got off early because of some problem with the equipment so they decided to have a barbeque. Called us to get the stuff to them."

"I see. Well, I should let you go."

"No, wait. I was wanting to talk to you. We've got a new idea and wanted to see if you could help us again."

"What is this new idea?"

"Drones."

"Drones?"

"Yeah, back home . . . I mean back in our old home, they were starting to use drones to deliver packages. We thought we should see if we could get a jump on that here. Can you check and see if we could get some?"

73

"Hmm, I'll look into it. But I'm not sure about having you girls flying drones around the town."

"Hey, Princess Catie was flying a Lynx when she was only twelve!"

"You do have a point. I'll look into what might be available and get back to you."

"When?"

"Why don't you set up an appointment with Melinda for next week."

"Sure thing. See you then," Katya said as she started to pedal away.

"The joys of being the governor," Marc sighed.

"Catie, do you have some time today?" Marc Commed his daughter.

"I'm free now. It's 2200 here."

"Oh, right. I should have checked."

"No problem. What's up?"

"I've got a request for delivery drones. I wondered what you guys have in the way of designs."

"Oh, speaking of drones, you should get some of our two-person hilos. We've started to sell them to the Delphi City police for their fast response teams."

"Two-person hilos?"

"Yeah. It's just a frame with a polyglass bubble. Two people can sit on it and fly it anywhere in the city. It runs on batteries and can go about ten miles. They're using them to get someone on the scene fast. Then they follow up with bigger vehicles and more people later."

"Interesting. I assume by your comment that ZMS is starting to sell them."

"Yes. I did a rough design, then Nikola worked with Ajda's team to finalize it. We covered all the patents so we have worldwide rights, and I guess interstellar rights."

"Send me the details on that and I'll send it to the three mayors. But back to my delivery drones."

"We can send you a design for those. We don't own all the rights, but we'd cover that in the licensing fee. They're pretty straightforward. Who wants them?"

"You remember the girls I told you about, Katya and Sebrina. Well, they're thinking about expanding."

"Staying ahead of the competition. You have to admire that."

"Yes, even if it creates more headaches for me."

"Hey, there's always Advil."

7   Picky, Picky

"Mr. Verity, Welcome to Delphi City," Siya told the man as she met him at the airport. Siya worked for the real-estate office, and her job was to meet new immigrants to Delphi City and get them settled into their condos.

Mr. Verity just looked at Siya.

"I'm Siya. I've been assigned to get you settled in. I'll take you to the condo you've been assigned so you can drop off your luggage, then I'll take you to Delphi Communications, so you can meet your colleagues, and they'll take over for the day and get you settled into your office. I'll meet you at the end of the day and show you more about how to navigate around Delphi City."

Mr. Verity nodded to Siya and pointed at his luggage. It was stacked on a cart, two suitcases, and a golf bag. Siya shrugged and grabbed the cart and guided it out of the airport terminal. "Right this way, I have a taxi waiting for us."

Mr. Verity followed Siya out of the terminal to the taxi. Siya put his luggage in the back of the taxi with the help of the driver. Mr. Verity just got into the back seat and waited for them. Once the luggage was loaded, Siya got into the taxi beside the driver.

"In Delphi City, nobody is allowed to own cars or other vehicles. Everyone gets around by walking, riding the subway, or taking a taxi. The city is not very large yet, so it's never too far from where you wish to go. Quite a few of our residents work from home most days, so they don't stray too far from their own neighborhoods. The neighborhoods all have a local grocery, restaurants, and other entertainment. So unless you're looking for something special, there's no need to leave it."

Mr. Verity nodded at Siya, then turned his head to watch the scenery go by as they drove out of the airport.

"As you can see, now that we've crossed the causeway and are in the city, there are parks every few blocks. It's laid out carefully so everyone has access to open space. There is a large central park that has a beach, and we also have a horse park where you can ride. It's a nice location and some people go there just to picnic and watch others ride," Siya continued to provide a commentary about Delphi city as they made their way to Mr. Verity's condo.

"Here we are. This is a nice location, right across from the park and just a few blocks from the main commercial district. Your condo is on the top floor, so you'll have a nice view. Once you've been here for six months you can purchase the condo, or choose another one if you like. We've just started selling condos so there aren't that many on the market, but your contract guarantees you the right to purchase this one."

Siya pulled a cart out of the taxi and unfolded it. It was just big enough to handle Mr. Verity's luggage and golf bag. With the help of the driver, she loaded the luggage and got the cart moving toward the building entrance. The driver rushed ahead and opened the door for her. Mr. Verity followed along quietly.

"Each building has its own supervisor. Their job is to handle the maintenance and deal with any issues that the residents have. Their number will be registered on your Comm."

"Comm?" Mr. Verity asked, it was the first time he had spoken.

"Why don't I give you yours now. That'll make it easier to explain." Siya paused in the lobby and pulled a box out of her purse. "There's a Comm in there, it's just like a cellphone, there is also a pair of specs like I'm wearing. They act like a 'Head-Up-Display', Google glasses, if you will. Then there is an earwig that you can put into your ear so you can hear your Comm when you're not wearing the specs or you want it to be private. They have amazing voice recognition and speech synthesis. I never have to type commands in unless I don't want someone to hear me."

Mr. Verity opened the box and picked up the Comm.

"You can clone your existing phone if you like, or just use the Delphi Communications interface. Most people only use their Comm, although you can keep your cellphone if you'd prefer; it works just fine down here. Now, back to the tour. There's a central courtyard through there. It's only for the residents of this building and has a pool and barbeque area. We'll take a quick tour once we drop your luggage."

Siya pressed the call button on the elevator. The door opened immediately and she pushed the cart in. Mr. Verity followed her and moved to the back of the elevator. Siya pressed the button for the top floor and waited while the elevator rose.

When they reached the top floor, the doors opened to a somewhat startled man standing in front of it. "Oh, excuse me," he said as he stepped aside to allow Siya and Mr. Verity to exit the elevator.

"Hello, Mr. Gantry, how are you settling in?" Siya asked.

"Just fine, thank you. I appreciated all of your help. Sir, you're lucky to be assigned Siya, she knows everything there is to know about Delphi City."

"Mr. Verity, this is Mr. Gantry, you'll be neighbors."

"How do you do," Mr. Gantry said.

"Hello."

Mr. Gantry shrugged at the short response. "I'll see you around," he said as he got on the elevator.

"What do you mean we'll be neighbors?" Mr. Verity asked after the elevator door closed.

"Mr. Gantry has the unit right across the hall from you."

"Are there more of them that live in this building?"

"More of them?"

"Blacks."

"You mean people of color like me?" Siya asked.

"Yes, whatever. I was told this was an exclusive condo."

"I don't know who told you that. You were assigned this condo because it is close to where you work. You were assigned the top floor as a perk since Delphi Communications really wants you."

"Fine, but are there more like him in the building?"

"You mean you would prefer a condo where all the neighbors are white?" Siya asked.

"Yes. I lock my doors, but I don't want to have to worry about my safety every time I leave my condo."

"I see. I'm sure I can help you find a condo that will meet your needs, just follow me." Siya used her HUD to summon a taxi and also entered some additional instructions. She led Mr. Verity down to the taxi and again, she and the driver loaded his luggage into the back.

Siya continued to work in her HUD as the taxi drove through the city. After a few minutes, they arrived at the marina. Siya grabbed one of the carts from the rack next to the curb. Then she and the driver loaded Mr. Verity's luggage onto it. She led Mr. Verity into the terminal building for the ferry.

"Where are we going?" Mr. Verity asked.

"We're not going anywhere," Siya said. "Here is a ticket for the next ferry to Rarotonga, and a ticket for the next flight that'll take you back to where you came from. I'm sure that they must have a residential area that meets your needs."

"What?! I've got a job here with Delphi Communications. I'm their new research manager."

"Not anymore. Your contract has been cancelled. If you have any questions, I suggest you contact their personnel office. Don't miss your ferry, your visa has been cancelled, so you won't be able to get a room here in Delphi City. You're welcome to keep the Comm, have a nice trip back to the dark ages."

With that, Siya pushed the luggage cart toward Mr. Verity then turned around and walked away.

"You can't do this to me!" Mr. Verity yelled as he started after Siya.

"Excuse me, sir," a constable said. "The system says your visa had been cancelled, you cannot leave the building."

"What?!"

"This is the port of entry for Delphi City. Things are so automated that sometimes people don't realize that's what it is, but my Comm says you don't have a valid visa. Therefore, you cannot enter the city. There's a ferry leaving in ten minutes that will take you away, or you're welcome to do some shopping and have a meal if you'd like. But you're restricted to the terminal."

"How dare you!"

"I'm sorry, but I'm just here to enforce the rules. You'll need to talk to someone else if you're unhappy with the situation."

Mr. Verity grabbed his cellphone and turned away. He let out a series of expletives as he moved to a sitting area so he could make some calls.

"I'm pretty sure I can guess why his visa was cancelled," the constable whispered as he returned to his station at the entry.

"Uncle Blake," Catie said as she knocked on Blake's office door.

"Hi, Catie, what brings you down here?"

"I just reviewed the Verity video. Good thing Siya kicked him out."

"Yes, I'm surprised they didn't catch the problem during the interview process," Blake said. "Did you have a problem with how Siya handled it?"

"No, but I wanted to ask you about racism," Catie said. "I can't understand it; it's so stupid."

"Isn't this a conversation you should have with your father, or your mother?"

"It's the middle of the night in Orion, and Mom's never good about explaining things like this. Besides, Daddy's always worked at the university, you've been out in the real world more."

"Okay, if you want, I can try."

"Please," Catie begged.

"First thing, it is stupid. But unfortunately, that doesn't mean it's uncommon."

"Why?"

Blake took a deep breath and let out a sigh. "Okay, here's how I explain it to myself. First, humans have a tribal instinct that's from back before the stone age when we had to worry about potential enemies or predators. So we naturally feel an affinity for other humans from our same tribe, people that look like us."

"That's stupid, you can't identify bad people by whether they look like you."

Blake waved his hand at Catie. "That's true today, but the instinct is still there. Now today tribes are defined quite differently, it might be all skateboarders, pilots, farmers; but the thing that is the most distinctive is skin color. It's just one of the first things you notice about someone."

"But that doesn't tell you anything about the person!"

"Not much. You can make some guesses, but especially nowadays you're likely to be wrong. Now back to my lecture. So you have this tribal thing going. Now, most people manage to ignore that. When they meet someone, they have a momentary tribal reaction to them from their low brain, but then their high brain takes over and they use logic to classify the person. Generally, a new person is classified by how they dress and present themselves, but of course, that can fool you too. Plenty of bad people dress nicely. It's important to learn to judge people by their actions not by their physical or social characteristics."

"That makes sense, so why is there racism?"

"That comes from two other deep-seated human needs: the need to be special, and greed," Blake said. "The need to be special is probably the most powerful."

"That doesn't make sense!"

"Come on, we all want to be loved, want to feel like we're special, even that we're better than somebody else. Anyway, the need to be special drives humans to divide everyone into different levels, somewhat like the caste system in India."

"That system is inhuman!"

"Yes, it comes from ages of racism or prejudice, but that doesn't justify it. Now back to the lecture. Every society has these castes, there are plenty of words to identify each of them: white trailer trash, Jews, immigrants, Blacks, gays, blue-collar, middle class, the list goes on. But the fundamental thing is that each caste wants to raise its status relative to the other castes. They want to be close to the upper castes which are the rich people, blue-bloods, folks like that. There are two reasons for that, feeling special and wealth by association."

"Wealth by association, what's that?"

"Well, if you're associated with a caste that's been accepted by one of the wealthy castes, then they'll hire you, loan you money, throw you a bone once in a while. It's the gateway to improving your personal lot. If you're associated with a caste that is not accepted by the wealthy castes, then you're discriminated against. The other castes don't want to associate with you lest your unacceptability might rub off on them and lower their standing."

"That's stupid!"

"Yep, but that's what happens when people don't think past their prejudices."

"So what drives the wealthy castes?"

"Greed and that need to feel superior to everyone else. That is easier to do if you identify a few classes that you target. The problem is that with so much money controlled by so few people, it's easy to isolate a group of people and discriminate against them."

"That's awful."

"It gets worse. By hoarding the wealth and privilege to the few castes they want in their elite circle, it sets up a positive feedback system that lowers the living standard of the other castes. The elite castes have better schools, better access to loans, jobs, food, housing. Not having fair access to those things drives down the living standard of the other castes and takes away from their ability to raise their standard of living. It becomes a vicious cycle."

"Argh!"

"And then that lower standard of living, lower education, is used as an excuse to extend the prejudice."

"That's so absurd. But what can we do about it?"

"What we're already doing. Delphi City and the companies controlled by MacKenzie Discoveries demand that people be evaluated only based on how they perform the jobs assigned to them. Personnel files only have job-related information in them. The ones that get exchanged between managers don't even have names or pictures. Nothing that would trip a bias. The companies use those files kind of like the military. The files go to a promotion board where all the companies' executives meet to figure out how to fill their slots. They select candidates based on the files. There is a round of personal interviews before the final promotions, but you'd better have a good reason for not going with the board's recommendation."

"I didn't know that. What else?"

"We have an excellent education system, and when you have a job, you automatically get access to a free college education. That means everyone has a chance to move up to more challenging jobs. When someone is down on their luck, they can go to one of the dormitories and live for free while they work to get back on their feet. Everyone gets a job."

"What about people who have limited abilities?"

"There's still a job for them. Sometimes their abilities can be raised, sometimes we have to accept what they can do. But hey, the streets need to be cleaned, dishes washed, there is always a job that they can do. You just have to give them a chance and provide access to the resources for them to learn and improve their abilities for better jobs if they want to."

"And kicking people like Verity out!"

"Yes, good thing we figured him out before he became a citizen."

"Ohh, what do we do with those who get through?"

"As long as they do their job, not much. But we have ANDI analyze all the personnel reviews, promotions, and bonuses to make sure there's no prejudice. Anything that looks odd is investigated."

"And if we find some racist on the staff, what do we do?"

"If they're discriminating against people in the company, then they're disciplined, or demoted."

"Demoted, to what?"

"An assembler on one of the production lines if we have to."

"What would someone like Verity do if that happened?"

"He might emigrate to someplace else, or he might learn something and work his way back up the ladder."

"Would we ever trust him again?"

"He'd have to earn it."

◆ ◆ ◆

"Fred, how are you doing?"

"Fine, Catie. Can I help you?"

"I came by to review the schedule for the jump probes."

"You can go over that with Alonso if you want."

"I know, but I wanted to talk with you."

"About something besides the schedule?"

"I was curious about what you thought of the Verity incident."

"I thought it was unfortunate."

"What did you think of the way Siya handled it?"

"I thought she did a great job."

"Did she get approval, first?"

"She told her boss what she was planning to do; she didn't really ask permission. She was following the established protocol after all. Her boss Commed her to go ahead and that she would take the heat if anyone didn't like it."

"Gutsy."

"Yep. Siya's personnel file had a green flag indicating she was a promising promotion candidate before the incident; now we see why. Pretty tough cookie for a seventeen-year-old."

"She's only seventeen? I couldn't tell from the video. I assume she's got a double green flag on her file now."

"Yes, she's pretty impressive. She and her mother are the main support for the family. She has four younger brothers and sisters. They moved here from India two years ago."

"What does the mother do?"

"She works in the caregiver co-op for the community. She's studying to be a teacher."

"That's nice. How old are the children?"

"Fourteen is the next down, the youngest is six."

"That's a lot to deal with. How long before the mother gets her teaching certificate?"

Fred looked the data up, "Two more years; she's going to start as a teacher's assistant this fall, so she'll get a bit of a raise then."

"Do they need help?"

"I don't think so. They're in the standard program. Free rent while the mother is in school. Between the two of them, they do pretty well. Siya might do a little better if she moved out, but it seems like she wants to stay with the family."

"Makes her all the more impressive," Catie said.

"Yep. Are you looking for someone?"

"I'll ask Marcie to look at her, but now that she's got two green flags, everyone will be looking."

"That's right."

"What about her boss?"

"You're too late. That woman was picked up the next day. She's now personnel director for . . .," Fred looked the answer up in his HUD, "interesting, Delphi Communications picked her up."

"Good for them."

8   Preparing for Guests

Catie and Liz met at Bettie's Diner for breakfast after their morning workout. Catie was feeling pretty good since she'd only been thrown once and had nailed Liz twice with strikes.

"Hey, don't go getting cocky on me," Liz said as she slid into the booth across from Catie.

"*Moi?*" Catie said with a big grin.

"Yeah, you. I just had a bad day."

"You mean it wasn't because I'm getting better?"

"That too." Liz gave Catie a big smile. "So, you're going to be spending the day with Dr. McDowell?" Liz asked, changing the subject.

"Yes. We're going to do some more tests on merging the wormholes. Are you looking forward to your day?" Catie asked, smiling.

"No, that's probably why I was distracted this morning. Having to tell fifty-two families that they have to move out of their prime spots in ring six isn't going to be fun."

"They don't have to move."

"Yeah, like they're going to like living there when we up the gravity to 1.4 Gs."

The MacKenzie board had decided to bring the Aperanjens to Delphi Station so they could prepare for their colony mission, but since their native gravity was 1.5 Gs, they had also opted to spin the second section of Delphi Station faster so that they would have 1.4 Gs in the outer ring.

"I'd start by telling them we have to raise the gravity and see if they suggest we move them," Catie said. "You might come off as their friend instead of the big bad wolf."

"That might work."

◆ ◆ ◆

"Dr. McDowell . . . Dr. McDowell!"

"Oh, hi Catie. Are things ready for our test?"

"Yes, ADI has placed the probes in the systems we specified and we've got four asteroids and our probes for test vehicles."

"Okay, then let's see how far we can extend a wormhole," Dr. McDowell said, rubbing his hands together.

It was the most animated that Catie had ever seen him. It had taken a week for the probes to be reconfigured on the Enterprise and to build the extra probes they needed. Apparently, Dr. McDowell was anxious to prove if his math correctly predicted what would happen. The two of them moved to the test consoles they had set up in preparation for the test.

"Okay, do you want to go for broke?" Catie asked.

"Why not. The math says this will work, we've already proved the wormholes will merge, let's go for it."

Catie hadn't expected Dr. McDowell to agree, she was just trying to get him to complain, to get a rise out of him. "Well, then let's open them up."

The six probes were arrayed in various systems close to Earth so they could simulate a jump between Artemis and Earth. They hadn't had the time to get the probes in place for the jump to Artemis yet, but this would be a good test example.

"Opening wormhole from Beta," Dr. McDowell said.

"Micro-wormhole established," Catie announced.

"Opening wormhole from Gamma to Beta."

"We have a wormhole from Alpha to Gamma."

They worked through the six probes until they had a wormhole snaking around the systems.

"Now that we have one established for the full distance, are we ready to power it up to max size?" Catie asked.

"Just another minute, I'm still recording the readings."

Catie drummed her fingers on the desk while Dr. McDowell went through the readings.

"Okay, power it up."

"Powering up."

"Readings match my expectations. Go ahead and push an asteroid through it."

"Pushing asteroid and one probe through," Catie said. "There it goes, . . . and there it is."

"Very good," Dr. McDowell said. "Just as expected."

"Yes, but we only did a three-jump wormhole when we first tested it. Before I go through one in the Roebuck, I'd like to see each configuration tested. Are you ready to see what happens when we make it bend around that blue giant?"

"Yes. The math isn't as clear there. It says it will just bend around it, but that is a very large gravity well."

"Okay, powering wormhole down to micro size. . . . Now opening a wormhole from Zeta to Epsilon."

"They've merged," Dr. McDowell announced. "Now wait while I finish my recordings."

After a minute, Dr. McDowell nodded to Catie and she immediately increased the power to expand the wormhole.

"Holding," Dr. McDowell said. "Another few minutes, please."

Catie had her pointer hovering over the engage button that would send the asteroid through for the entire four minutes and thirty seconds Dr. McDowell used to collect his data. As soon as he gave her the nod, she clicked it.

"Asteroid is through," Catie announced.

"Impressive. The wormhole has to be making a forty-degree bend around that blue giant."

"Nice. And you know that will take four days off the passage to Artemis, eight off of a round trip," Catie said.

"Yes, yes," Dr. McDowell muttered as he moved to his display board and started working on the equations.

◆ ◆ ◆

"How was your day?" Liz asked as she sat down at their table at Giorgio's on Delphi Station.

"Good, we simulated a jump from Earth to Artemis, no hitches. We even had the wormhole bend around a blue giant."

"That's a pretty big deal. When will we be able to get the jump points placed so the Dutchman can use them?"

"We have to talk with Daddy to confirm. Then we need to make the probes. We can use the seven we have now to seed the jumps to Artemis. They might be in place in time for Derek to use them for his trip home."

"What about between Artemis and Paraxea?"

"We'll have to see what Uncle Blake and Daddy agree to. I think we're ready. But we have to finalize the issue about Paraxea knowing about the jump gates."

"After dinner?"

"Sure. And we really should talk to Derek tomorrow. He's got to feel like we've abandoned him."

"He's a big boy, he should be handling it just fine."

Catie chuckled. "I guess. How did you make out with the residents of ring six? You don't look like any of them attacked you."

"No. Forty-six immediately begged me to move them to ring five."

"And the other six?"

"They demanded that we not change the gravity. When I told them that we didn't have a choice, they demanded that we pay for their move and reserve their cabin for them so they could move back into it when we reset the gravity."

"Daddy, Uncle Blake, I want to finalize the jump points design and deployment," Catie said as she started the meeting.

"Are we ready to send the Paraxeans their asteroid?"

"Almost. I think we should do a final test. We need to set the jump points first, then I think we should group the chunks Jimmy cut off of their asteroid when he resized it and send them through with a few empty stasis chambers on them as a final proof," Catie said.

"You're not just trying to get another colony run to Mangkatar are you?" Blake teased.

"Why would you think that?" Catie demanded.

"Well, you guys really made out on that last run," Blake said sheepishly, realizing that he must have hit a sore spot.

"We did, and we'd love another, but I would never do something like that," Catie said, obviously hurt that her uncle would think so poorly of her.

"Sorry, I was just teasing," Blake said. "And I agree, with over a million people on that asteroid, we should err on the side of caution."

"Okay," Marc interrupted the tiff. "Set it up with the governor and whomever you need on your side."

"What about the colonists from the battleship?" Catie asked.

"Damn, I forgot about them. Ask the governor how he wants to handle that. We're keeping that section of the battleship, so we have to either wake the colonists or move the stasis chambers; and we'll want those back."

"I'll talk to the governor about how he wants to deal with that," Samantha offered.

"Thanks, Sam. Now, what do we need to have so we can decide on the jump points?"

"Each jump point needs a quantum relay. Uncle Blake wants them all to be able to open a wormhole large enough for them to jump through to the next system, which will cost more and use up more platinum metals, but simplifies deployment."

"So what's the issue?" Marc asked.

"I was getting to it. Uncle Blake and I discussed the final jump point. We were discussing whether to have a non-jump probe in the system to track what was going on and just jump the jump-probe in from an uninhabited neighboring system when we need to open a wormhole. But that begs the question of whether we should also have a non-jump probe in the alternate system so we would know what's going on there before we jump back."

"Why would we want to do that?" Marc asked.

"Well, the whole point of putting the jump-point into the neighboring system is so that no one can study it. What if someone were to enter the neighboring system while we were away," Blake said.

"That seems highly unlikely. We can always add a probe later. Let's just stay with the two. We need to be careful with how many quantum relays we use."

"Okay, then the priority of deployment? Right now, we have Earth to Paraxea, Earth to Artemis, and Artemis to Paraxea, Earth to Mangkatar, Mangkatar to Artemis, and Mangkatar to Paraxea."

Liz interrupted, "What about Earth to the Onisiwo system? I think we need to be prepared for whatever happens there. Who knows what the Fazullans are doing to them now?"

"When does the Solar Explorer get to Onisiwo?" Marc asked.

"It's still a week out," Catie said.

"Okay, let's prioritize getting a set of jump-points from Earth to Onisiwo, then Earth to Artemis, then Mangkatar, and finally Paraxea. We can worry about the between-colony jumps later," Marc said. "Blake, does that meet with your approval?"

"Yes, we can move things around later if we need to. What's the story on our frigates?"

"The design is done, Ajda is starting to extrude the first hull," Catie answered.

"Okay, timing is slower than I'd like, but I guess that would be true no matter when they were going to be done."

"It takes time," Catie said. "I'll work with Ajda on the schedule. Maybe we can figure a way to speed it up."

"Yes, and it takes priority over your next StarMerchant," Marc said.

"I know," Catie groaned. "I'll start moving the probes we used for our test and place them along the path to Onisiwo. We're already making the additional probes, so we should be able to start sending them out. It'll take four or five weeks to deploy them."

"Why so long?" Liz asked.

"They can only power a wormhole that's four or five light-years distant. They can open one farther if they're not going to jump through it. But since they have to jump through it, it takes two or three jumps to reach each jump point. We can cycle through the probes to expedite the jumps, using a different one for each jump, but they need eight hours to recharge, so we can just cycle through them once every eight hours, and the number of probes drops for each jump point since we'll be leaving one behind."

"Okay, okay, I'm sorry I asked," Liz said.

"Liz, are you ready to come pick up the Onisiwoens and Aperanjens?" Blake asked.

"I'm heading out on Sunday."

"Are the accommodations ready?"

"We've got people moving, starting Monday. Should have the ring cleared by mid-week. Then they'll spin Section II up to the higher speed. I'm not aware of any modifications to the cabins."

"No, they've been happy with the accommodations here on Gemini Station, so that should work. Liz, how many Oryxes are you bringing out?" Blake asked.

"We're going to use ten," Liz replied.

"So you're planning on four trips?"

"No, we're going to set up a relay, so they show up at Delphi Station one at a time."

"Smart, that will simplify the effort to bring them all out of stasis, and we don't have room for that many here anyway," Blake said.

"Okay, sounds like we have a plan," Marc said. "Call if something comes up, otherwise we'll chat when the Solar Explorer reaches the Onisiwo system."

◆ ◆ ◆

"Was that Lena I heard?" Liz asked as she came into the living room of Catie's and her condo.

"Yes, she came to do my hair. She just left."

Catie turned around to show off her hair. It was in a French twist. She'd opted to wear her evergreen party dress to the jazz club. Yvette had really liked it, so Catie thought she'd see if her wearing the dress would make Yvette jealous. It hit just above her knees, a snug fit that flared from the waist.

"You had her come to do a French twist? I could show you how to do it yourself."

Catie gave Liz a glare.

"Oh, right, I forgot who I was talking to. Anyway, I love the dress. When did you get it?"

"Grandma-ma gave it to me."

"I wish I had people giving me dresses," Liz said.

"We're the same size, if you need something else, grab one from my closet. I've got way more than I'll ever wear. That's a new one," Catie said, nodding at Liz. Liz had opted for a blue cocktail dress that really hugged her body.

"I picked it up last week. I really like the new dress shop Ms. Shammas opened."

"It is nice. Who would have thought making knockoff ship suits would lead her to owning the most exclusive dress shop in Delphi City."

"She has an eye for style. Let's go, our taxi is waiting."

"Where's Morgan?"

"At the club. She's having Maxi guard us on the way over so she can scope out the club before we get there."

"And that means she gets to enjoy the music," Catie said with a small laugh. "That Morgan is always working the angles."

As Catie and Liz entered the jazz club, she nodded to Morgan, who had grabbed a seat close to the door. It didn't give her the best view of the stage, but it gave her a view of the room and control over the door if necessary. The room was arranged in an arc in front of the stage. There were two levels, so the back tables had a nice view as well. A bar was along the side wall so the people there could sit sideways and see the stage.

"Wasn't that Azem at the door?" Catie asked Liz.

"Yes, Morgan must have persuaded the club to let him be the doorman for tonight."

"I'm sure no one is going to mess with him." Azem was 190 centimeters of solid muscle, and with his shaved head, he looked wicked.

"It's kinda crowded," Liz said as she observed the closely spaced tables.

"Are you worried about social distance?"

"Yeah."

"Shouldn't be a problem. They just converted the airflow system in here to downflow. If you look, you'll notice that some of the floor tiles are porous. There are return air vents along the bottom of the wall and along the step up to the back tier. Everything is designed to keep the flow moving downward. It actually makes it nicer, no drafts since the airflow is well distributed."

"If the floor is porous, how do they clean it?"

"They mop it with muriatic acid. Then bots clean out the ducts."

"How did you know about it?"

"MacKenzie Real Estate is paying to convert all the restaurant and bar spaces. So it came across my desk to review the design," Catie said.

"No more shop talk, here they are."

"You ladies look lovely," Freddy said as Liz and Catie joined the trio at the booth they'd managed to grab. It was just off-center of the stage.

"Why thank you," Liz said.

"I forgot to steal that dress before you moved out," Yvette said as Catie sat down.

"If you want it, I'll send it over next week."

"Please, I'd like to wear it at least once."

"You should come check out her closet," Liz said. "Her grandparents like to give her dresses but Alex hates to wear them."

"Drat, Yvette is always the lucky one," Miranda said with a frown. She had a slightly thicker build than Catie, so wouldn't be able to fit in her dresses. "Alex, did you finish your project?"

"Mostly," Catie said. "Liz has to make a trip to Gemini Station next week, and I have some follow-up work to do. Why, do you have other plans?"

"No, just wondered. We'll be back in training on Tuesday, so there won't be time for much."

"I'm still free," Yvette said.

"Do you want to fly an Oryx?" Liz asked.

"Hmm," Yvette mused. "Fly an Oryx for a week, or lounge around and go out to parties at night?"

"You mean you're going to turn down the opportunity to fly to Gemini Station?" Catie asked, dumbfounded.

"You are so young and enthusiastic," Yvette said. "I will be able to fly an Oryx in the future, but there are only so many days when I can go to the spa."

Catie shook her head, she couldn't believe Yvette would pass up the opportunity for free training.

"Young and enthusiastic?" Freddy asked in a whisper.

"Alex is much younger than the rest of us," Yvette said. "She skipped most of high school. So we try to watch out for her."

"Oh, so you three are like her aunties," Freddy said.

"I think our Freddy has a death wish," Liz said as she slipped her hand over Freddy's. He smiled as she caressed the webbing between his thumb and forefinger. Then his eyes went wide in pain and terror as Liz pressed on the pressure point there. Sweat beaded on his forehead as he used his right hand to steady himself.

"Ah . . . I . . . meant . . . older sisters," he stammered.

Liz eased up on the pressure point, but only a little.

"Her beautiful and sexy older sisters," Freddy added.

Liz looked at Freddy with a smile but didn't ease up on the pressure point any.

"Waiter, please bring a round of drinks for the ladies," Freddy said. A little extra pressure from Liz and he added, "And please put all their drinks for the night on my tab."

Liz patted Freddy's hand. "You are truly a generous man."

Catie was struggling to suppress her giggles. She felt sorry for Freddy, she knew how much pain that pressure point delivered. She suspected that Freddy would find a way to avoid sitting next to Liz in the future. And he probably would be moving as soon as he could get away with it.

"Here comes the band," Yvette announced.

The band made its way on stage. There was a bass player, a drummer, a guitarist, a sax player, and a trumpeter; a piano stood along the side, but there wasn't anyone at it yet. The musicians played a few notes as they tuned their instruments. Then the sax player came to the microphone.

"It's my pleasure to introduce Miguel Cordova."

The crowd applauded as a tall man came out on stage. He was wearing a dark suit, and he had that two-day shadow look on his face. He smiled at the crowd as he grabbed the mic. He sang 'Embraceable You' in a low sultry voice.

"He sounds like Nat King Cole," Liz whispered.

"Shhh!"

The band finished the set with 'Route 66'. After the applause, Miguel walked over to their table. "Miranda, it was nice of you to come."

"I wouldn't miss it for the world. Guys, this is my cousin Miguel; Miguel these are my friends, Alex, Liz, Yvette, and Freddy."

Freddy stood up and extended his hand. Miguel grasped it for a handshake, but Freddy held onto it just a bit longer, giving Miguel a bright smile.

Miguel laughed at Freddy. "Not me, but the bass player is looking for someone to show him around town."

Freddy immediately excused himself and went to find the bass player.

"How was your trip?" Miranda asked.

"Nice, they brought us here on one of those supersonic private jets. Now that's the way to travel," Miguel said.

"How long are you here for?" Liz asked.

"Two weeks."

Catie was smiling at Miguel and sighing to herself before Liz pinched her.

"Oh, where are you going after that?" Catie asked.

"Nothing's booked yet."

"Are you going to play on Delphi Station?"

"We weren't booked for there, but that would be nice."

"ADI," Catie messaged.

"Cer Catie, would you like me to arrange a booking?"

"Yes."

"They can play for four days after the end of their engagement here."

"There's a booking available right after you finish here," Catie said.

"How do you know that?" Miguel asked.

"Oh, our Alex has her ways," Miranda said. "Rest assured if she says there's a booking available, there is. You will stay and play, won't you?"

"I'd love to. How will we get there?"

"Alex will probably fly you there herself."

"You're booked, the hotel will make the arrangements," Catie said.

"Hmm, you're quite mysterious," Miguel said. "What do you do?"

"Liz and I work for StarMerchants. We pilot their cargo ship."

"More like captain it," Miranda said.

"Interesting, you'll have to tell me more. But right now, I think they want me on stage."

Catie watched as Miguel walked away.

"Alex . . . Alex . . . Catie!" Liz hissed.

"Oh la la, the pheromones are just dripping off that man," Yvette said.

"Huh," Catie said, her face turning red. She had never had her body react to someone after just meeting them. She hoped her friends hadn't noticed.

"It's called having the hots for someone," Yvette said, waving her hand in front of Catie like a fan. "I'm glad to see you're not immune. I was beginning to worry about you."

"Alex, don't feel bad about it, I think Miranda was the only one immune to him," Liz said.

"You guys, he's my cousin!" Miranda said.

"That's good, less competition," Yvette said with a smirk.

Fortunately, the band started up. They began the set by playing 'Fly Me to the Moon'.

At the end of the set, Miguel came back to their table, and Freddy headed off again.

"Are you enjoying the show?" Miguel asked.

"Yes."

"Immensely."

"Good. So, Miranda, you have a couple of days off?"

"Yes. Since we came today instead of yesterday, I traded Friday duty with a friend, so I'm off until Tuesday."

"The guys want to go fishing, any chance you know where we can charter a boat?"

"Doesn't the hotel offer them?" Liz asked.

"Yes, but they're full. Apparently, six guys is a big group for most of the charter boats they have available."

"ADI?"

"Cer Catie, the Mea Huli is available," ADI reported.

"I know a guy who can take you out," Catie said.

"You do? You really are a miracle worker," Miguel said.

"It's a big yacht, you can even go overnight if you want. I'll send you his contact information."

"What will it cost?"

"Just pay for fuel."

"Are you talking about the Mea Huli?" Liz asked.

"Yes."

"Then fuel will be real cheap," Liz said, alluding to the fact that since they had installed a fusion reactor in the Mea Huli last year, it didn't use any fuel.

"Caesar will present you with a fuel bill. But like Liz says, it shouldn't be too much," Catie explained. "Caesar compensates himself for 'free' cruises by making up a modest fuel cost to be compensated by the guests."

"That's my kind of deal. What else should we bring?" Miguel asked.

"You'll need to bring your own beer. The boat is stocked with food, so Caesar will be able to feed you. Caesar is the guy who manages the boat."

"And he cooks?"

"He's versatile. He lives on the Mea Huli. Of course, he gets kicked off once in a while when someone wants to take it out for a private cruise," Catie explained.

"Will you come with us?" Miguel asked.

"I can't, I've got things I have to do Sunday and Monday," Catie said.

"And I'm flying to Gemini Station tomorrow," Liz said.

"Miranda?"

"Sure, can Freddy come?"

"Why not. Will you guys come back for another show?" Miguel asked.

"We can probably come next Saturday," Liz said.

"I'll leave tickets for you at the desk."

"Tickets?" Miranda asked.

"Yes, we're a big-deal band. They charge money for people to come in and see us. How'd you get in?"

"I just told them we were with Alex and they showed us to this table."

"Hmm," Miguel mused looking at Catie.

"I know the event manager, Sandra Bishop. She's dating a friend of mine."

◆ ◆ ◆

"What are you busy doing tomorrow?" Liz asked Catie as the two of them left the jazz club.

"Not being stuck on the Mea Huli with six jazz musicians that are trying to figure out how to fish while drinking beer."

"What about Miranda and Freddy?"

"I don't think Freddy's going to be on deck that much, and Miguel is Miranda's cousin, they'll be able to talk about family."

"You could have kept her company. And that Miguel is pretty hunky."

"He is, but he's too old for me. And Miranda is a big girl, she can manage it by herself."

◆ ◆ ◆

"Hi, Ajda," Catie said as she walked into Ajda's office on Delphi Station. The office was a big room with Ajda's desk and models of various ships mounted on the wall. It had a big work table in the center where she was working.

"Don't tell me. Marc wants the frigates sooner."

"Good guess."

"Not a guess. Doesn't he understand that things take time?"

"He understands; he just doesn't like it. I told him that we would spend some time looking at the process to see if we could come up with a way to speed things up."

"I guess it can't hurt to try. We might learn something."

"What's the bottleneck? Wait, don't tell me, the gravity drives."

"Yes. They're so huge and they have to mount to the hull, so it's hard to do anything. They have to fit snug against the hull, so you can't spin the hull around them."

"Can't you just spin the girth, then slide each gravity drive into place and weld it there? Then you could spin up the rest of the hull with them in place."

"Okay, let me map this out. We build the drives and reactors. There are four of each and they're laid out in quadrants anyway; so we put the gravity drives in first, then build the reactors around them while we continue to spin the hull out. Doing it that way instead of printing the gravity drives in place will save four weeks, though it'll cost a lot more since you're adding work. But it does let you parallel a lot of it."

"That sounds good. Can you do the same with the cabins and the bridge?" Catie asked.

"Sure, won't save that much extra time since there are not that many cabins. Most of the ship consists of the three flight bays and the cargo hold."

"I know, but every little bit helps."

"Okay, let me send this off to the team and they can work out a detailed plan. I think we'll just finish the hull we started while we do all this. Then we can push it aside while we make the next three. We'll work on it as things allow, but it'll probably be the last one done."

"If we get the next one faster, it'll be worth it."

"You got it."

"Okay, I'll tell Daddy that you're going to be nice and mess up your plan just for him."

"Thanks. You sure you don't want to come work here? You've turned into an exceptional engineer and project planner."

"I don't know. I'm not sure I'd be able to stay focused when things settle in. It was easy when it was all new to me, but now it seems . . ."

"Boring?"

"Not that exactly."

"Hey, I know what you mean. You can only run a detailed stress map on a ship a few times before you want to pull your hair out. Fortunately, ANDI does a lot of the work for me, so I get to keep my hair."

"How's he doing?" Catie asked. ANDI was the DI they had built to replace ADI on the Sakira so they could move her to Delphi Station. He was now in Delphi City, having been replaced by an AI that wouldn't become sentient. All the ships now had AI, since there was a high probability that becoming sentient would drive a DI insane.

"He does pretty good. He still requires very exact instructions, but hey, it's way faster to set a problem up with him than with a computer."

"What else are you working on?"

"I haven't started the project yet, but the Four Seasons has asked us to figure a way to get passengers to Delphi Station without having to go through microgravity."

"What?!"

"They have people that want to come up but do not want to have to deal with microgravity. Apparently, they are afraid to embarrass themselves by getting sick."

"And that's worth designing a new entry port?"

"Well, we have some cargo that people swear doesn't like microgravity as well. And for small stuff, it would be more efficient."

"So what are you thinking? Adding a docking port on the outside of ring three?"

"Yes, and that lets them on board without going through microgravity, but how do they get into orbit without the transition?"

"Oh, that's easy," Catie said.

"If it's so easy, then why don't you explain it to me?"

"Design a shuttle with gravity drives, then it can take off, go to the north pole while still experiencing full gravity. Then it just starts circling at a two- or three-k radius, speeding up as it climbs out of the gravity well. It should be able to balance the speed and the gravity strength from Earth to maintain a constant internal gravity. Once it reaches the right altitude, then the pilot just starts to extend the orbit until it's on the same orbital plane as the station. Balancing the Earth's gravitational pull and the rotation shouldn't be too difficult. Definitely not as complex as syncing up with the station's rotation while in orbit.

With the gravity drive, you don't even have to actually set the shuttle down on the station. Just hover a few centimeters up, that way the station won't have to deal with the big change in mass."

"Oh, that is easy. We can use that iris you and Dr. Zelbar designed. Then the passengers can move from the shuttle into the station with a minimal wait and avoid using an airlock."

"You could use a boarding gate like at the airport that seals against the shuttle and leads directly into the interior. That would give you an extra layer of safety against sudden decompression."

"Nice. What made you think of this?"

"I'm thinking about a luxury liner to tour outer space. Avoiding microgravity seemed more important for something like that. The starship could cruise by the rings of Saturn, then bring you home. What do you think?"

"Do you want a partner?"

"Hmm. I'll ask Liz. We should probably make it be a separate company from StarMerchants."

"Definitely. You don't want cargo to be associated with your cruise line in anyone's mind. Not when you're charging them up the wazoo for a cruise around the solar system."

"I'll let you know. We'll probably look at doing something next year."

"I'll start saving my money," Ajda said.

9   Welcome to Delphi Station

Catie spent the next two days making sure things would be ready for the Aperanjens to arrive at Delphi Station. The last of the residents were moved out of ring six by Tuesday and they started to spin up the gravity on Wednesday. They rigged up a temporary docking port for the Aperanjens on the top of the hub for Section II. This would keep the aliens out of sight of the other residents on Delphi Station as well as shorten their transit into ring six.

On Wednesday, Catie met with Captain Clark and Ajda to review the design concept for the docking bay on the outer rings. Captain Clark approved the design phase for the project.

"Catie, are you ready for us?" Liz asked. She and Catie were reviewing the status before the first Oryx of Aperanjens docked at Delphi Station.

"I guess. Section II is spun up so ring six has a gravity of 1.4 Gs."

"You're sounding uncomfortable. What's up?"

"Oh, I'm just worried about meeting them," Catie said.

"Why?"

"They're kind of ugly and I don't want to offend them by reacting weird when I see them."

Liz laughed.

"It's not funny."

"Sorry. I know what you mean, but here, look at this guy," Liz said as she threw a video up so Catie could view it. It showed a little Aperanjen kid running away from his parents and the elevator at Gemini Station. His arms were pumping hard as he ran. He ducked under a rope and dove under some seats. His parents pinned him between them, and after trying to crawl away, he finally surrendered and allowed his parents to take him by the hand and lead him back to the elevator.

Catie laughed. "What was he running away from?"

"I don't know, something about the elevator spooked him. But he's so innocent, and isn't he cute?"

"Yes."

"Just remember every adult Aperanjen has a cute child just like that inside them. All races and species seem to have cute babies and tiny tots; you just have to visualize the little guys when you meet the adults until you get used to them."

"Okay, I'll try that," Catie said. "See you in two hours."

"Whew," Catie let out a deep breath.

"Are you nervous?" Captain Clark asked. He and Catie were waiting in the gravity side of the hub to meet the leaders of the Aperanjens as they arrived at Delphi Station.

"Just a little. This is the first time I've greeted an alien dignitary."

"But you met some of them on Gemini Station."

"Yes, but then I was just Catie. This time I have to be Princess Catherine."

"I'm sure they're just as nervous as you," Captain Clark said.

"I hope so."

"Here they come." The elevator door opened and the first six Aperanjens and Liz stepped off.

"Counselor Faroot, may I introduce Princess Catherine of Delphi Nation. Princess, this is the senior leader of the Aperanjens, Counselor Faroot."

Counselor Faroot clasped his right hand into a fist and thumped it against his left pectoral in salute. He gave a slight bow of his head as he did so. "Thank you for having us."

"Counselor Faroot, we are delighted to have you. Welcome to Delphi Station," Catie said. "With me is Captain Clark, the commander of Delphi Station." Captain Clark gave a slight nod of his head and returned the salute.

"We've designated this section of Delphi Station for your people," Captain Clark said. "Let us take the elevator up to ring five. Delphi

Station has two sections, each with three rings. Ring five is the second ring of Section II. We've increased the spin so that ring six, the outer ring, will have 1.4 Gs. But for the comfort of the Princess, we'll be conducting our meeting in ring five."

"We are very happy that you've been able to accommodate our need for higher gravity," Counselor Faroot said. "With children, it is important that they experience the correct gravity so their bones develop the proper strength."

"We were happy to do that," Catie said. "The gravity on ring five is only five percent higher than our usual gravity. Since Section II is just starting to be populated, it was easy to direct our people to ring five instead of ring six. We just hope the accommodations meet your needs."

"We were told that they would be the same as on Gemini Station."

"That is correct."

"Then they will be luxurious compared to what we are used to. Even on our homeworld, most of us would not have such nice accommodations."

The delegation quietly followed Captain Clark and Catie to the lift that would take them to ring five. It was only a couple of minutes before they entered the conference area that Samantha had told Catie to configure. It was luxurious by Delphi standards; it mirrored Marc's office in Delphi City. It had a mahogany conference table which complemented the mahogany wainscoting and mahogany crown molding around the walls. The table was surrounded by real leather chairs, all of it sitting on a huge Turkish rug. The center position of the table had been given an extra treatment to highlight Catie's position, with the Flag of Delphi behind her seat.

"I'm sorry I'm late," Samantha said as she entered the room.

"But Sam's on Artemis, and she's eight months pregnant," Catie thought.

"Gotcha!" Samantha texted both Catie and Liz. *"Penny will be my avatar."*

"ADI!"

"I was sworn to secrecy."

Penny walked over and sat next to Catie and whispered, "Did you get the message?"

"Yes!" Catie messaged.

"Stay focused. This is your show," Samantha messaged Catie.

"Counselor Faroot, Ambassador Newman is our interplanetary ambassador," Catie said. "She's here to provide counsel and answer any questions of a diplomatic nature." Rhino and a few of the Aperanjens that had been awakened early had selected several of the members of the original crew and a couple of the more experienced descendants to be their representatives.

Counselor Faroot introduced the other members of their party while Masina served coffee to everyone. The Aperanjens treated coffee like manna from heaven. They loved the cream just as much, mixing it fifty-fifty. Fortunately, Liz had warned Masina to bring lots of cream.

"Again, I want to welcome you to Delphi Station." The Comms provided an interpretation to everyone as Catie talked. "I'd like to point out a few things that I believe will help avoid confusion later on. First, Earth, our homeworld, is not under a unified government. Delphi is an independent nation among many on Earth. Because of this, we would like to keep your presence on Delphi Station a secret. We have not informed the other governments of Earth about details of our encounter with the Fazullans, other than that we won the encounter. We fear that if the press were to learn of your presence, they would create a panic among the people. I hope you understand."

"We do. I suspect that the gutter press is a galaxy-wide plague. An unfortunate side effect of having a free press."

"We agree," Catie said, suppressing a snicker as she thought about how Sophia would react to the comment. "Also it is important to know that Delphi Station and Earth's space fleet are actually owned by MacKenzie Discoveries, a private corporation, and it is that private corporation that has made the offer to provide you with a planet suitable for your colonization."

"A private corporation?" Counselor Faroot asked. "Is this translation correct, that private individuals own that company and control all that you described?"

"That is correct. My father is the majority stakeholder," Catie said. "It is the goal of our company and Delphi Nation to create a league of planets in this galaxy that will trade with each other and work together to ensure their combined prosperity and safety."

"That is a lot for a private company to do."

"Yes, but with a fractured government on Earth, it was felt that it would be the only way. MacKenzie Discoveries owns all the technology that allows us to explore and colonize space, so the burden is upon us to do it."

"An admirable goal. And you, you are a princess?"

"Yes, Delphi Nation was founded by MacKenzie Discoveries and set up by my father to be a model nation on Earth. He is the Monarch of Delphi. We hope that in time the governments on Earth will realize that their common bond is greater than their differences and form a united government, that they will create a unified voice from Earth that will further our expansion into the galaxy."

"I see; that explains why Admiral Prince Blake was able to be so confident in his offer. Please, may we move to that discussion?"

"Of course. MacKenzies has been searching for habitable planets for almost a year. We have eight probes out searching. However, the parameters of the search were set based on Earth and Paraxean physiology; so we have been ignoring planets with a gravity that is more than 25 percent higher than ours. We have noted their existence, but have not made any surveys of them."

"So you have found some?"

"Yes. We are sending the probes back to look at five candidates. But it will take several weeks before they are able to circle back to them. Once we have done a preliminary survey, we'll send out a team to do a more detailed survey. Your people are invited to participate in the survey."

"That is most gracious. Can you explain what you know about the planets so far?"

"The five we have selected all have gravity between 1.4 and 1.6 times our gravity. They all have oxygen atmospheres and significant bodies of water," Catie explained.

"Then what else do you need to know about the planet? Couldn't we just go to our original destination?"

"We still don't know where that planet is. For other planets, we would want to know that there is no sentient life on the planet, the percent of oxygen in the atmosphere, that there are no pathogens that would be harmful to your people, that food that will sustain you will grow there, and that there are sufficient quantities of the minerals and elements necessary to build a modern society."

"To us, that knowledge would be a luxury. We had expected to terraform the world we were going to, taking as much time as necessary."

"We understand. But with our jumpdrive, that level of risk is unnecessary. Now Ambassador Newman will go over the various details of the offer."

"Thank you, Princess," Penny said. "Counselor Faroot, MacKenzie Discoveries will provide you with a suitable planet and sufficient resources for you to establish yourselves there, . . ."

"But?" Counselor Faroot said.

"Yes, but, we would like to establish a more beneficial arrangement. We would like to provide you the resources to accelerate your transformation into a modern civilization. To accomplish that will require a significant investment."

"And for this investment, you would want?"

Penny and Samantha were clearly frustrated at the counselor's continued interruptions, but Penny maintained her calm. "We would want a mutual defense agreement and two percent of the value of your exports for the next fifty years."

Counselor Faroot pushed back in his chair, staring hard at Penny. "Two percent for fifty years. What about our imports?"

"We feel that it would be difficult for you to manage a tax on your imports, it could limit how you attract investors and other colonists. We see the tax on exports as sufficient."

"I see. And what do you imagine the trade would consist of?" Counselor Faroot asked with disdain.

"I'm sure your world, like ours, has a dark history of colonialism," Penny said. "We would like to avoid any repeat of that situation. As you know, trade flows from plenty to need. In the beginning, you will have plenty of land and natural resources, so we would expect the trade to consist mainly of foodstuffs and high-value minerals. However, over time, we will assist you in establishing your own manufacturing capabilities. That will allow the trade to move up the chain and involve the exchange of manufactured goods as well as natural resources."

"What about our right of government?"

"We would provide advice, but how you manage and govern your colony will be up to you. Our only requirement is that you respect the rights of all sentient races to the same extent you do your own citizens."

"The Princess mentioned mutual defense earlier."

"Yes. We will provide a frigate which we will station in your system. We would ask that you allow the crew some access to the planet, although, with the high gravity, that might not occur very often. They will provide a first line of defense should some natural disaster happen, such as an asteroid in a high-risk orbit, or should some different race enter the system. We will also place probes around the fringe of the system to warn other races that the system is occupied and protected," Penny explained.

"Would our people be expected to serve in your military?"

"It would not be a requirement, but we would welcome it," Catie interjected. "It would also increase your people's awareness of some technology that you might learn to leverage to your advantage."

"What about education?"

"Much of our education is facilitated by an AI. We would provide you with an AI for your planet; it would have access to all of our unclassified information. We would also provide you limited access to our DIs which have more cognitive ability, but that access would be limited. That will provide you access to technical training and allow you to set up an education system that spans our knowledge and yours. We would also provide access to scholars on Earth to augment where needed," Penny said.

"I see. We were told that we are here for training. What does that mean?"

Penny nodded to Catie.

"Our machinery and technology will be different than what you're used to. We need you to work with it, learn how to use it. That way you'll be familiar with it when you establish your colony. Also, we need you to identify changes that might be necessary to accommodate any specific needs your physiology requires or even those you would prefer. Also, you may wish to have us replicate technology or machines that you're more familiar with. We have a design team and scientists who can help to facilitate that. When we established Artemis, we only shipped critical components. They built the bulkier components on-site, so we would want to train your people how to do that."

"That is interesting. Somewhat more complex," one of the other members of the Aperanjen delegation said.

"We could send a few of your people to Artemis to study what they have done. But minimally you will be able to observe what they've built, ask questions, and study their documents and videos about what they've done and learned."

After another hour of discussion, Catie ended the meeting. "We will let you go. I'm sure you wish to get settled into your new accommodations and facilitate the arrival of the rest of your people. As I'm sure Commander Farmer has told you, your people will be arriving on three flights per day over the next two weeks. Let us know if there's anything we've missed. We'll talk again in two days."

◆ ◆ ◆

"You did good," Samantha said as Catie got up to leave the meeting.

"Thanks. And very funny springing Penny on me." Catie swatted at Samantha's image.

"I know how you like surprises. The Aperanjens put a lot of stock in personal appearances, so using Penny was the easiest way."

"I was shocked when she showed up and wasn't pregnant. Speaking of that, when am I going to be an big sister?"

"Any day now."

"Am I having a baby sister or a baby brother?"

"You'll be getting a sister or a brother, I'm the one having the little imp."

"Don't talk that way about my baby brother!"

"Your baby sister or brother likes to kick me at the most inopportune times. And 'e's got my bladder squeezed down to the size of a pea."

"So it's a he!"

"I said 'e. That goes for either he or she. You'll find out the sex right after your father does, which will be right after e's born."

"Do you know the sex?"

"Of course. Dr. Marrock and I are the only ones who know."

"And me!" ADI chimed in.

"I should have known you would know," Catie said.

"Of course I would. And don't try to get me to tell," ADI said.

"I'll talk to you later," Samantha said.

"So she wouldn't tell you the sex," Liz said. She'd been trailing behind Catie and had overheard the conversation.

"No! Nattie says she's as big as a house, so I'm guessing a boy," Catie said.

"Birth weight isn't a good indicator of sex," Liz said.

"We'll see. Where do you want to go for dinner?"

"The Four Seasons or Deogenes."

"Let's do the Four Seasons."

Once the waiter had finished serving the wine, Liz proposed a toast.

"To our new colonists!"

"Cheers," Catie said as she tapped her glass to Liz's.

"Why are you so glum?"

"Oh, I'm just frustrated," Catie said. "I feel stuck here babysitting the Aperanjens."

"Remember, you should be stuck on the Dutchman delivering cargo," Liz said. "This has to be more interesting."

"I guess, but we're going to do a test run on delivering the asteroid to Mangkatar next week. I wanted to be there."

"You can run the test from here. Don't tell me you would really spend two weeks to get there?"

"I guess not. But this seems . . . boring."

"Hey, it can't be all fun and games all the time. And you'll get to learn more about the Aperanjens, that should be interesting."

"I guess."

"Come on, what's really bothering you?"

"I feel trapped. Everywhere I go, I'm Princess Catie, or '*That* Lieutenant McCormack', or '*That* Catie McCormack'. I never thought I'd miss the Academy."

Liz laughed. "I knew you would. Those were some of the best years of my life. You form such tight bonds with your mates. But you can visit Yvette, Joanie, and Miranda anytime you want. They won't treat you like a princess."

"I know, but everyone else does. I manage to slide by a little as Alex MacGregor, but that's pretty thin. Half the people recognize me. Sophia and her damn book."

"Hey, if it wasn't that book it would have been another. If you want, we can create another alias for you."

"But what do I do when I have to be Catie McCormack, like today? It would blow my cover."

"We can work on that. There should be a way to come up with a disguise that you can slip into and out of without anyone figuring it out. People do it all the time."

"But people figure it out. Just like Commander Griggs. I'm too young to do what I do, so that calls attention to me, then people start guessing."

"Well, you're almost seventeen. Dr. Metra can probably do something to make you look older. We could even come up with a body double for you like Penny. That would make it better, if you're in Delphi City, then people won't expect you on Delphi Station or Gemini Station. Or on the Dutchman."

"Maybe."

"Is this about wanting to do stupid teenage stuff?"

"What's stupid teenage stuff?"

"Never mind. Forgot who I was talking to," Liz said. "Damn!"

"What's the matter?"

Liz nodded toward a family that was being seated at a table across the restaurant. "I do not understand why people bring young children to expensive restaurants. They're too young to enjoy the food, so all they do is make themselves and the rest of us miserable."

Catie looked over at the family. The two little ones didn't look very happy, and the two-year-old definitely looked mad. "They're probably tourists, where would they leave the kids?"

"Come on, don't you think this hotel offers a babysitting service?"

"Yes, but they probably don't understand how to monitor the service. So they'd be nervous about leaving their kids with strangers."

Right on cue, the two-year-old started squalling.

"Great!"

"Don't' worry, the maître d' will take care of it," Catie said.

"How?"

The maître d' returned to the table carrying one of the candle holders that each of the tables had in its center. He smiled at the couple who were looking embarrassed as they were trying to shush the two-year-

114

old. He replaced the candle holder on the table with the one he had brought, stepped back, and waved at the hostess. The sound coming from the two-year-old brat faded.

The maître d' smiled and made a few comments to the couple before leaving.

"What happened?" Liz asked.

"The restaurant has a noise-canceling system."

"Then why don't they have that thing on all the tables? Why wait until there's a problem?"

"We just installed it. The team will come back next week and equip all the tables. You have to get a reading of all the acoustics before you make the receivers," Catie explained.

"We?" Liz asked.

"Yes, ZMS. This is our first commercial installation."

"ZMS?"

"Zelbar, McCormack, and Sloan."

"Did you design it?"

"No, Nikola thought it up. I worked with her on the software. Pretty cool."

"Like a Cone of Silence."

"A what?"

"*Cone of Silence*, it's from a movie, <u>Get Smart</u>."

Catie looked at Liz, still confused. Then ADI ran a commercial clip of the movie on Catie's HUD.

"Oh."

"Yeah, I'm sure business people will love it. They can discuss secrets over martinis without having things overheard."

"Yeah. We think bars will like it too."

"But won't that mess up the ambiance?"

"You can set it for a noise level. So you get a sense of a big crowd without it becoming so loud you can't hear the person sitting next to you."

"How much does it cost?"

"You don't want to know."

"Sure, whatever. Hey, you do notice that nobody is hassling you right now," Liz said. "You're not being treated like a princess."

"Are you sure?" Catie asked. "Morgan is sitting over there in the corner. My two shadows are outside. And those two at the table over there are reporters."

"Reporters? I thought they were part of your security detail."

"Nope. And Morgan has already threatened one person that was paying too much attention to us."

"Okay, we'll talk to Dr. Metra next week."

"Okay. Here come our salads."

10 Catching Up

"Derek, how's it going?" Catie asked once she and Liz established the Comm link to the Dutchman.

"Doing fine," Derek said. "We're dropping into the Paraxean system, just passed their first gas giant."

"Are you staying busy?"

"Busy enough. I've caught up on all my TV series, I've read *War and Peace*, and I finished requalifying on the Fox."

"You did not read *War and Peace*," Liz said.

"No, but I could have."

"What else have you been doing?" Catie asked.

"We built some grav shuttles like Natalia designed. They'll make maneuvering the cargo pods go faster. We've got four, so each load specialist can handle a section."

"That's cool. So how long do you think you'll be at Paraxea?"

"We're not going to do shore leave, so just about fifteen hours. We'll do an extra day at Artemis to make up for it."

"That's nice. It'll be easier for the crew if they can have a whole day dirtside."

"Yep, that's what Davey told me. He's a good first mate. You know he could have captained this voyage," Derek said.

"Yes, but then who'd be first mate?" Liz said. "Don't worry, he'll get his chance to sit in the big chair."

"Did you hire another engineer? Arlean says once she hits Earth, she's not leaving for at least one month, even if she has to sabotage the ship to manage it."

"We're working on it. We have to hire two. The second StarMerchant will be ready to sail pretty soon."

"Is there going to be enough cargo for two of these babies?"

"Sure, we're adding another colony for the Aperanjens, and we hope to be trading with the Onisiwo system soon."

"The Aperanjens and the Onisiwo?" Derek asked.

"The aliens we rescued from the Fazullans."

"Oh, I heard a rumor that there were other races on that ship."

"Oops, I guess Daddy was keeping that a secret. Don't tell anyone."

"Just like you didn't."

"You were there, I'm surprised you didn't know."

"I was just there when we stopped the Fazullans. After that, it was need-to-know."

"Well, you need to know since we plan to trade with them."

"Are you staying in shape?" Liz asked.

"Yes, the 1.25 G profile isn't too tough, so I work out. And we still do the six-hour 1 G accel every two days," Derek said. "It's still pretty boring. Exercise is one of the only releases you have."

"So you're suggesting we come up with more entertainment for the voyage?"

"Maybe, even if you cut out the middle four days like you're saying, then it's still four weeks between planets. That's a long time to be stuck in a tin can."

"Hey, the Navy sends sailors out for longer than that between port calls," Liz said.

"I know, but they have bigger crews, so more activity. There are only thirty-five of us, and we're on alternating shifts, so it gets lonely."

"Alright, we'll look into expanding the entertainment package. Maybe we should set up a live stage so you can do karaoke," Catie suggested. "Maybe some open mic comedy."

"That might work. I can probably have the chief convert a couple of cabins."

"Take the four at the end of E-deck," Catie said. "It's by the cargo hold, so you won't bother anyone."

"Sure."

"Are you talking to the Paraxeans about the exchange?" Liz asked.

"Talked to the captain yesterday. He says our load is in orbit waiting for us. So we'll drop off all this grain, do the database update for their entertainment system, and load up the fixtures and appliances for Artemis, and be on our way."

"All that in fifteen hours?" Liz asked.

"That's what my loadmaster tells me. I'll believe her until she proves herself wrong."

"Smart man. We'll talk to you later," Catie said.

"Dutchman out."

"Cer Catie, Pollux is preparing to enter the Onisiwoen system," ADI informed Catie. Pollux was the Solar Explorer probe they'd sent back to Onisiwo.

Catie rolled over and looked at her clock. "0300, couldn't you have waited until 0400?"

"You gave me instructions to notify you when the probe was preparing to jump. You did not mention anything about beauty sleep," ADI said.

"Very funny. Okay. Don't let it jump until Dr. McDowell and I are in his lab to observe. Did you wake him up yet?"

"No, I thought you might want to do the honors."

"Oh, no you don't. Wake him while I take a shower, but record whatever he says so I can listen to it later."

"Chicken," ADI chided Catie.

"Good morning, Dr. McDowell," Catie said as she joined him in his lab.

"Night is more like it," he replied. He was holding onto a mug of coffee like it was his lifeblood, using both hands to bring it to his mouth so he could take a long sip.

"I brought more coffee," Catie said as she set the thermos on the desk.

"Good. Are we ready?"

"Yes, do you want to configure any of the instruments differently?"

"No, I configured them last night, actually just a few hours ago."

Catie brought up the monitors of the various systems on the Solar Explorer. Once she had everything ready, she said, "ADI, have the probe jump."

"Jumping in three," ADI said. "One . . . two . . . three!"

"Everything looks normal," Catie said. "I'm not reading any of the energy signatures that we see when a wormhole is present."

"We're a long way around the system," Dr. McDowell said. "It's possible that we wouldn't pick up the reading. We jumped the explorer into the Onisiwoen system ninety degrees away from where I estimated the Fazullan wormhole would be. I'm not sure what would happen if that thing was open when we opened our wormhole."

"I know, they might merge."

"Or they might collapse each other. Who knows, we've never seen one with that much power," Dr. McDowell said.

"Do you think we should risk a microjump around the system, or should we just fly the explorer there?"

"I think we should risk the microjump. We're awake, we might as well learn all we can."

"ADI, can the probe do a microjump?"

"Yes, Cer Catie. It has enough power to do two microjumps since it did a short jump from a neighboring system."

"Okay, then let's jump it to our target location."

"Jumping . . . Jumping again."

"I see a satellite sitting there," Dr. McDowell said.

"It makes sense that the Fazullans would put one there so they could observe the system."

"But it's silent."

"Hmm. Maybe they send a probe through the wormhole when it's open, and it activates it and pulls whatever passive readings it has recorded. That would minimize the chance of the Onisiwoens discovering it."

"That makes sense. Well, there definitely isn't a wormhole here. What do you want to do now?"

"Drop a small surveillance probe of our own to watch things and send the Solar Explorer back around to the other side of the system. I think ninety degrees still sounds right."

"I agree."

"ADI, will you take care of that? And have the explorer record what else is happening in the system. It'll be interesting to see what kind of civilization the Onisiwoens have."

"Yes, Cer Catie."

"Hi Catie," Alyssa called out, waving to Catie as she got off the Lynx. Alyssa's family had moved in just across from Catie's grandparents in Boston. She and Catie had first met when Catie was in Boston for Christmas four years ago.

"Hey, it's good to see you. I still can't believe your parents gave in and let you come," Catie said.

"Well, I did put up a big fuss. And how could they say no? Delphi University is well accredited and I do know the Princess of Delphi."

"Don't think that knowing me will get you anywhere," Catie said.

"It got me here, didn't it?"

"I guess. Let's go, Sophia is meeting us at Macey's diner. We'll have lunch, then you two can go check into your condo."

The two girls joined the line of passengers moving to the subway line that would take them over the causeway and into Delphi City. It was a short trip on the moving sidewalk and then a few minutes before the train showed up.

"Why doesn't the train come all the way to the terminal?" Alyssa asked.

"Because the causeway will break apart right here if there's a big storm. We wouldn't want the train to fall into the ocean. This section of the causeway is isolated from the airport. It will remain attached to the city, and once the storm passes, we can move the airport back into position. And they rotate the airport around this point."

"You could have just said for safety," Alyssa said. "Storms, rotating the airport, that's a lot of weird to take in."

Catie laughed. "Sure, we're weird, but you'll get used to it. Macey's is the second stop, it's right next to your condo. The university is the next stop after, but you'll probably just walk or take a taxi."

"I'm sure I'll be walking. You're overestimating how much my parents are financing me. Taxis are too expensive."

"They're free," Catie said.

"Free?"

"Just like the subway. Unless you reserve a private cab. All the little minibus cabs are free."

"How does that work?"

"They're supported by taxes. You cannot own a private car here, so the taxis are just part of the public transport, and everyone gets to use them."

"Boy, that would go over like a lead balloon in Boston. You'd have riots."

"Why?"

"People like their cars."

"Even if they're stuck in traffic all the time? You don't need a car here."

"That's just because you're so small."

"Hey, we passed one hundred thousand this year," Catie said as she grabbed Alyssa's suitcase and started toward the exit. "This is our stop."

Alyssa followed Catie off the train. She looked back at the car. "At least they're clean."

"They cycle the cars out of service every four hours and have a bot clean them."

"How can they do that? Do the trains just stop?"

"No. Each car is independent. Watch." Catie pointed to the last two cars on the train. As the train took off, those two cars stayed stationary for a bit then they followed. When they reached the end of the boarding area, both cars turned toward the right, taking another branch in the system.

"Where are they going?"

"Those cars are going to the next line over. They'll take the passengers over to the northwest side of the city and start making stops along that line."

"Won't some people get mad? What if they were going to the university?"

"Their Comms would have told them which car to get on. Their Comms also tell them when they need to switch cars. That way you don't have to crawl through the subway station to get to a different train."

"Sounds complicated."

"It's not if you're the passenger. It was a lot of work to configure, but once we got it working, it's been reliable."

"You guys really are weird."

"You said that already. Here's Macey's, we can leave your bag here in the front. Nobody will bother it."

"Are you crazy?"

"No, there are cameras everywhere. If anyone messes with it, they'll get nailed right away." Catie didn't mention that in the unlikely event that someone did try to grab the bag, the two bodyguards Morgan had following them would be standing right outside the diner to grab them. And Morgan had set herself up at the table right next to the door anyway.

Catie nodded to Morgan, then pushed Alyssa toward the back of the diner. "Sophia's waving at us, so keep going."

"I see her," Alyssa said. "Who's that with her?"

"More friends for you to meet."

"Nice," Alyssa said as she made her way to the table. The diner wasn't too crowded since it was two o'clock, but for Alyssa, it was ten p.m., her stomach had been growling since she got off the flight. She hadn't eaten on the flight since they had this late lunch scheduled.

"Hi, you must be Alyssa, I'm Sophia, your new roommate," Sophia said as she made room for Alyssa to sit. "This is Annie Halloway and Chris Tate; we'll probably have some classes with them. The two over there are Yvette LeClair and Joanie McCoy. They go to the Academy, so we'll only see them on weekends, but they can be a lot of fun, especially Yvette."

"What! I'm not fun?" Joanie complained.

"You are, but you know what I mean. Yvette is just crazy."

"*Mon Chéri*, that just means that I have lots of imagination," Yvette said.

"As you can tell she is French, you'll soon find out that she's a man-eating tigress," Catie said as she slid into the booth next to Yvette.

"Does that mean there won't be any men left for the rest of us?" Alyssa asked.

"I only eat one at a time," Yvette said, "so I don't mind sharing."

"She might only play with one at a time and share, but she flirts one hundred percent of the time," Catie said.

"That's because you have to keep in practice," Alyssa said.

"Oh, a girl after my heart," Yvette said. "I understand you are from Boston."

"Yes."

"A long way to come to college."

"It is, but I really wanted to go somewhere warm. *And to tell the truth, someplace far from my parents*," Alyssa whispered the second part.

"I can understand that. My mother ruined my summer cruise. Our only port was Nice, and she had to meet me at the ship and dominate all my time."

"Yvette is just mad because she couldn't flirt on the ship, so the tigress was hungry and her mother wouldn't let her have a snack while she was in Nice," Catie said.

"Very funny, but accurate," Yvette said. "Now we need to order before we get kicked out for loitering."

After they ordered they just chatted about what it was like at the Academy. Joanie and Yvette provided dramatic descriptions of what Basic was like as well as the now much more normal life at the Academy.

"Alyssa, were you able to get the classes you wanted?" Joanie asked.

"Yes, it's a bit weird starting in the second trimester, but I guess the university expects that so they have the first class in a lot of the series start then."

"Yes, having the calendar skewed does make it difficult. The Academy stays on the same calendar as the U.S. and Europe, but the university aligns with the school schedule down here in the southern hemisphere."

"That's because the Academy wants to stay synced to the U.S. and European Academies," Catie explained. "The university has to stay synced to the school calendar since Delphi High syncs to the calendar down here and lots of their graduates go to New Zealand or Australia for college."

"What do they do if they're going to the Academy?"

"They either go to a prep class that the Academy runs, or go to one of the universities for a term. Isn't that what David did?"

"Yes, he's in Guatemala right now for part two of Basic," Sophia replied.

"He's welcome to it," Joanie said. "I'm glad we only have to go through that once."

"Saved by the bell," Yvette said as their food arrived. She was obviously not interested in talking about Basic or Guatemala.

"Wow, these burgers are huge," Alyssa said. "We should have split our orders."

"I should have thought about that," Sophia said.

"You guys can split yours," Joanie said. "I'm eating all of mine."

"It's too late."

"No it isn't, they can box one up and I'll take it with me," Joanie said.

"What?"

"Yeah, I'll eat it tonight for dinner."

"How can you eat like that and stay so slim?"

"We do PT every day."

"You mean you have to do PT every day?" Alyssa asked.

"Except for the weekends," Joanie said.

"If my mom knew that she'd have made me go there."

"Why?"

"She wants me to lose weight. In fact, I promised her I would and she says if I don't, she's going to move here and make me train with her."

"You don't need to lose weight," Catie said.

"Oh yes I do," Alyssa said. "The women in my family tend to carry extra weight. My mom works hard to stay trim. I didn't have to worry about it until I turned fifteen. Now whenever I eat, it seems like the weight either goes right onto my hips or my boobs."

"I'd take your boobs over mine any day," Chris said. "I've been thinking about having mine augmented."

"You're crazy," Catie said. "Why would you do that?"

"Because guys like big boobs."

"So, screw them."

"Says the c-cup who's also a princess," Chris said.

"If you need bigger boobs to catch a guy, then he's not much of a man," Yvette said. She arched her back a bit to highlight her b-cup size breasts.

"You've got that sexy French accent working for you."

"Next weekend, you and I will go out and I will show you how to catch men," Yvette said.

"Can I come?" Alyssa asked.

"Me too," Annie added.

"Hey, you're dating Jason," Catie exclaimed.

"So, that doesn't mean I can't learn a few tricks."

"What about you, Joanie?" Chris asked.

"I've already had my lessons," Joanie said. "Besides, I'm pretty busy right now trying to get ahead in the simulation class."

"Oh, you're taking that this semester."

"Yes, and there is a *lot* of reading."

"Good morning Dr. McDowell," Catie said as she and Nikola walked into his lab.

"Good morning, Catie. I assume our asteroid is ready."

"Yes, they've strapped the pieces together."

"And put the stasis chambers on it?"

"Of course."

"Who's in the stasis chambers?" Dr. McDowell asked.

"Seamore," Catie replied.

"Poor Seamore," Nikola said.

"He's alright. They sedated him before they put him in the chamber and we're pretty sure there won't be a problem with the transition, but we have to verify it," Catie said.

"Are the Paraxeans prepared to deal with an upset spider monkey?"

"They've promised to take good care of him until we can send him back. The crew of the Enterprise has grown pretty fond of him. He's become their mascot."

"Are we ready?" Dr. McDowell asked, impatient with the chit chat.

"We are," Catie said. "The relativistic velocities of the jump ships on both sides are matched, and we're ready to start the cascade."

"My instruments are ready to record, so let's begin."

"Starting cascade," Catie reported as she began opening the wormhole starting in Mangkatar. "Wormhole is established."

"Readings look good. Power it up," Dr. McDowell said.

"Powering it up."

"It looks stable. Are you ready to push your test asteroid through?"

"Yes, pushing it through now," Catie said.

"Hmm, that's unexpected," Dr. McDowell said.

"What!"

"A large power spike. Did the asteroid make it through?"

"Poor Seamore," Nikola said.

"The asteroid made it through, the instruments on the stasis chambers show normal," Catie reported. "I've told the Paraxeans to hurry up and check it out since we had an unexpected anomaly."

Dr. McDowell left his station and went to his display boards and started writing equations.

"What caused the power spike?" Nikola asked.

"He won't hear you," Catie said. "He'll tell us when he's figured it out. I've asked the Paraxeans to give us a status update as soon as they get to Seamore."

"Oh, I hope he's okay," Nikola said.

"I do too. Let's go. They won't reach him for another hour, and Dr. McDowell won't be back with us for a day or so."

"That long?"

"Yes, we have to have someone come in and force-feed him," Catie said. "His Comm has an alarm on it to tell him to drink water."

"He's worse than Leo; at least Leo is smart enough to take breaks."

Two days later Catie found Dr. McDowell enjoying lunch in his lab.

"Dr. McDowell, did you figure out what caused the power spike?"

"Yes."

"Well?"

"What?"

"What caused the power spike?" Catie asked, perturbed at the twenty questions.

"Oh, we didn't fully account for the difference in the star's velocity around the galaxy. Mangkatar is lower in the plane than Earth which means you need to add a bit to the radius from the core. That means it is traveling at a lower velocity. We need to compensate for that."

"It's never been a problem before."

"We've never moved that much mass before. The wormhole had to push its velocity up to match, hence the power spike."

"So can we compensate for it?"

"Yes, I've already entered the new figures. We can move the real asteroid whenever you're ready."

"Thanks, I'll let the Paraxeans know."

The actual delivery of the asteroid was anticlimactic. Everyone reacted more strongly to the return of Seamore to the Enterprise. The Paraxeans simply thanked everyone and started moving the asteroid toward their Mangkatar. It would take them five weeks to get it into orbit given the limited ability to accelerate so much mass with the gravity drives mounted on the asteroid.

"How was the fishing trip?" Catie asked when she sat down with Miranda and Yvette.

"Pretty funny," Miranda said. "Most of those guys have done lake fishing, but they didn't do a very good job of calibrating the difference between catching a five-pound bass and a two-hundred-pound tuna. Maybe it was the beer. Anyway, a couple of them almost fell in."

"Did they land the tuna?" Catie asked.

"Oh, yeah. Caesar was expecting the problem. He had cameras set up to catch the fun and was there to haul their asses back to the deck before they went over. I'm not sure if he's selling the video to them as a memento, or if he's blackmailing them not to post it on the web."

"I'll have to watch it," Catie said. "Where's Joanie?"

"She can't make it. Strategy class simulation," Yvette said.

"Oh. Did you talk to Lieutenant Farnsworth?"

"I did. I thought I was in big trouble, he dragged me to his office and interrogated me. I told him you had told me to talk to him, but it wasn't until I said, Catherine McCormack instead of Alex MacGregor that he relaxed."

Catie and Miranda started laughing. "It wasn't funny," Yvette said.

"You would think a master spy would have handled it better," Miranda said.

"Maybe that's why he's recruiting instead of spying," Catie said. "But what was the upshot?"

"I have an extra class," Yvette said with a pout. "No good deed goes unpunished at the Academy."

"What's the class?"

"Psychology."

"That shouldn't be too difficult for you."

"But you have to write four papers, and then there are extra labs."

"Poor baby. Maybe you should reconsider doing surface ships," Catie said.

Yvette flicked some water at Catie. "*Non,* this does sound like fun."

"Here come our college freshmen," Miranda said as she waved to Alyssa and Sophia.

"Where's Chris?"

"She has a date," Sophia said.

"Oh, so Yvette's lesson worked."

"Oh, yes," Alyssa said. "It was so fun."

"What did you do?"

"The four of us went to Club Mirena and got a table. We sat there chatting and telling stories. Yvette had us totally ignore all the men who came in. A couple sent drinks over, but she had us send them back. Some guys came over to say hello and ask to join us. We told them it was nice to meet them, but we were doing fine by ourselves. Two guys asked Chris for her number. One of them called her the next day and they had lunch."

"Men always want what they can't have," Yvette said. "You can't go looking for men, you have to make them look for you."

"Did anyone ask for your number?" Catie asked Alyssa.

"Three guys."

"And?"

"I have a date on Saturday. Pizza at Giorgio's."

"That's a nice place."

Alyssa looked around, "Is Liz coming?"

"No, she's covering for me now, I'm covering for her tonight," Catie said. "We're pretty busy right now."

"Doing what?" Miranda asked.

"Handling some colonists," Catie said. She didn't mention that the colonists they were handling were aliens.

"Sophia and Alyssa, now that we've talked about boys, how were your classes?" Miranda asked.

"Interesting," Sophia said. "We're in the same calculus class and the same journalism class."

"What does a reporter need with calculus?"

"That's exactly what I said to my parents. They told me that I should write an article about that after I've finished the class."

That comment elicited chuckles around the table.

"Alyssa, what else are you taking?"

"I'm taking statics and dynamics, which made me ask the same question. I'm a computer science major, but my father said it is good to know how the things you're programming actually work."

"Well, maybe you'll shift to robotics," Catie said. "Then you'll know how to program a bot to lift something without breaking its arm or putting a hole in a bulkhead."

"Very funny, but maybe. Robots would be cool. Why aren't there robots running around Delphi City?" Alyssa asked

"We have lots of bots," Catie said. "But we don't make human form robots. Too expensive and difficult to maintain."

"Really?"

"Yep. The Paraxeans tried it and found it very uneconomical. We're trusting them so far. I've had economic models run and they agree with them. Why? Are you thinking a robot for a boyfriend would be better?"

Alyssa blushed while the other girls laughed.

"Well he would certainly have plenty of stamina," Yvette said.

"You have a filthy mind," Miranda scolded.

"I'm just stating the facts."

"Alyssa, how are you finding Delphi University?"

"It's very different than I expected. It's weird that there aren't any dorms or sorority houses."

"You can blame my Uncle Blake for that. He, the prime minister, and the university president talked about that and they decided that having the students stay close to the university was important but opted for putting them into condo buildings in the area instead of designating some buildings as just for students."

"But how do they make sure there are enough rooms for the students?"

"They designate certain condos for students; they're spread out over the various buildings close to campus. Any overflow just has to take a condo farther away; it's not like the university is that far from anyplace in Delphi City."

"But doesn't that diminish the college experience?"

"That's the plan. There are clubhouses on campus for various sororities and other student organizations to use, but they intentionally avoided having dense clusters of student housing."

"Why?"

"Uncle Blake says that the stupidity factor goes up directly in proportion to the number of individuals between fifteen and twenty-five that occupy a building. They're trying to avoid that. Studies have shown that sexual assaults, drunken parties, and other problems associated with college students are lower when students are distributed among more mature residents."

"I'm sure that's right," Miranda said. "But then why are the cadets in dorms?"

"Because they're under discipline," Catie said. "At least that's what Uncle Blake says. The rules are stricter than at the U.S. Academies, and also easier to monitor and enforce."

"That is true," Yvette said. "I haven't seen any stupid parties or things like that. Nothing like at the Academy back in France."

"I guess the stupidity factor is a part of the college experience I can do without," Alyssa said.

"Me too," Sophia added. "Besides, we do get the roommate experience. And I like having a neighbor that I can trust. Someone who will remember to water the plants when I'm gone."

"Hey, Uncle Blake," Catie called out as she met Blake at the docking ring of Delphi Station.

"Hey, nice of you to come welcome me."

"I came to welcome Charlie," Catie said. "He and his friends are the guests. Come on, move, they're probably getting tired of the microgravity."

They'd used an Oryx to bring the eight Onisiwoens to Delphi station. It was a hover Oryx, so it had been able to maintain gravity the whole time. But now that it was docked at the docking ring, they were under microgravity.

"They're trained astronauts, they can handle it," Blake said.

"That doesn't mean they like it; now come on, move it."

Blake led the way into the docking ring, and up to the hub. It only took them ten minutes to reach the elevator that would take them to the gravity section.

"Hi, Charlie, you guys doing okay?"

"We're doing fine. Doesn't seem like that long ago since we were in microgravity. We were almost a year into that mission without gravity."

"I guess you'd be used to it. It's easy to forget how things are when you can't put a fusion reactor in your spaceship. I guess we're spoiled."

"I'd say so," Charlie said as he looked around the elevator.

The elevator car held eight people, the other two Onisiwoens waited with Blake's aide while Blake, Catie, and the first six headed down.

"Gravity coming up as ordered," Blake said as he hit the button to start the elevator moving. The feeling of gravity was immediate but gentle. By the time they reached the end of the ride, it was up to .2 Gs.

"This is nice," Charlie said.

"Where are we putting them?" Blake asked as he let the elevator head back up for the next load.

"We've cleared a space in ring three. We were reserving it for retail space, but they can stay there until we take them back to Onisiwo."

"And when will that be?" Charlie asked.

"We're still waiting until we have probes along the way so we can make it in one jump," Catie said. "Plus we need a starship."

"Your father plans to send you in the Roebuck," Blake said.

"That's what I guessed. So it shouldn't be long."

Constable Aisha's Comm announced her at the door to the condo. She waited patiently for the resident to answer the door. It was two minutes before someone finally came to the door.

"Can I help you?" the man asked.

"Yes, I'm Constable Aisha. Are you Cer Tasker?"

"I'm Mr. Tasker."

"Well, Mr. Tasker, I'm here because yesterday you put a trash bag into the recycle chute that was not separated. As you should know from your lease agreement, all trash must be separated to facilitate recycling."

"It wasn't me."

"I'm sorry sir, but it was you."

"How dare you?! How could you possibly know?"

"The system records each person who uses the trash and recycle chutes. It also takes an x-ray of the bag and labels it so we can track it.

At 1920 you were recorded disposing of a bag with both paper and food products in it. The bag was intercepted, inspected, and separated."

"Okay, so maybe I did. I don't remember."

"Sir, this is your first violation, so you are only being fined the seventy dollars it cost to separate the trash and for me to come issue this warning?"

"I have to pay for you to come hassle me?!"

"Your neglect led to the expense."

"Whatever, just put it on my monthly dues."

"We will. However, I must warn you that the next fine is twenty Auroras."

"That's over five hundred dollars!"

"Yes it is. It is important to separate your trash. We do not use a landfill, so everything has to be recycled."

"That's ridiculous."

"This is a floating city and Delphi is very environmentally conscious. Surely you were made aware of the various restrictions associated with living in Delphi."

"You've warned me. Now can I get back to my breakfast?"

"Yes sir. Have a nice day," Constable Aisha said as Mr. Tasker closed the door in her face.

11   Board Meeting – Sept 5th

"Let's bring this meeting to order. I see that everyone is in Delphi City except for Admiral Michaels, Sam, and myself. Fred, how is our new airline doing?"

"It's doing great. We're adding one plane every three weeks as they finish their certification. Ticket sales are solid, people love the service and the short flights."

"Los Angeles to Paris in just under three hours, who wouldn't like that?" Liz asked.

"Is it making enough to pay for the planes yet?" Marc asked.

"Yes, the last three planes were paid for by the company, so our cash flow is starting to recover," Fred replied.

"Anything else with the airline?"

"We've hired a marketing director. Marcie helped us find one from British Air. She will start next month."

"What about a president?"

"I'm going to promote one of my people," Fred said. "I just sent you the résumé. If you approve, I'll make the announcement tomorrow."

"Good; batteries and fuel cells?"

"We're doing great. Next year, all cars sold around the world will be all-electric or fuel cell – electric hybrids. Several countries are talking about forced retirement for old cars."

"We should come up with a conversion kit for the older cars," Catie said.

"Why?" Marc asked.

"Style. People like the way they look."

"Why don't you work on that," Marc said.

"As a separate company?"

"Hey, you still work for MacKenzies," Fred squawked.

"Oh, so you think it'll be a moneymaker."

"Maybe, but it'll probably be too small for MacKenzies to worry about," Fred said.

"So I can start another company?"

"You get my vote as long as I get to be a partner," Blake said.

"Go ahead," Marc said. "Fred, anything else?"

"Nothing you won't learn by looking at the monthly report for ten minutes."

"Okay, then let's talk about Onisiwo," Marc said. "Catie, what does the probe show us?"

"No wormhole yet. We haven't had much time to really study the system, but it looks like the Onisiwoens have a pretty well-developed space industry, even without gravity drives. We detect at least two space stations in their asteroid belt and two around the planet. Their planet is on the opposite side of their sun from the probe, so we can't really tell that much yet."

"Are the Onisiwoens ready to go home?"

"Definitely," Liz said. "They're being polite, but they are a bit antsy. I think they're starting to wonder what's taking so long."

"Well, we didn't want to head that way until we had a probe in place, and we have been busy getting the Aperanjens settled in. Catie are you up for captaining the Roebuck to Onisiwo?"

"Sure. Uncle Blake said that was your plan. It'll be about as interesting as what I'm doing now," Catie said.

"It's *not* all about having fun," Marc scolded.

"Sorry, I didn't mean it that way," Catie said. "I'm just not doing anything that requires me to be here except being hospitality director for the Aperanjens."

"Liz, I assume you can step in there," Marc said.

"Sure."

"Okay, back to normal business. Kal, how's the real-estate business?" Marc asked.

"Hey, my guys are happy," Kal said. "You have to ask Fred for the details."

"The sales seem to be doing well," Fred said. "We've sold five thousand condos the first month."

"That's a lot, how many did we finance?"

"Forty-five hundred."

"So we got cash for five hundred condos?" Marc asked.

"Yes, I think it was 320 million dollars."

"Wow, I'm sure that made Herr Pfeifer happy."

"Yes, he was impossible to put up with. He thinks we'll sell that many every month," Fred said.

"Well?"

"It looks like we will for the next few months. But eventually, we'll run out of customers or condos."

"We can add another half-ring to the city."

"We already are."

"Okay. Are the prime minister and Chief Nawal ready to come in?" Marc asked.

"I'll message Masina," Blake said.

"I should go prepare for my mission," Catie said.

"Sit back down," Blake said. "This will be good for you."

Catie frowned at her uncle but sat back down. Blake was happy that she didn't stick her tongue out at him.

Everyone stood as Masina led Prime Minister Nazeri and Chief Nawal in. Once everyone was seated again, Marc nodded to Kal.

"There have been a couple of incidents that have led Prime Minister Nazeri to question some of our investigative techniques. She asked that we have this review to discuss them and, I hope, validate their usefulness and appropriateness," Kal said.

"This will be interesting," Catie messaged Liz. "What incidents?"

"We have just arrested a man for running an illegal prostitution ring," Kal said.

"But prostitution isn't illegal," Blake said.

"It is when the prostitutes are ten years old."

"Oh my god," Catie gasped.

"How did you catch him?"

"That goes to one of the techniques we use," Kal said. "We insert members of the Marine Corps investigative team into Delphi City as, let us say, less than upstanding citizens. Their job is to drift along at the bottom of society and to infiltrate any illegal activity."

"You mean spy on our citizens," the prime minister said.

"They are not *peeking* into people's bedrooms," Kal said, somewhat exasperated. "They are simply engaging with the margins of society."

"Exactly where and how do you insert these agents?" Admiral Michaels asked.

"We have the youngest looking ones attend the school here as either juniors or seniors. They take classes, make marginal grades, and hang out with the rougher crowd. Generally, they pick up on different methods the kids come up with to cheat on their tests, but occasionally they are brought into more seriously illegal activities. That's how we first learned about Hooligans, the teen bar. Then we inserted an agent there to work as a bartender."

Chief Nawal had been nodding her agreement as Kal told the story. "That was important. Their agent helped us to realize that we should leave Hooligans alone. It was serving a good purpose, giving teenagers a place to blow off steam. She was able to influence the club to further restrict the use of hard liquor and focus on beer."

"So how did you tumble onto this prostitution ring?"

"A prostitute, who was earning extra money doing private parties for this ring, noticed the young girls. She mentioned it to one of our guys."

"That's horrible," Catie gasped.

"How did she know one of your guys well enough to trust him with something like that?" Admiral Michaels asked.

"Well, various prostitutes in the city occasionally have trouble with one of their customers. They want to keep these problems quiet, so they use our guy to sort them out."

"And how does he do that?"

"He is very skillful at arranging accidents for these problem customers."

"What kind of accidents?"

"Some of them have been known to stumble down a flight of stairs when they bump into someone else, others seem to trip on the sidewalk, things like that. He's managed to accomplish all of the accidents without being caught by Chief Nawal's constables."

"With all of our cameras around, that is pretty remarkable," Blake said.

"Well, not many of his victims complain, and he is remarkably good at it. Anyway, he checked it out. Determined that there was a problem. He got the prostitute to get one of the girls to come forward. Then we were able to set up surveillance. We picked up seven johns and then we grabbed the ring. Three girls were involved. We've moved them to Delphi Station to protect them."

"Okay. Prime Minister, what is your problem with the methods?" Marc asked.

"Due process."

Marc nodded to Kal.

"Our agents have to observe a crime being committed or have someone come forward who's observed a crime being committed. That allows us to get a warrant to move further. In this case, it took two rounds before we had a broad enough warrant to roll up the operation."

"Two rounds?"

"The judges typically issue a pretty narrow warrant with limited use that allows us to surveil or wiretap an individual. That means we cannot use things we observe that are not related to the warrant in order to expand the case. But once we prove that there is a broader conspiracy or organization involved, we go back and get a broader warrant," Kal explained. "Then we install more surveillance probes into the situation to gather more intel."

"And the problem with that would be?" Marc asked, looking at the prime minister.

"I'm not sure."

"Would you have a problem if a regular citizen came to the police and reported a crime, and after that, the police instituted the same procedure that Kal described?"

"I don't think so."

"Then, what we have here is that Kal and Chief Nawal are simply inserting regular citizens into situations where they are more likely to observe a crime being committed."

"What about that enforcer of yours?"

"Chief Nawal, what do you think?"

"If we catch him, we'll arrest him," the chief said.

"Agreed, but would you refuse to accept evidence from a known criminal?"

"No, not if it was credible."

"Then it seems that we are following due process and not violating anyone's rights."

"Except the enforcer."

"Yes, he is breaking the law. But it doesn't seem that the justice system is being subverted. Kal, is that correct?"

"Yes, the agents know they're on their own if they break the law. If they get arrested and it goes to conviction, we would step in and pull them out, but they know we will not intercede before that."

"Have any of your agents gotten into trouble?"

"A couple have run into other enforcers," Kal said.

"And what happened with those other enforcers?" Blake asked.

"Well, so far they haven't been able to demonstrate the level of training our people have, so they've been forced to find another line of work. Sometimes after a brief stay in the hospital."

"Okay, now back to the original case. What's going to happen with the prostitution ring?"

"The johns have all confessed. They'll receive treatment while they serve out their sentences."

"How long are their sentences?" Catie demanded.

"Ten years, plus lifetime monitoring," Chief Nawal said.

Catie grimaced but decided that that was enough.

"And the members of the ring?"

"We expect the low-level guys to hold out until after the top guy is convicted. They'll get the same sentence as the johns when convicted. The ringleader will get twenty-five to life, and lifetime monitoring if he ever gets released."

"What is he hoping for?"

"He's trying to intimidate the witnesses."

"How is he managing that?"

"It appears he has associates who are doing that for him. They may have prior instructions or he has a way to give instructions through his lawyer. We monitor that, but no system is perfect. We're still backtracing all the incidents to see if we can determine the source of the instructions," Chief Nawal said.

"How are the witnesses being intimidated?"

"The use of enforcers against friends. We've moved a couple of *friends* up to Delphi Station to protect them."

"By friends, you mean other prostitutes?"

"It's not illegal, here or on Delphi Station."

"But a cabin on Delphi Station is usually out of their income bracket," Blake said.

"Blake, you can't be that naïve," Liz said.

"Oh, so not out of their income bracket."

Liz just shook her head.

"Back to the witnesses," Marc said.

"Yes, the constabulary has arrested a couple of enforcers, and a few others have discovered it is an unhealthy business to be in. We're now waiting to see what happens next."

"You mean, now that he realizes he cannot easily intimidate the witnesses?"

"Correct."

"And when is the trial?"

"In two months."

"When did you arrest him?" Samantha asked.

"Last month," Kal said.

"So three months to prepare for trial."

"Do you think that's too long?" Chief Nawal asked.

Samantha laughed. "It seems pretty short."

"Hard for him to make a case that he couldn't get an attorney full time right away," Chief Nawal said. "And our judges lean toward speedy unless you can show why you can't be prepared."

"So what are we going to do with all these prisoners?" Samantha asked.

"We'll finish building the prison. We'll have to accelerate the expansion to include workspace for these guys since we wouldn't want to let them out into the community for work."

"What kind of work will you have them do?" Samantha asked.

"We won't be trusting most of them, so we'll start out with recycling. We have to do a lot of disassembly, and we're not too worried about sabotage there. We'll see what else we come up with as time goes on."

"Prime Minister, are you happy with this?" Marc asked.

"I'm still not comfortable."

"What would make you comfortable?"

"I think I'd like someone to be reviewing all the warrants and activities."

"You could set up an independent judicial committee to review the operations and warrants."

"That would make me feel better."

"I have no objection. Kal, Chief Nawal?" Marc asked.

"We're fine with that."

"Okay, then are we done here?"

The prime minister nodded, and Marc closed the meeting.

"Kal, I want to talk to the girls," Catie said as she followed Kal out of the meeting.

"I thought you might," Kal said. "They're in cabin 3-7-180. The security people taking care of them will be expecting you."

"Thanks."

"You do know that you need to leave the counseling to the doctors."

"I *know*. How are they doing?"

"The doctors say they're doing reasonably well. They're frustrated that they cannot do as much as they want to until after the trial."

"Why?"

"We cannot touch their memories before they give their testimony."

"Oh," Catie said.

"Yeah, it's a raw deal, but we have to do what we have to do."

"Push!" the doctor ordered.

"I am pushing!" Samantha yelled.

"Come on you can do it," Marc said. "Ouch," he winced as Samantha dug into his wrist with her fingernails.

"Sir, it's best if you stick to 'I'm here,' and 'do you want some ice chips?'" the doctor said.

Marc nodded as he continued to wince as Samantha squeezed his wrist.

"Remind me to explain to Dr. Metra what painless means in English!"

"Oh, you wanted the pain-free option?" the doctor asked.

"What! You mean there is a way to avoid this!" Samantha screamed.

"Here she comes! ... There's no pain-free option, but that comment usually gives the patient the energy for the final push I need," the doctor said as she handed the baby to the nurse.

"I am going to make you pay . . ."

"Here's your baby," the nurse said as she brought the newborn over to Samantha. The nurse had been trying to clean the baby up but figured that Samantha needed to be distracted right away.

"Ohh, she's so beautiful," Samantha said.

"Yes she is," Marc said. He now finally knew the sex of the baby.

"Yay! A baby girl!" Catie squealed over the Comm.

12   Tres Amigas

The guard at the door snapped to attention as Catie entered the cabin.

"Ma'am."

"Relax, call me Catie."

"Yes, ma'am. . . . uh, Catie, I'm Sergeant Ferra."

"How are they doing?"

"They seem to be doing pretty well. They've really taken to the video games. They're playing with the Fox simulator right now."

"That's good. So are they eating okay, sleeping?"

"Yes, ma'am. They've got good appetites. Of course, who wouldn't when you can have whatever you want. They're sleeping together, but no night terrors that I'm aware of. The doctor comes every day to do some counseling. They've been especially happy since Celia came to stay with them."

"Celia?"

"The woman who first reported them."

"Oh, the prostitute," Catie said.

"Yes, ma'am. She's in the kitchen making dinner. She does a good job keeping the place clean, we don't even need to bring a maid in. And she's a very good cook."

Catie winced as one of the girls squealed, *"É a Princesa Catie, pessoal, é a Princesa Catie!"* Catie's Comm translated it to, 'It's Princess Catie, guys look, it's Princess Catie.'

"You've been made," Sergeant Ferra said with a grin.

Catie moved into the room and sat on the couch as the three girls stood up and chattered with each other in Portuguese.

"Hi," Catie said. "Can we talk?"

The girls took a second to respond, then nodded their heads, *"Sim."*

"Their English isn't that good," Sergeant Ferra said.

"How can that be?!"

"They're looking into it. It's gotten better over the last week, but obviously, they haven't been doing the training."

"ADI, how long have they been here?" Catie asked.

"I assume you mean in Delphi," ADI said. "If so, then they've been in Delphi for three months. They're from Brazil, Sao Paulo."

"So why isn't their English better?"

"They have not been going through the acclimation program."

"How is that possible?"

"Someone has hacked the system," ADI replied.

"Who?"

"I cannot tell you."

"Cannot or will not?"

"Cannot, it would violate the due process rule."

"I don't care about due process!"

"I still cannot tell you."

"Have you fixed the hack?"

"I can."

"Then do it."

"Yes, Cer Catie. But I must tell you it is likely to result in bodily harm to the hacker when his clients are caught violating the system."

"That sounds like perfect due process to me!" Catie said.

"Done," ADI replied.

"Com quem você está falando, who are you talking to?" one of the girls asked.

"I'm talking to my friend, ADI. She tells me that you were not studying English before," Catie said. Her Comm translated and vocalized her words.

"We don't like school anyway," the girl said.

"Why not? And what's your name?"

"I'm Lílian, that's Teresa, and she's Benedita," Lílian said.

147

"So why don't you like school?"

"It's boring."

"Boring? Don't you like to learn about stuff?"

"Why? We know everything we need to."

"Can you read?"

"Yes, we read your book!" Teresa squealed.

"You did. See, if you hadn't gone to school you wouldn't have been able to read the book about me."

"We could have watched the movie."

"There isn't a movie. They don't make a movie about all the good books, so if you can't read, you miss out on a lot of things."

"But we can read, so why should we go to school?"

"Well, can you do math?"

"We can count, add, and subtract."

"What about multiply and divide?"

"We can do that, but it's not as easy."

"Do you know how to draw?"

"They teach that at school?"

"Yes. They even teach you how to paint."

"Do you go to school?"

"Dummy, she's a princess, she doesn't have to go to school," Lílian said.

"Yes I do. And I did. I told you I liked school."

"Is that where you learned how to be a princess?"

"Yes, I learned that at school and my friends taught me."

"Is it hard being a princess?"

"Yes! You have to sit up straight all the time. You have to clasp your hands and talk fancy. Like, 'Mr. President, we are delighted to have you come to our city.'" Catie gave her best impression of the English Queen.

The girls giggled at her. "That doesn't sound too difficult."

"Well, it can be very tiring. I'd rather fly Foxes and Starships around."

"Cool, we like flying the Foxes."

"Sergeant Ferra told me you guys were doing really well on the simulator. You know what I like to do as much as flying a Fox?"

"No, what?"

"I like to design them."

The three girls looked at Catie skeptically.

"You don't believe me?"

"No!"

"So you don't believe I can design them or don't you believe that I like to design them?"

"How can you design them?"

"I went to school," Catie said. "Here look." Catie brought up a wire diagram of a Fox on the big display the girls had been using for their simulation. "This is a Fox. It's just like the one you've been playing with. You can see that there are two seats, one behind the other. The front one is for the pilot and the back one is for the weapons officer; he's the one who guides the missiles when you're using them."

The girls nodded as they studied the Fox.

"Now if you wanted to make the Fox able to fly faster you would make it skinnier like this." Catie changed the Fox so that the cross-section of the cockpit was half the size.

"Oh, that's cool."

"But if you did that, then you would have to find really skinny pilots. And if you wanted to let really fat pilots fly it, you would make it really wide like this." Catie expanded the cockpit dimension to 50% bigger than the design.

"Then you could have the pilots sit next to each other," Teresa said.

"To do that you would have to make the cockpit even bigger." Catie changed the design to show side-by-side pilots in the cockpit. "But if you did that, then it would be too slow."

"Why?"

"Air resistance."

"What?"

Catie looked around for something to demonstrate. She grabbed the tray that was sitting on the table, probably it had held a snack for the girls. She removed the plates and glasses and handed the tray to Lílian. "Wave that around," Catie instructed.

Lílian grabbed the tray and started fanning it in front of Catie.

"Now, hold it horizontal, like this," Catie instructed, using her hands to demonstrate. "Now wave it. ... No side to side like before."

"Oh!" Lílian said as she started to wave the tray horizontally.

"Can you tell the difference? Which way was easier to wave the tray?"

"This way," Lílian said as she waved it horizontally.

"Let me try," Teresa and Benedita shouted together.

Catie waited until each girl had waved the tray before proceeding. "Now which way was easier to wave the tray?"

"This way?" Benedita said as she demonstrated waving it horizontally.

"And why is that?"

"Air," Benedita said hesitantly.

"Correct. When you wave it the other way, the tray has to push a lot more air out of the way so that it can move. This is called the cross-section, and it just means how big a space the tray takes up when you hold it like that."

"So?"

"So, the Fox has a cross-section just like the tray. And when you change it so that you can have two pilots next to each other, then you have to make the cross-section bigger. That means it has to push more air out of the way when it wants to go fast."

"But isn't that why it's pointy?" Teresa asked.

"Yes, but look at it this way," Catie said as she rotated the wire diagram so it showed the cross-section head-on. "It doesn't matter how pointed it is, it still has the same cross-section, so it still has to move more air than the skinny version." Catie brought up the original Fox design next to the fat one.

"Making it pointy helps. That was real smart of you to know that. It takes a lot of complex math to prove it, but it just makes sense, doesn't it?"

"Yes."

"So, when you design a jet that you want to go real fast, you try to make it have the smallest cross-section," Catie said. "You look for every place where you can squeeze a little bit of space out, you even require that the pilots can't be too fat."

"So that's what you learn in school?"

"That and lots of other things. Sergeant Ferra had to go to school to learn how to be a Marine."

"She did?"

Catie motioned Ferra over.

"Yes, I did." Sergeant Ferra said, speaking in Portuguese. "They call it Basic Training. After that, I had to go to school to learn how to be a security guard."

"A security guard? What do you need to learn to be one of those?"

"Lots of things. How to spot the bad guys, how to beat them up," Sergeant Ferra said.

"She had to learn threat assessment. You'll notice that her partner is standing by the door now."

The girls looked over at the door and spotted the second security guard standing there.

"When I asked her to come over and talk to you, she immediately signaled her partner to come out and take up her post by the door. That way nobody could sneak in on us."

"So you have to go to school to learn how to do stuff like that?"

"Yes. At first, they'll teach you things like math, reading, art. Stuff you need to know for most jobs. Then they'll teach you how to do the things you need for a specific type of job. And of course, you can take classes to learn some stuff just for fun."

"Like what?"

"Dancing, horseback riding, painting, playing an instrument, even acting," Catie explained.

"I'd like to do horseback riding," Lílian said.

"Silly, we're on a space station."

"Well, one day you'll be able to go back to Delphi City. There's a big horse park there where you could learn how to ride."

"Why do we have to have a security guard?" Benedita asked.

"They want to make sure bad guys don't bother you," Catie said. "I have to have a security guard with me all the time."

"You do? Where is yours?"

Catie signaled Morgan to come in.

"See? That's Morgan. She's my main security guard. There are others since Morgan has to be able to take time off, but she's in charge of them."

"Wow. That means you get to go to all the royal balls," Teresa oohed.

"Princess Catie doesn't go to many royal balls," Morgan said. "She likes to do other things."

"Like what?"

"Flying; of course if she's flying a Fox, she doesn't need me to protect her."

"What else?"

"She went to the Academy."

"The Academy?"

"It's the school where we send all the people who want to learn how to be officers. There they learn how to boss people like me around," Morgan said.

That got a laugh out of the girls. "What do they teach you at the Academy?"

"Oh things like this," Morgan said as she brought up a video on the display. It showed Catie crawling through the mud at the base in Guatemala.

"Oh, yuck. Is that you?"

"Yes it is," Catie said. "How did you get that?"

"Hey, I was your security even when you were at the Academy. I was always around. Here is the princess learning how to climb a rope." Morgan changed to a video showing Catie jumping up to climb the rope and being told to go back and start without jumping. You could clearly hear the sergeant yelling at her.

"And here she is learning how to fall." Morgan showed a video where she managed to throw Catie to the mat.

"Hey! I threw you way more times than you threw me."

"Yeah, but those aren't as fun to watch," Morgan said. "And here she is learning how to maneuver in microgravity." Morgan showed a video of Catie when one of the twins pulled an exceptionally good juke on her and Catie wound up doing a face plant into the wall.

"Hey, you weren't even my bodyguard back then."

"Natalia and I share everything," Morgan said.

All three girls were giggling uncontrollably by this time. Their laughter enticed Celia out of the kitchen.

"You're all having fun out here?" Celia asked in Portuguese.

"Yes!"

"Would you two care to stay for dinner? It would be no trouble to set two extra places."

"We wouldn't want to intrude," Catie said.

"Please!"

"Okay."

"I'm on duty," Morgan said.

"Come on!"

"Okay, I'll call my backup."

"Hello, I'm Catie," Catie said as she stood up and offered her hand to Celia.

"Yes, I heard. Thanks for coming. I think it's made their day, probably their month," Celia said.

"I'm happy I did. I really came to see what they want to have happen after the trial. I want to make sure they get a good start on their new life."

"That's nice of you. I'm sure people like you don't usually worry about the likes of us."

"Why not? You were a good citizen, and nobody can blame them for getting into the situation they were in."

"It's nice of you to say that, but . . ."

"Hey, tell me about yourself while Morgan entertains them with more unflattering videos of me."

"Do you really want to know?"

"Yes. One, I'm curious and two, you're obviously important to them, and I'd like to know you better."

"Well, my story is nothing like theirs. I came to Delphi City when I was seventeen; we were refugees but we had a pretty good life in Brazil until the gangs took over our neighborhood. I finished school that year and move out of my parent's house. I was lazy. I didn't like the job they gave me, so I started hooking. It was easy money. I got to go to parties. It was okay. But then that creep brought the girls to Delphi City. I worked parties for him sometimes, and that's how I met them."

"I heard you told a friend, an enforcer," Catie said.

"Oh yeah. Eduardo. He's a nice guy. At least to us girls. I guess he's not too nice to the johns we tell him are being vicious. He straightens them out for a small fee."

"What do you want to do when this is over?"

"Do you mean, will I go back to hooking?"

"Yes, will you?"

"I don't know. I'm not sure what options I have."

"The same ones you had when you got out of school," Catie said.

"I don't know, I really don't have any skills."

"Ferra says you're a good cook. You could get a job in a diner."

"You think they'd hire me once they saw my résumé? Past experience, hooking."

"I'm sure they'd overlook it. It all depends on what you want to do. You could even get a job in Deogenes here on the station and learn to be a chef."

"Oh, I'd like that. But they'd never give me a shot."

"Oh, I bet they would. I know the owners, and they wouldn't hold your past against you. They had nothing when they opened their restaurant. I could set up an interview for you."

"Would you? Oh, but I can't. I've got to stay with the girls."

"I'm sure they would be able to deal with you going to work for a few hours," Catie said. "We can bring in someone to watch them. And they will have to go to school. It starts next week."

"Oh, you're going to put them in school? Do they have one up here?"

"Sure. It's set up in multi-grade level pods since there aren't that many students, but that will work better for them anyway. Their level of skills will be all over the map. So do you want the interview?"

"Sure, set one up."

"What do you girls want to do when this is all over?" Catie asked once everyone had filled their plate.

"You said we have to go to school," Lílian said.

"That's right, but do you want to say up here on Delphi Station, or do you want to go back to Delphi City, or would you want to go back to Sao Paulo?"

"No! We want to stay here!"

"On the station or in the city?"

Lílian Looked around at the other two. Seeming to get confirmation by telepathy she turned to Catie. "Here on the station?"

"Do you have any family who could come and take care of you?"

"No."

"What kind of family would you want?"

"We don't want a family. We're all we need," Lílian said.

"So you want to stay together?"

"Yes, with Celia," Benedita said.

"Oops," Catie gasped. "But Celia isn't your parent."

"But she's our best friend. She's the only one who cared about us."

"I didn't see that coming," Catie said to Celia as she helped her clear the table after dinner.

"Neither did I."

"Well, we won't know what they really want until after the trial and the doctors can really treat them."

"Really treat them? What does that mean?"

"Once the trial is over, the doctor can go in and dull the memories associated with the abuse. They might even be able to erase them," Catie explained.

"That sounds dangerous."

"It's not, I've had it done. And my friend Liz finally had it done to dull an assault she suffered. She kept having nightmares. Once she finally got treated, the nightmares went away. She told me she wished she'd gotten the treatment as soon as she learned about it instead of waiting."

"Will they forget me?"

"No, the doctor will only modify the memory associated with the trauma. You're a good memory, so they won't touch it."

"Oh, that's good. Maybe we will stay together. But I'm not sure I'll make enough money to support them."

"Delphi will pay for their support until they finish school," Catie said.

"Really. They won't just put them in an orphanage?"

"No, it's better and less expensive to support them inside the community."

"Well, it might work then. Of course, we'll have to find a smaller place to live."

"No you won't. If you take care of them, you could stay here until they finish school."

"But how?" Celia asked, then when she saw Catie's face she laughed. "I guess you kind of own the station."

"Only part of it. But I can take care of the rent. One of the perks of being a princess."

"Uncle Blake," Catie called out as she caught him leaving his office.

"Hi, Catie. Do you need something?"

"I wanted to talk about the Belousov case. Do you have time?"

"Sure, let's go back into my office. I was just heading down to Delphi City, but there's nothing pressing. What did you want to discuss?"

"How can someone like him get into Delphi City?"

"I think I know what you're asking, but be more specific."

"We screen our immigrants for criminal records. How did he slip through?"

"He doesn't have a criminal record. He has a second cousin that's been involved with prostitution before, but that's a pretty loose connection. If we excluded everyone with an unsavory second cousin, we'd have a hard time getting anyone to come to Delphi City."

"So he just shows up and decides to form a gang that prostitutes ten-year-old girls?"

"We assume he came here specifically to start a prostitution ring. Likely he and his cousin or someone else he knows were talking about how Delphi City is this nice, innocent place. Kal says they can connect him with a few attempts to force prostitutes to work for him. Didn't work since it's not illegal here. After a few failed attempts to intimidate them, he apparently decided that pimping minors would be more cost-effective. Fortunately, we caught him."

"But how can someone do something like that? What did he do before he came to Delphi City?"

"He ran a bar. It was a normal bar; if it had had a history of illegal activities, we would have turned down his immigration request."

157

"But . . ."

"Look, there is no way to exclude all unsavory people from any population. Someone who's been here a few years might just decide that they could do better getting involved with illegal activity. It happens all the time in any sizable population. It happens here. Kal's team is pretty good at identifying them early, but for some people, morality is an option. They're going to do whatever gets them ahead. We can't screen them all out."

"So we just have to accept it?"

"No, we have to accept the risk of it happening. We have Kal and Chief Nawal to keep an eye on things and root them out. People are just flawed; you have to accept that. You're going to have some flawed people on your ships. There were probably a few on the Sakira when you commanded her. The only thing you can do is create an environment where everyone knows that they can get help if one of these flawed people tries to take advantage of them."

Catie grimaced and Blake laughed a little. "It's just life. You'll get used to it."

"I hope not!"

"You will. That doesn't mean you should get jaded. It's always a disappointment to find someone like that. But if you pretend they don't exist, then you make it easy for them to get away with it. If you accept the reality of it, then you'll more likely pick up the warning signs."

"Thanks," Catie said, still frowning. "I guess I still have a lot to learn about people."

"Yes, despite all of your adventures, you've lived a sheltered life. Most of the people you've associated with have been successful. It's tougher on the margins. Here in Delphi, we try to avoid having too many people in the margins, but there are always some."

"But we have the barracks for people to restart. They're not that bad."

"No, they're not. But some people just don't want to do more than the minimum. Do you know that thirty percent of the people who live in the barracks are permanent residents?"

"No way!"

"Yep. They just do enough to stay out of trouble, but they refuse to do enough to get their own place. Some of them actually do pretty well, but they seem to be stuck in place. Like teenagers, they like living someplace where they are not responsible for anything. We had to start a cleaning service there. Of course, it's the residents that do the job, but if we didn't institute the service, some of them would never have cleaned their rooms."

"Gross!"

"Flawed people."

"Thanks, I guess," Catie said.

"No problem. Now back to work, are you ready to head out?"

"We leave tomorrow."

"Good luck. Should be simple, but any sign of trouble, you head for the fringe and jump out."

"Yeah, you already told me."

"And I'll probably tell you again. Now, I've got to go if I'm going to make my dinner date."

"Say hi to Jackie for me."

"I will."

13   A Ride Home

The Roebuck was sitting at one of the bays in the docking ring. It nestled right in with the Oryxes that were docked. Even the Sakira would fit. It was only the carriers that were so big that you couldn't get two of them in adjacent bays. But if you spaced them out, anything as small as the Sakira could fit in next to them.

"Welcome aboard," Catie said to the Onisiwoen group. They still looked skeptical, but they were happy to be going home. "As soon as you're settled into your cabins, we'll push back. We'll have gravity ten minutes later. Please call the steward if you have any issues getting settled in."

"Thank you, Captain," Charlie said. "We are very happy that you're going to take us home."

"Let me know if there's anything I can do for you. I'll see you tomorrow at dinner," Catie said. She'd invited the Onisiwoen group to dine with her in her cabin. Samantha wanted her to do as much as she could to butter them up, hoping it would lead to a better relationship with the Onisiwo system.

"We look forward to it."

First Mate Koko Suzuki had been finalizing the details of their departure with the Delphi Station crew. Catie saw her coming up the gangway and decided to wait for her.

"Good morning, Princess," Suzuki said as she made her way onto the Roebuck. The spacer that was stationed at the entry barely suppressed his snicker. Catie was shocked at being referred to as Princess instead of captain.

"Good morning First Mate, would you join me in my cabin before we depart," Catie said.

"I need to get to the bridge and input our departure parameters."

"I'm sure it can wait five minutes."

"Yes, ma'am."

Once the hatch was closed, Catie led the way to her cabin.

"Have a seat," Catie said as she sat down behind her desk. Catie knew that First Mate Suzuki hadn't been happy when Catie had taken over as captain of the Roebuck. Suzuki had been acting captain ever since Lieutenant Payne had finished his tour. Obviously, she had been hoping for the position to be made permanent.

Catie left Suzuki hanging for a few minutes, specifically to create tension.

"Was there something you wanted to say to me, ma'am?" Suzuki asked.

"Yes there is. I was just trying to make a decision first. But I think I'm ready. First Mate Suzuki, you will address me as Cer, Ma'am, or Captain while you are aboard my ship, do I make myself clear?"

"Yes, ma'am," Suzuki answered, feigning confusion.

"To be clear, if you ever address me in any other way, specifically as princess, you will be spending the rest of the trip in your cabin. And if I find you making comments to the crew that undermine my position or authority, you will also be spending the rest of the trip in your cabin as well as being brought up on charges when we make it back to Earth. Is that clear?"

"Yes, ma'am. Sorry, ma'am, I just heard one of the Onisiwoens calling you princess, I guess it just slipped out."

"We both know that is not true. And if you ever lie to me again, we'll use the same remedy," Catie said.

"Yes, ma'am. I apologize."

"Enough said. Please get us prepared to push back."

"Yes, ma'am," Suzuki said. She stood up and made a crisp about-face and left the cabin. Catie hated being so heavy-handed, but she couldn't afford to allow Suzuki to imply to the crew that the only reason she was captain was because she was Princess Catie.

Suzuki slammed her palm into the bulkhead opposite Catie's cabin. "Damn her," she hissed. "I should challenge her to a sparring match!"

"Are you alright, ma'am?" Morgan asked.

"Oh, sorry, I'm fine," Suzuki said.

"She can be trying."

"Who?"

"The captain. If you decide to challenge her to spar with you, give me a day or two to lay down bets."

"You would bet on the match?"

"Oh, I'm sure the whole crew would." Morgan gave First Mate Suzuki a reassuring nod.

"Maybe I will," Suzuki said as she straightened out her uniform and headed toward the bridge.

Catie gave Suzuki five minutes before she followed her to the bridge. When she arrived, everyone was at their stations, preparing for the push back.

"First Mate, you parked her here, I'll let you do the honors of getting us underway," Catie said.

"Yes, ma'am," Suzuki said.

Catie noticed a knowing glance between the second mate at the communication console and the navigator. She wondered if he was implying that she might not be competent to issue the correct orders to get the ship out of the dock. She grimaced; she'd have to figure out how to undo any damage that Suzuki might have done in the past week.

Once the Roebuck was free of the dock, Catie looked at the navigator. "Do you have the course laid in for our jump point?"

"Yes, ma'am."

"First Mate, you have the bridge. Make an announcement before we accelerate so the Onisiwoen will know to expect gravity. I'll be in my office."

"Yes, ma'am."

◆ ◆ ◆

"I'll take the conn," Catie said as she arrived on the bridge. They'd been underway for three days, and the tension between her and Suzuki was still palpable. Catie had tried to find a way to bridge the gap, but Suzuki was maintaining an ice-cold demeanor.

"You have the conn," Suzuki said.

"Anything to report?"

"No, ma'am. Everything is running smoothly. I'm going to head to the gym and get a workout in before lunch."

Catie smiled. This was the first time Suzuki had said anything personal since they started the voyage. "I like to get a run in first thing in the morning."

"Oh, you run. I prefer doing a few katas," Suzuki said.

"Oh, you practice Aikido?"

"Yes, do you know it?"

"I've had some training," Catie said.

"Maybe we could do a sparring session together. I'm always looking for a new sparring partner," Suzuki said with a smile.

"Sure. Let me know when a good time would be."

"How about tomorrow afternoon. We both have the third watch off."

"Sounds good," Catie said as she brought up the ship's log on her display and started to enter the change of command.

The next afternoon, Catie met Suzuki in the gym. "Kind of crowded," she said as she looked around. About one-third of the crew was crammed into the space, just leaving room in the middle for the sparring ring and a half meter safety zone around it.

"Some of the crew thought it would be instructional to observe your technique," Suzuki said.

Catie was wearing grey yoga pants with a loose white blouse. Suzuki was wearing a white gi with a black hakama, a huge billowing pair of pants, over it. Catie slipped out of her sandals as she stepped into the ring. She did a few stretches as she looked around at the crowd. Apparently, Suzuki was planning on showing her up. So, she was still mad about losing command.

Suzuki stepped into the ring and started doing a slow warmup. "Let me know when you're ready."

"Any time," Catie said, shaking her head. She grabbed her headgear and put it on.

"Headgear?"

"A requirement," Catie said. "Either of us can do our jobs while healing from anything except a brain injury. I don't want to risk losing you for two weeks."

Suzuki smiled as she went to the rack and grabbed her headgear. "I don't think you need to worry about losing me."

"Of course not, but accidents do happen."

Morgan stepped into the ring and asked the two women to square off and bow to each other.

"Did you get some bets laid on?" Catie messaged.

"Lots of bets," Morgan whispered. "Okay, no strikes to the eyes. If one of you hits the ground and cannot get up before the count of eight the match is over. If one of you is pinned to the ground by the other for more than a count of ten, the match is over. You may begin!"

Catie relaxed and started circling Suzuki. When Suzuki stepped in, Catie threw a soft punch at her. Suzuki blocked it easily and tried to grasp Catie's arm to get her into an armlock. Catie circled out of it and stepped back. Suzuki stepped in, throwing a three combination punch series. Catie blocked the punches and kept circling.

Suzuki started moving faster, punching harder, using a more complex series of punches and blocks. Catie kept blocking the strikes, but her blocks were coming later and later. Suzuki got in a couple of glancing blows as Catie continued to back up and circle away from her.

The noise from the crowd grew louder and Suzuki became even more aggressive. Catie kept blocking and circling away. Occasionally she would throw a combination at Suzuki, but Suzuki would easily block it. Suzuki became even more confident and aggressive. She attacked Catie almost constantly. Catie's blocks continued to lag. Suzuki couldn't get in a solid hit, nor was she able to grasp Catie's arms or shoulders when Catie launched one of her infrequent counter attacks.

Suddenly Catie stepped in, throwing a hard right at Suzuki's head. Suzuki sidestepped it and grabbed Catie's arm. She slid her arm along Catie's until it was pressed against Catie's armpit. Catie flailed and twisted her body. Suzuki stepped forward with her right leg coming behind Catie's legs. Catie lurched and circled her arm from Suzuki's grasp and fell backward on Suzuki's leg. Suzuki thrust her weight forward trying to push Catie's body to the floor. Catie continued to flail and threw her weight backward, spinning her body on top of Suzuki's leg, her head angling toward the floor. Catie kicked out with her left leg which Suzuki easily blocked upward. As Catie was falling toward the floor she kicked out desperately with her right leg. Her heel caught Suzuki right in the solar plexus. Suzuki collapsed to the floor as Catie rolled back into an upright stance.

"One . . . Two . . .," Morgan counted. Suzuki tried to stand up, but she was almost paralyzed by the blow. "Six . . . Seven . . . Eight!" Morgan finished the count. "The captain is the winner!" Morgan shouted.

Catie walked over and helped Suzuki to her feet. "Are you all right?"

"I'll be fine," Suzuki gasped. "Lucky shot!"

"Better lucky than good," Catie said as she helped Suzuki over to the bench. The gym was emptying quickly. "You'll be fine in a minute. Morgan will stay with you until you've recovered."

Catie left the gym, followed by the stragglers. Soon there was only Morgan and Suzuki in the gym. Suzuki's coloring was returning and her breathing was becoming easier.

"Sorry about that," Suzuki said. "Lucky shot."

"Why are you sorry?" Morgan asked.

"I cost you money."

"Nope, I made eight thousand Aurora."

"You bet on the captain?"

"Of course," Morgan said.

"But I nearly beat her. If it wasn't for that crazy kick, I would have won."

"You think? She used to pull that trick on me all the time. It took me six months before I could train myself not to go for that move."

"She did that on purpose?"

"Oh yeah."

"But she was barely blocking my strikes."

"Barely is still good enough. Did you ever tag her? If you did, I didn't see it."

"No way!" Suzuki jumped up, clearly almost fully recovered.

"She suckers you in by letting you think you're winning."

"I don't believe you!"

"Kaia!" Morgan shouted.

Suzuki stepped back and blocked Morgan's strike. Morgan launched another combo tagging Suzuki on the head, not too hard, but hard enough that she knew she'd been hit. In four more exchanges, Morgan tagged Suzuki twice more and then got her in a shoulder lock, releasing her just before Suzuki would have hit the floor.

"So you're her sensei."

"No, I'm her sparring partner. When we spar, the captain usually crushes me," Morgan said. "She let you save face this time. If you challenge her again, she'll humiliate you."

"You think?"

"I know. You've got two strikes. Catie doesn't give anyone a pass after the third."

"Thanks for the heads up," Suzuki said. "I think I'll go sit in the jacuzzi and meditate."

◆ ◆ ◆

"We've reached the fringe, Captain," the navigator reported.

"Are you ready to open the wormhole?"

"Yes, ma'am."

"Then start the cascade," Catie ordered. Using the preplaced probes, the navigator opened a wormhole one jump away, then continued to open one from the next system back to the last one, allowing the wormholes to merge. Finally, the last wormhole from Onisiwo was opened. When it merged with the previous wormhole, there was a single wormhole snaking from Earth to Onisiwo.

"Cascade complete."

"Prepare for transition," blared on the ship's speakers.

Catie gave everyone one minute to prepare. "Take us through," she ordered.

The Roebuck adjusted its jump engines so the wormhole became stationary instead of being projected in front of the Roebuck. "Entering wormhole now."

"And welcome to Onisiwo," Catie announced as the Roebuck exited the wormhole seconds later.

"Flipping the ship in one minute," the pilot announced.

"Navigator, plot a course that brings us to the edge of their asteroid belt. I want us to orbit outside of their farthest space station. We'll start contacting them once we're inside the second gas giant."

"Yes, ma'am."

14   We Have a Problem

"The wormhole has just appeared in the Onisiwoen system!" ADI alerted Catie. They were just two days into their journey to the Onisiwoens' planet.

"Put the ship on yellow alert," Catie ordered as she made her way to the bridge. Yellow alert put the Roebuck into active military status.

"Captain on the bridge," the ship AI announced as Catie entered.

"Oh, I wanted to say that," ADI said.

"I can't believe you let the AI beat you," Catie messaged back. "First Officer, please bring up the weapons station," Catie ordered. First Officer Suzuki got out of the captain's chair and moved to the weapons station.

Catie sat in the captain's chair and brought up the navigation screen; after a few strokes and calculations, she sent the data to the navigator. "Navigator, execute the turn I just sent you. Comms, announce we'll go to max acceleration in one hour."

"Yes, ma'am," the comm officer and navigator announced together.

"Admiral McCormack is on the Comm."

"Put him on the main display. ... Admiral."

"Captain, I hear the wormhole has opened. Are you moving back to the fringe?"

"Yes, it'll take us three days to get back to the fringe. The wormhole has been stable for two minutes; I suggest we push our probe through."

"I agree."

"ADI."

"Moving the probe," ADI replied.

Kasper entered the bridge and immediately moved to the flight operations station. "Captain," he acknowledged Catie.

"Please put your pilots into their Foxes," Catie ordered.

"Yes, ma'am. Should we depressurize the flight bay?"

"Let's hold off on that until we know more," Catie replied.

"The probe is through," ADI said.

"Sorry I'm late, you caught me in the shower," the sensor operator said as he made his way to his station. Until the Roebuck went to active status, the sensor station was handled by the comms officer.

"Not a problem. Please bring up the reading from the probe."

"Yes, ma'am. On the main display now."

"Oh my!" Catie said as she saw a flotilla of Fazullan ships in the space around the wormhole's entrance. "What is the speed and time to the wormhole for those ships?"

"The ships are at dead stop relative to the wormhole. The closest one would take forty-two hours at 4Gs to reach the wormhole," ADI messaged Catie.

"Let's let him do his job," Catie messaged back.

"Ships are at dead stop relative to the wormhole," the sensor operator announced. "Calculating distance now. . . . The closest ship is approximately four hundred million kilometers from the wormhole, approximately forty-two hours at 4Gs."

"Have they sent a probe through?" Blake asked.

"Sensors?" Catie asked.

"No sign of any activity on our side of the wormhole. Our probe doesn't show any activity close to the wormhole"

"Thank you. Kasper, you can stand your pilots down, but keep them on alert."

"Yes, ma'am."

"First Officer, you have the bridge. I'll be in my office. Kasper, please join me," Catie said as she got up and left the bridge with Kasper immediately behind her.

"No rust on the captain," the navigator said once Catie had left the bridge.

"Hey, I thought she ordered you to flip the ship," the second officer said.

"No, she had me make a 30-degree turn. It'll get us to the fringe the fastest. I've never done a turn like that without going through microgravity, but it keeps the ship under gravity while changing course. It takes an hour, but we're two days in from the fringe, so who cares? It allowed the pilots to get to their Foxes and avoided the mess of an emergency flip. We'll hit the fringe in three days."

"Nice. Hey, why don't we do something like that when we exit the wormhole?"

"I don't know. I'll ask the captain when all this is over."

"Uncle Blake, quite a gathering around the wormhole, don't you think?" Catie said as she brought up the main display in her office and shared it with everyone.

"Yes it is. Your father, Sam, and Admiral Michaels should be here any minute. Liz just joined us."

"Hi, Catie. You always get all the exciting missions."

"I think too much excitement," Catie said. "What do you think they're up to?"

"Studying the ships, some of them don't seem very space worthy," Liz said.

"I noticed that. Why would you put so many marginal ships into space? It looks like they activated anything that could make orbit," Catie said.

"We're here," Marc reported as he and Samantha joined the conference.

"We've been listening in, so we're up to speed," Samantha said. "And to answer your questions, my guess is that they are planning to move."

"Move?!"

"Yes. I'm just scanning your report on the wormhole. Based on my reading, this is the first habitable system that the wormhole has connected to."

"I think that's correct. We can't be sure, but based on the analysis that Dr. McDowell and I did, none of the other likely systems had planets in the habitable zone."

"Right. And Captain Lantaq said that the Fazullans' planet was harsh. Maybe they decided to move to a system that was more hospitable."

"That's a huge investment. They've put at least one hundred years into colonizing that planet."

"But," Liz interrupted, "maybe it's gotten worse over time. You said it's in a binary system. Aren't planets in those kinds of systems susceptible to orbital changes?"

"It's possible," Catie said. "So, Daddy, what are we going to do?"

"I don't know," Marc said. "We still need to figure out what the Fazullans are up to."

"Captain, we just received a ping from the wormhole," the comm officer announced on Catie's private channel.

"Thank you," Catie replied. "They just pinged for their satellite, but wait, they can't do that. Sensors, how did they ping their satellite?"

"What do you mean they can't do that?" Blake asked.

"You can't transmit a signal through a wormhole. You probably forgot because we use the quantum relays."

"Okay, so how did they do it?"

"They must have sent a probe through," Catie said.

"But didn't you just say there was no activity around the wormhole on their side?"

"We must have missed something."

"I can explain," the sensor operator announced.

"Please do."

"Reviewing the logs, we can detect a very small probe, approximately twenty centimeters in diameter, exiting the wormhole. It sent a ping, waited approximately one minute then reentered the wormhole."

"How can they move a probe that small?" Blake asked. "There's no way they have a gravity drive that would fit."

"You wouldn't need one," Catie said. "All you have to do is have the probe enter the wormhole. As soon as its entire mass is inside, it transitions to the other side. You could do it with thrusters."

"So what did they learn?" Marc asked.

"That the wormhole is open, that wherever it's open to, their satellite is either not present or is inactive."

"Wouldn't they have picked up more information?" Liz asked.

"I think a probe that small would be just a comm relay. It probably transitions the wormhole, pings the satellite, waits for a data dump, and then returns."

"So they don't know it's in the Onisiwoen system?" Blake asked.

"They just know that the wormhole has temporarily stabilized on a system. Our calculations showed that the wormhole skips around for a while before it really stabilizes on a system," Catie said. "Sensors, any movement on the enemy fleet?"

"No, ma'am."

"I'm here," Admiral Michaels announced. "ADI just gave me an update. I had to beg out of a meeting with the German ambassador."

"What do you suggest we do?" Marc asked.

"Do you intend to stop them?"

"I do."

"Then we need a lot more firepower than the Roebuck. We should send the Victory and the Enterprise."

"We can have them both there within a day," Blake said. "We just need to position the jump ships."

"Then let's move them," Marc ordered.

"Is there a possibility of getting the Galileo there as well?" Admiral Michaels asked.

"We'll have to contact Mangkatar and ask the Paraxean governor," Marc said.

"I'm working on it now," Samantha said. "What about asking the Paraxean home planet for some help?"

"We could," Marc said. "How do we convince them that it's in their interest?"

"I would suggest we send the Princess of the Realm there," Samantha said. "Face-to-face negotiations will impress them."

"What?!" Catie demanded.

"Face it, you're still our best asset when it comes to goodwill," Samantha said. "Besides, you haven't been there."

"What about you?" Catie asked. She was skeptical about why they'd decided she needed to go to Paraxea.

"It would take twenty days for Sam to reach the fringe, we wouldn't want to put the baby through a high-G profile," Marc said.

"Not a good idea," Blake agreed.

"Oh, I guess that would be bad for little Allie," Catie sighed, resigning to her fate. "Will you start the negotiations?"

"I'll work with Governor Paratar to come up with an approach. We'll have something ready before you jump."

"What about Uncle Blake?" Catie made one more desperate attempt to get out of the assignment.

"I'm bringing the Sakira to Onisiwo," Blake said. "Suck it up, Lieutenant."

"Okay, we'll make the jump in three days," Catie replied.

"Good. We'll keep analyzing our options. We'll meet again after your jump," Marc said.

"Charlie, sorry about the excitement," Catie said when the lead Onisiwoen joined her in her office.

"We have been very curious about what is going on," Charlie said.

"I'm sure; have a seat and I'll try to explain. You remember Ambassador Newman," Catie said to introduce Samantha on the main display.

"Yes, a pleasure to see you again," Charlie said.

"My pleasure as well."

Once Charlie was seated, Catie brought up the image of the Fazullan fleet. "Do those ships look familiar?" Catie asked.

"Not all of them, but most of them look like the ship that attacked us."

"They are. The wormhole opened. We sent a probe through it and discovered this fleet there. We believe that they are planning to move their entire colony to Onisiwo."

"Their colony?"

"Yes, the Fazullans in this system," Catie pointed to the Fazullan system on the star map, "are a colony sent from their homeworld. We do not know where their homeworld is."

"Okay, and why do you think they're coming to Onisiwo?"

"We had assumed that they would send other ships to raid your system, but since they're sending what looks like everything they have, we believe that something has made their colony world sufficiently uninviting that they're willing to spend four or five years relocating everyone and everything to Onisiwo," Catie explained.

Charlie nodded his head in understanding, although he didn't look like he really believed her. "And what will happen now?"

"Ambassador," Catie said to turn the meeting over to Samantha.

"We need your help. The Roebuck has been redirected to Paraxea to ask them for help. It will take you about ten days to get there. We'd like you to stay with Princess Catherine and act as the Onisiwoen ambassador. We have only been trading with Paraxea for about nine months. We've actually only been in contact with them for about two years. We need you to help us convince them that helping to defend Onisiwo is in their best interest," Samantha said.

"And how can I do that?"

"By being honest with us and them. I understand that you don't trust us. But we need to get over that. We need help if we're going to turn back this fleet. Your system doesn't have the technology to do it. We do, but we can only get three carriers and a big frigate to Onisiwo in time. We need help. The Paraxeans will have carriers and fighters like ours, we have to convince them to help."

"What do we have that would interest them?"

"Trade," Samantha said. "The Paraxeans have essentially three colonies that they now have access to thanks to our jumpdrive. Those colonies will have abundant raw material that Paraxea can use. Your system will have raw materials as well as advanced manufactured goods that the colonies can use, and Paraxea will have more advanced manufactured goods that you can use. It sets up a perfect triangle trade. Plus, Delphi hopes to expand the number of colonies we have and we are willing to help your people and the Paraxeans to do the same. That requires stability. The Fazullans are a destabilizing influence."

"Okay, then what do you need from us?"

"More information about your technology as it would relate to trade. You seem to have done a lot of expansion into your solar system. That implies you may have technology that those of us who have not done as much local expansion may not have developed yet."

"And what technology would you be willing to share with us? Your jumpdrive?"

"The jumpdrive is our most closely held secret. We are not willing to share the technology with anyone. But we can provide you with access to gravity drives which will greatly improve your ability to access your solar system. We can also provide access to fusion reactors."

"We have fusion reactors."

"But are they small enough to power a starship? What about a spaceplane or an ocean liner?" Samantha asked.

"You have them that small?"

"A fusion reactor powered the Oryx that you flew to Delphi Station," Catie explained. "The Fazullans are using fusion reactors and gravity drives to power their starships. Our reactors and drives are more efficient and smaller."

"I see. This could be of great benefit to us," Charlie said. "But how can I speak for my entire planet? We haven't even contacted them yet."

"We'll tell the Paraxeans about the situation, but what we need is knowledge about your system. The Paraxeans will recognize the opportunity if we present it correctly."

"Okay, so what do you need me to do?"

"Help me create a proposal," Samantha said.

◆ ◆ ◆

"Captain, the Victory just jumped in," the sensor operator reported.

"Comms, hail them," Catie ordered.

Captain Clements' image came up on the main display.

"Captain McCormack, sitrep?" Clements ordered.

"Nothing has changed in the twenty seconds it has taken you to jump here," Catie reported.

"Good. How long before you reach the fringe?"

"Twenty-seven hours and forty seconds," Catie answered.

Captain Clements smiled. "Point taken. Is Admiral Blake available?"

"We'll ping him," Catie said as she nodded to her Comms officer.

Blake's image joined Captain Clements on the display. "I assume the Victory jumped in," Blake said.

"Yes, sir."

"The Enterprise should be there shortly," Blake said. "They're waiting for Captain Desjardins."

"Good day, Admiral," Captain Clements said. "Have you decided how you want to deploy us?"

"By the wormhole," Blake said.

"Admiral, just so you remember, the wormhole will wander around," Catie said.

"What?! I thought it only wandered between systems."

"No, it also wanders within a system. It will change position every ten to twenty hours," Catie explained. "As things in this system change, the zero point that the wormhole latches onto will change. The new location can be anywhere from one to six million kilometers from the last position."

"So we can't just sit on the wormhole," Blake said.

"It will work for ten to twenty hours, then you would need to move to wherever it wandered to.'"

"Has there been any indication that the Fazullans are preparing to transit the wormhole?" Blake asked.

"No, sir. They will probably send their relay probe through again."

"How many times do you think they'll try before sending a bigger probe through?"

"I don't know. Hopefully, they'll think that when the wormhole wanders, it's wandering between systems or around a previous system. The wormhole has probably been doing a lot of jumping before it settled here. Initially, they'll wait. But sooner or later they're going to notice that its moves aren't causing big power spikes. So they'll know it's stabilized in a system," Catie explained.

"If they send a big probe through, I think we should destroy it," Blake said.

"I agree, but eventually they might get smart and send one through right after the wormhole wanders to a new location. They have to be a little nervous about the Onisiwoens learning about the wormhole."

"Okay, we'll see how much time that buys us. You need to go get us more help," Blake said.

"Yes, sir."

"Why hasn't the probe been able to communicate with our satellite?" the Fazullan Admiral demanded.

"I assume that the wormhole is not in the system yet," the sensor operator replied.

"It must be. The energy readouts say it's no longer jumping systems."

"Possibly it's wandering around a different system before it finally jumps to Onisiwo."

"It's never done that before."

"It could be that the wormhole is too far away from our satellite for the probe to pick up the reply to the ping," suggested the navigator. He shrank back from the Admiral's glare.

"Send the relay again and have it wait for an hour," the Admiral ordered.

"The Fazullans sent their relay probe again. It was in system for one hour," Blake said to the assembled team.

"That means they're suspecting that the wormhole must be at Onisiwo," Catie said. "They'll be sending an active probe through next."

"Based on what you said, as long as we destroy it before it transitions back, they will still be in the dark."

"Unless some part of it transitions back through the wormhole," Catie said.

"Then we'll use plasma cannons to vaporize it."

During all the drama, the Dutchman was steadily making its way to Artemis, completing the first leg of its trade loop.

"Artemis Control, this is the Dutchman."

"Dutchman, Artemis Control, we have you on radar."

"Artemis Control, we'll be entering orbit in two hours. We're planning on a stationary position over your North Pole."

"Dutchman, Artemis Control, just don't hit the moon and you'll be good to go."

"Thanks for the advice. Can you switch us over to the mayor's office?"

"No problem. Here you go, Artemis Control out."

"They forgot to warn us about the satellites," the navigator said.

"Probably because they're so small," Captain Payne replied. "Communications, do we have the office?"

"They're on now."

"Hello, this is Captain Payne of the Dutchman. We have a load of colonists for you guys."

"We're waiting on them. We assume you will be unloading them first."

"Yes, we're going to see if we can keep them under gravity while we unload them. Some of them have expressed a distinct dislike of microgravity."

"Let me guess, they express that dislike by hurling their last meal all over your clean deck."

"Yes, they do. Anyway, Catie came up with a concept of a stationary orbit over the pole while loading and unloading to keep them under gravity. We're going to give it a try. Will you please instruct your Skylifters to meet us there?"

"We're on the channel, we'll see you there. Sounds like fun."

Derek had the helm steer them in a looping orbit so they were backing down toward the North Pole on their final approach to Artemis. At four hundred kilometers, they halted their descent. Hovering at that altitude gave them a gravity of 99% standard, hardly a noticeable difference.

Now they had to slide the cabin pods out of the Dutchman without banging them up. Derek had them put two grav lifters on each pod as they slid it out. Once there was room for the Skylifter to attach to the pod, they were able to slide it free of the Dutchman and start the descent to Artemis, releasing the grav drives to go deal with the next pod. Derek had been shocked when he'd calculated the time to land the pods. It only took 14 minutes at 0.1G of acceleration and deceleration to get each pod down to ten thousand meters. Of course then it took five hours to fly the thing from the North Pole to Artemis, supersonic speeds were not an option for the bulky cargo pods.

So with only three Skylifters, it took thirty hours to move all the colonists down. They couldn't unload the other pods, since with the Dutchman sitting on its tail in a stationary orbit, those pods would start falling as soon as they were free of the ship.

Most of the colonists in the inside cabins found space in a cabin aboard the pods so that they would be able to make an under-gravity transition to the planet's surface. That meant that there wouldn't be too much effort to finish unloading the Dutchman once the cabin pods were down. A couple of Oryx trips would handle all the colonists' luggage.

Once the last cabin pod was released, Derek had the helm ease the Dutchman into an orbit at 400 kilometers. They had to be extra careful since without half her pods the Dutchman was structurally weak. Thinking about it afterward, Derek decided that it might have been just as fast to unload the cargo pods the same way. The slow transition to a normal orbit had taken eight hours. It would be interesting to go over the whole thing with Liz and Catie.

Finally, after three days to unload the Dutchman, Derek was able to declare shore leave for the crew. Half would remain on the Dutchman and secure the outbound cargo, switching with their mates after two days.

15   Some Help Please?

"Kasper, would you join me in my office," Catie messaged.

"I'll be right there, Captain."

It was only a minute before Kasper knocked.

"Enter."

"Captain, what can I do for you?"

"We're alone, call me Catie."

"Okay. So what do you need?"

"As you know, we're going to Paraxea to ask them to send a couple of space carriers to Onisiwo. And as part of that, Sam has changed my status to Princess of Delphi to make it a state visit."

"Yeah, I know that."

"Well, anyway, besides designing a fancy uniform for me to wear, she wants me to have an aide de camp. I was wondering whether you would be willing to play that role."

"Why me?"

"Because I know you. And I'm embarrassed by this whole princess thing and I'm hoping you won't use it against me later."

"Why? You didn't have a problem embarrassing me back when I was in flight school," Kasper said. He was referring to the time that Blake had Catie go against Kasper in a mock dogfight in order to develop a little humility in him. Catie had killed Kasper three times. She thought they'd become friends afterward.

"You can't be holding that against me. You even used it in your speech to the new pilots."

"So . . ."

"Sorry I asked," Catie said.

Kasper laughed. "I'll do it. I just wanted to make you sweat. Since I can't do it in a jet, I couldn't resist this opportunity."

"I should get even for that . . . but I won't. You'll have to wear a fancy uniform too. It's mostly the same as your regular one, just a sash and some extra stuff. The quartermaster has the design."

"I'll go get fitted then," Kasper said. "When is our first performance?"

"We are supposed to join a video meeting tomorrow. Then we'll have a big welcome to Paraxea ceremony when we make orbit in four days."

"Okay. Should we practice?"

"I'm sure Sam will want us to. I'll ask her."

"Let me know," Kasper said as he exited Catie's office.

That night when they practiced, Samantha simply pointed out that Catie needed to make Kasper do all the work. He should be the one to look things up, even if Catie could do it faster. She made the point with Kasper that he had to act solicitously toward Catie at all times.

"Like a toady?" Kasper had asked.

"Exactly," Samantha had replied.

The next day, they convened in Catie's office for the video meeting. Morgan joined them acting as Catie's squire. Catie was wearing the standard dress uniform, black tunic over dark grey slacks. She had her medals pinned and her beret tucked under the epaulet on her left shoulder. Kasper's uniform was the same except he had a thick gold braid on his right shoulder, indicating he was the aide de camp.

Once the Paraxean minister joined the meeting, Morgan made a show of serving tea to everyone.

"Minister Malashka, I understand that you and Ambassador Newman have made a lot of progress," Catie said after the introductions were over.

"Yes, Princess, we have," Minister Malashka said. "We hope you and your father approve of our efforts."

"I'm sure we will," Catie said. She smiled at the thought of Marc disapproving of Samantha's efforts.

"It is awkward talking about an alliance without having your homeworld directly involved," Minister Malashka said.

"I'm sure that Ambassador Newman has explained the urgency of the situation. We have been working with the governments of Earth to formalize an interstellar alliance, but the impending invasion of Onisiwo makes it urgent that we reach out to you now. Waiting for the completion of the discussion on Earth is not possible," Catie said.

Kasper made a show of providing Catie some information before she continued.

"Our latest estimate is that there are forty-two combat starships preparing to enter the Onisiwo system. We have to act now before they come to the realization that the wormhole is fully established in Onisiwo."

"Yes, I see. And we appreciate the fact that you're willing to make a personal visit to appeal to us," Minister Malashka said. "Our government has been meeting nonstop to forge an agreement. It is just so outside our experience that we are struggling to come up with the right format."

"Ambassadors!" Admiral Michaels said, almost shouting. "We do not have time for petty politics. Princess Catherine and Ambassador Newman are meeting with the Paraxean government as we speak."

"Under what authority do they propose to form an alliance?" demanded the Chinese ambassador.

"Under the authority of the Colony of Artemis and the Colony of Mangkatar," Admiral Michaels replied. "We have also aligned with the Aperanjens who we will be helping to establish another colony. And of course, we will be talking with the Onisiwoens as soon as we establish contact."

"You are exceeding your position!"

"We are responding to the situation we have. If Earth wants to continue to argue among ourselves, then we will form an interstellar alliance without her. But if you want to step forward and lead, then do so. Now, we were discussing the terms on page thirty-two."

"Sam, why do you need me to attend these conferences?" Catie whined.

"Because we need to build up pressure on the Paraxeans. You will be the first alien to set foot on their planet, and it will be a state visit. They're going to want to make that special. So hopefully they'll agree to the treaty to commemorate your visit."

"But Liz was there before and the Dutchman was there just three weeks ago."

"But nobody visited the planet. It's not the same."

"How do you stay awake while they drone on and on about such little things?"

"Hey, at least they're not crying," Samantha said.

"Are you hinting that my baby sister cries too much?"

"Wait until you come visit and get to babysit for a few hours. You'll be desperate for adult conversation."

"But you can talk to Daddy anytime you want."

"He seems to be very busy, especially when Allie is fussy."

"And you let him get away with that?"

"I'm breastfeeding, there's not much he can do."

"You know they invented these things called bottles and breast pumps."

"She's too young. I'll start her on a bottle next month. Don't worry, I won't let him hide for long. Now study the treaty so you're ready for the next meeting."

◆ ◆ ◆

"Hi, Uncle Blake," Catie said as she and her uncle connected.

"Hey, squirt. How are you doing?"

"I'm bored."

"Negotiating treaties doesn't excite you?"

"No!"

"Well, you would be bored here. The Fazullans haven't sent a probe through yet."

"They will. Have you contacted the Onisiwoens yet?"

"Not yet. The probe you launched will be in place tomorrow. We're going to wait until it's in a solar orbit before we send the first message."

"Ping me before you signal them. I want to listen in."

"You sure you'll have time?"

"Uncle Blake!"

"Okay, I'll work it around your schedule. Bye."

"Bye."

"Do you want to play a game?" ADI asked Catie after the call closed.

"Oh, hi, ADI. Do you have an escape room set up?"

"Yes."

"Don't tell Sam. Now, what's the first clue?"

"Why do I have to wear a skirt?" Catie whined.

"Because we want to remind them that you're a princess," Samantha said. "Now quit acting like one and finish dressing."

"Okay, is this good enough?" Catie asked once she finished dressing.

"Put on the sash."

"Really?"

"Yes. Prince William wears one."

"Who cares what he wears."

"You realize the British Royalty must have a hundred rules about how to dress. You don't have much to complain about. Now put on the sash."

Catie finally made it to the flight bay, fully dressed. Kasper and Morgan were waiting for her along with the two biggest Marines they had on board the Roebuck.

"After you," Kasper said, pointing to the Lynx.

"Nope, last on, first off," Catie said, quoting the rules about captains boarding boats.

"Yes, ma'am."

They took the Hover Lynx. Although the Paraxeans had Lynxes, they'd invented them after all, they hadn't invented a Hover Lynx. Samantha was hoping to further impress them. It was a short flight to the Paraxean surface. Marta, their pilot, made a point of bringing the Lynx into a hover at the end of the runway, then floating it over to the waiting grandstand area the Paraxeans had set up.

As Catie exited the Lynx, the Paraxean band started playing the Delphi National Anthem. There were banners welcoming her to Paraxea and the troops in front of the grandstand stood in ranks ready for inspection.

"They're worse than the French," Catie whispered under her breath.

"I'm telling Yvette you said that," ADI said.

"She'll probably agree with me," Catie messaged.

"We'll see."

Catie walked up to Paraxean President Plaxmar, "Mr. President, thank you for welcoming me to Paraxea."

"Princess Catherine, it is our pleasure. Would you do the honor of inspecting our troops with me?"

"Of course."

◆ ◆ ◆

"Nice digs," Morgan said as she placed Catie's now-empty bags in the closet.

"Well, it is the presidential palace. You would expect it to be nice."

"You guys might need to upgrade the palace in Delphi City."

"What palace?"

"That's my point. How can you host these alien dignitaries if you don't have a palace?"

"I think the French will let us use theirs."

"Won't that piss the Americans off?"

"Probably. But what wouldn't?"

"Holding it at the White House."

186

"Hmm, that'd piss off the French."

"And Germans, British, Chinese, and Russians."

"Everything pisses the Russians off."

"So you guys need a palace."

"I'll mention it to Sam."

"Sure, you do that. Now, you've got two hours before the state dinner. Will you need help getting dressed?"

"I might. You've seen that dress Sam is making me wear."

"I've never known anyone who complained so much about being treated so well."

"I'm not into dressing up," Catie said.

"Hey, I remember that red dress."

"So do I, and so does Daddy," Catie laughed. They were referring to the first sexy dress Catie had ever worn. Blake had goaded her into wearing it to an event her father was hosting. He'd sprayed his drink all over the table.

◆ ◆ ◆

"So that's what was in that bag Sam had sent from Earth," Morgan said, motioning to the tiara and jewels that Catie was wearing.

"Yes. Can you believe she thought of it in time? Then had ADI fly a Fox out here with it." The Fox, without a human passenger, was able to accelerate at a high enough G force to catch up with the Roebuck.

"I have to say it was worth it. You sure have grown into a beautiful woman," Morgan said. She stood back admiring Catie in the gown. It was midnight blue, highlighting Catie's blue eyes and tan skin tone. At five-eight, Catie had lots of leg for the gown to flare down around. "When did your boobs get bigger than Liz's?"

"What?"

"You heard me."

"About six months ago," Catie said. "Liz was not happy."

"Yeah, I'd guess not. She had this gangly teenage friend to look after, then all of a sudden, her friend is better looking than she is."

"I am not."

"You are too. Not that Liz is bad looking, mind you. But you're more elegant."

"I think it's the tiara," Catie said.

"Keep telling yourself that. It's why we all love you."

"Well, is everything on straight?"

"It is, now put on the sash," Morgan said as she handed Catie the red sash.

Catie stared at Morgan.

"I brought an extra one," Morgan said, explaining how the sash was clean and dry after Catie had stuffed it in the toilet tank.

"Damn you!"

"Just put it on, and we can go. Kasper is waiting in the hallway."

"Wow!" Kasper said when Catie exited the room. "I mean. You look exquisite Your Highness."

"Suck-up," Morgan whispered.

Kasper extended his arm for Catie. She took it and they made their way down the stairs to the reception.

At the dinner, Catie was seated next to the president while Kasper was seated next to the president's daughter. Catie frowned at the idea, but cross-species relationships didn't seem likely so she assumed the president was just trying to give Kasper someone younger to chat with. By the end of the dinner, Catie was jealous, Kasper probably got to talk about something besides government policy.

Admiral Michaels showed the video of the state dinner to the ambassadors of the UN Security Council. "That is President Plaxmar of Paraxea sitting next to Princess Catherine. The president of the entire planet, not of one country."

"How can you have this if Paraxea is so far away?"

"We have a ship at the fringe. It jumps back and forth delivering a data dump each way. It then takes eight hours for the data to reach us here."

"So, what does it mean?" the Russian ambassador asked.

"It means that by tomorrow the Paraxeans will have signed the alliance treaty and Earth will get to be a late signatory."

"We can't have that," the American ambassador said.

"Well, that's what will happen. You've been stalling, complaining about minor details while the Paraxeans have been negotiating in good faith."

"Princess, I hope you will share the design of this Hover Lynx as you call it," the Paraxean President said. "It is so much more versatile than our FX9. I'm amazed we never thought of it."

"I'm sure that can be arranged," Catie said. She thought that Marc would be okay with just giving them the design. It wasn't that much more complex when compared to a regular Lynx and would obviously delight the president. She messaged her idea to Samantha.

"As you know, most of our population is now concentrated in the cities due to the constraints of power distribution and our eco-conscious laws. But with the solar panel design we got from you, we're able to build communities off the grid, as you say. That's where we're going, to see one of our new communities."

"That sounds like what we've done on Artemis," Catie said.

"Yes, we're modeling these new communities on the design that your father showed us. It's quite ingenious. And I understand that that design is based on your Delphi City. A floating city, what an amazing concept. We might have to build one of those. Paraxeans love to be close to one another, but lately, people are wanting to have more space around them."

"We dedicate thirty percent of the area in a city to open space," Catie said.

"I wish we'd done that. But in the previous industrial cycle, they were so focused on utilizing the space efficiently to minimize resource consumption that I think we overdid it. We need to find a way to break these cycles, and I think spreading people out a bit will help."

"Why would that help?"

"If people can get away from everyone else for a bit, I think it will take away the pressure to conform. Then people might be more comfortable with the variations in society and the variations in wealth."

"I'm not sure about that. People on Earth are very nonconformist and they're not happy about the disparity in wealth."

"But you people take it too far," the president said. "We would never allow the level of poverty that you do. No, Paraxeans would never accept that. Now you can just see the new city over there."

The president asked the pilot to circle the city before they landed. Catie found it interesting. There was a nice, two-lane highway going into the city from the direction they'd come from. No other roads left the city, making it look a bit like a lollipop stuck out from the main city.

"How far is this from the capital?"

"It is three hundred twenty kilometers from the capital. Long ago there was another city here, but previous generations reclaimed all the resources from it and returned it to nature."

"Why?"

"Efficiency. They were using up all of our resources and couldn't afford to have cities all around the planet. They had to concentrate everything into supercities to accommodate the population and maintain their standard of living. Of course, now that we have interstellar trade, we can make different choices. And our population has continued to shrink, so we're not taxing the planet so heavily.

"Here, now we're landing. I hope you're as excited as I am to see this new wonder," the president said as he undid his restraints and prepared to deplane.

As Catie followed the president with Kasper on her heels, she got the sense that she was in Delphi City. The layout was eerily similar. The airport was connected to the city on the same corner. Like Delphi City, there was a large warehouse district, although no wharves. Then the city grew as you looked past the warehouses. There were a few tall buildings but most of them were on the order of eight stories like Delphi City. But instead of being surrounded by an ocean, it was surrounded by a sea of grass.

"Our welcoming committee," the president said. "The one on the right is the mayor, a nice fellow. The one on the left is the governor of this province; he's a suck-up. I like that word your people have, suck-up."

"President Plaxmar, welcome to Dermarxia, and you as well, Princess Catherine," the governor said as he greeted them with a slight bow.

"I wanted to show the princess how we were using the Delphinean design here to build this community," the president said as he led Catie past the governor and to the open car waiting for them. Kasper and Morgan hurried after them and made it clear that they would be in the car with Catie, which left the governor having to grab a seat in the next car. The mayor decided he would drive, so he managed a seat next to the president.

"We've adopted your design of cargo delivery," the mayor said. "Much more efficient than putting it on the subway or having trucks deliver it. They would just clog up the street. The people here walk fifty percent more than the people at the capital. It's much healthier."

"We see the same thing," Catie said. "When the streets aren't crowded, people like to walk. Also quite a few ride bicycles. We're having to figure out how to manage that, the bicyclists are almost as dangerous as the cars."

"I can see that. We don't have many people willing to ride a bicycle. I guess Paraxeans don't trust themselves on two wheels."

The mayor wandered around the city showing off some of the important buildings. He provided a commentary on the progress as well as the significance of each of the decisions they'd made. Finally, he pulled into a parking lot in the center of the city.

"And here is our biggest luxury." The mayor led them into the large central park. Catie could just see the sail of a sailboat over the hill.

"You have a big lake?"

"Yes, it is a favorite place for young people to come and spend time. The children love to play on the beach. We didn't put in a wave machine like yours because we wanted it to be friendly for boating. Of course, you have all that ocean around for boating, so the wave machine makes more sense."

"They've got a large lake in Orion as well," Catie said. "Of course, the city still has to grow around it."

"Yes, it takes longer to bring in colonists to a planet than it does here. People just book passage on the bus and have their belongings shipped out. They can complete a move in just one week."

"Wow, that is fast."

"Yes, we've been growing quickly," the mayor said proudly.

"How big a city are you planning?"

"We are targeting three hundred thousand via our planned migration. We should reach that in another year. Then we expect the city to grow to about one million over the next ten years. We'll try to stabilize it there."

"How will you stabilize it?" Kasper asked.

"We'll start another city," the governor said.

"Is this the only one so far?" Catie asked.

"We have started one on each of our four continents," the president said. "Eventually each province will have one. We'll have to see how it goes after that. Of course, by then we'll have a new president and it will be their problem to work out the details."

Catie caught Morgan deftly cutting off a Paraxean who was rushing to join the group. The woman was forced to slow down and go around Morgan, which took her to the governor instead of Catie.

"President Plaxmar, can we get a statement?"

"I'll let the governor and mayor answer any questions, I'm on an unofficial break with our guest," the president said as he headed back toward the cars. "The press, we have not found a solution for them. You wouldn't have discovered one, would you?"

"Nope, they're a necessary evil," Catie said.

"Yes, yes, free press and all that, but I wish they would just stick to attending the press conferences. We'll leave those two to it and have a driver take us back."

"Thanks for the tour," Catie said. "It was interesting and relaxing."

"Just what we needed. Now we need to go back and make an appearance at the negotiations. It will encourage the ministers to make progress. Of course, I understand your Ambassador Newman doesn't require much encouragement. My people tell me that she's quite tenacious."

"She is that."

16   The Galaxy Keeps Spinning

"The Fazullans have sent a probe through the wormhole," Blake announced once everyone had joined the meeting.

"And?" Marc asked.

"We destroyed it as it emerged."

"How did you destroy it?"

"Plasma cannon," Blake said. "We wanted to avoid any debris passing back through the wormhole."

"That might buy some time," Catie said. "They might just assume it wasn't at a good location yet. They're not going to expect anyone to be all the way out at the fringe."

"We'll have to just wait and see."

"The Paraxeans have agreed to send two carriers," Marc said.

"Does that mean they're ready to sign the treaty?" Catie asked.

"Not quite," Marc said.

"Daddy, you cannot keep me and the Roebuck here. I know you want to, but it's not fair. It's bad leadership to leave a critical asset off the table."

"The Roebuck is not that critical."

"Yes it is, you only have two jump capable ships, the Sakira and the Roebuck. Who knows how vital that might turn out to be?"

"Sam?" Marc asked.

"I'm sure we're close enough to a final agreement, and the Paraxeans understand the situation," Samantha said.

"Okay," Marc said, he clearly hadn't gotten the answer he wanted. "You can head back tomorrow."

"Governor, we have a situation," Mayor Mallory messaged Marc.

"Marc here, what kind of situation?"

"One of our citizens has started building a home in the middle of the land we've designated for a future resort. He says he's going to claim the land for his allotment next year."

Marc laughed then sighed, "And you can't deal with it?"

"I could, but I'd have to use force. He refuses to listen to reason."

"And you think I can do better?"

"I hope you can. I think he will at least listen to you."

"Alright, I'll be there in an hour," Marc said. "Melinda," he called his assistant.

"Yes sir."

"I need a chopper to take me to the coast."

"When?"

"Right away."

"I'll have one here in five minutes," Melinda said.

"Thanks."

An hour later Marc was landing at the fishing village they'd established at the coast. Mayor Mallory was waiting for him.

"I'm sorry about this, but we need to deal with it before he gets too established. Others are already talking about staking their claims."

"Where did they get the idea that they could arbitrarily pick out their allotment?"

"Who knows how their minds work."

"Okay, lead the way," Marc said.

He and Mayor Mallory got into a jeep and the driver started off. Marc's security detail followed in another jeep.

"I hope you don't have to deal with him like you did O'Brian," the mayor said. She was referring to the time Marc had knocked O'Brian down when the big Aussie foreman had decided that Marc should step aside and let the real men figure out how to run the colony.

"Why? That worked out okay," Marc said with a chuckle. "Don't worry, I think we're beyond that."

"Good," the mayor said. "Here we are."

They'd driven off-road to a spot on the cliffs overlooking the bay. It was a beautiful location, which is why they'd set it aside to develop a resort community in the future.

"Mr. Haggasey, I'm sure you recognize our governor, Marc McCormack."

"Yeah, I sure do."

"Mr. Haggasey, you do know that you're not allowed to just pick your allotment, much less do it a year early," Marc said.

"Sure I do. But we had that problem with those new colonists you guys sent over here. Didn't have a place to put them, so I said I'd give up my condo and start building me 'ome. Seemed like a good solution."

"And why did you pick this spot?"

"'Cause it's close to the village and it has a nice view, reminds me of me 'ome in Kent."

"Did you know this area is allocated for a resort village?"

"The mayor told me that, but why should they get the best spots? They're not even here yet. We're the ones doing all the work."

"Because that's how we're funding the colony," Marc said. "We're selling land for development, and giving allotments to those like you who help. But we can't allow you to just pick your lots on your own."

"Why not? First-come, first-served is what I says."

Marc laughed and shook his head. "If that's what you think, then the first to come was MacKenzie Discoveries, over one year ago. We mapped out the planet and set aside various locations for colonists and for future development. This was one of the areas we allocated to future development."

"Well it don't seem fair, you guys grabbing all the best locations."

"Isn't that what you're doing? You're grabbing this spot a year before anyone is allowed to pick their allotment. And claiming a farmstead in a place designated as residential seems a bit much."

"Maybe, but what will I do? It looks just like me old 'ome. If I wait, then it won't be here. I'd be willing to settle on just a town lot. I guess a farmstead was me being greedy."

"How about this? You can pick out a lot on the community plot and when we develop this area, you can trade your allotment for it."

"You'd do that?"

"But it's just one lot, and it can't be one of the front row ones. Row eight or farther back."

"That seems fair. I could agree with that."

"Okay, the mayor will take care of you tomorrow. You have my word."

Marc and the mayor walked back to the jeep. "What am I to do if everyone wants to do that?"

"Let them. Not everyone is going to want to live in a community where you barely have a yard. If we have the front eight rows, that'll be enough to make what we were planning to gain from the resort."

"It's your land."

Once they got back to the mayor's office, Marc asked, "Mayor, how did we get into a situation where we had colonists without a place to stay?"

Mayor Mallory sighed. "It's quite a complicated story. But the bottom line was, one of our guys drove his excavator into the corner of the new condo building. It's taken us a month to repair the damage."

"Why didn't the autopilot take over and prevent that?"

"He'd disabled the autopilot. It seems the autopilot refused to let him take the shortcut he liked to use. Of course, the shortcut took him by the condo building. We've changed the protocol so that it takes a supervisor's approval to disable the autopilot."

"What happened to cause him to lose control?"

"One of those wasp things got into the cab, he panicked and tried to swat it away before it stung him. He momentarily forgot he was driving a twenty-ton excavator."

197

"He does know that if he gets the sting treated the same day, there's no problem."

"He does now, and probably did then, but those things are nasty looking. One can understand his panic."

"So what are you doing with him?"

"The community's taking care of that. Many of our big, burly guys have suddenly developed a phobia about those wasps. Usually, they panic right when he's standing next to them. He's had three trips to the ER in the last month. And he did give up his condo to a family with small children. His bar tab for the month is probably bigger than his wages as he's trying to make up for it."

"Is he going to be alright?"

"We'll see. I think they're starting to lighten up on him. If it doesn't get better, we'll have to look at moving him to another area."

"Okay," Marc sighed. "The things we have to deal with. Now I need to get back and see what's happening with our war."

"War?!"

"Oh, we think we have it under control, but remember the aliens that were coming here? They're threatening another system."

"I'm sorry to have bothered you with this."

"The galaxy doesn't stop turning just because some idiots decide they want to start a fight."

◆ ◆ ◆

"Have you talked with Tracey lately?" Catie asked Morgan as they were circling the mat. They were doing a type of sparring where you couldn't use kicks or hand strikes. It was a mix of Aikido and Tai Chi. Liz and Catie always chatted when they did it. It taught you to recognize opportunities subconsciously. She and Morgan had just started sparring that way.

"Are you trying to distract me?"

"No, just curious if you've forgiven her for punching you."

"Oh, we laughed that off over beers the next night."

"Good, so have you talked to her lately? You know you can use the quantum relays."

"It's a privilege I try not to abuse. But I talked to her a couple of days ago."

"How's she doing?"

"She's up on Delphi Station. Her team is training on ship boarding using that partial ship Kal had made."

"Does she like it?"

"She says she's loving it. She just got promoted to squad leader so she's pretty excited."

Catie took a small opening and pulled on Morgan's forearms as she slid in, turning sideways so her shoulder caught Morgan's solar plexus and her right foot slid under Morgan's right thigh, her knee connecting and pushing Morgan to the side.

Morgan hit the mat rolling. She sprang back to her feet rubbing her solar plexus.

"Nice move."

"Thanks. Are you and Tracey going to do anything special when you get back?"

"Tough to plan that since I don't know when we'll be back. Let's talk about your love life."

"What love life? All the guys I know are either in my chain of command or are put off by the Princess Catie thing."

"That's just an excuse. You're just not interested."

"I am too!"

"Oh, I heard that Miguel Cordova got your juices running. Why didn't you hit on him?"

"He's too old for me. Besides, I'm pretty sure Liz is hitting on him."

"Oh, you know something? Spill."

"I'm not sure, but by triangulating on their locations the week when Miguel was on Delphi Station, I'm pretty sure they spent three or four nights together."

"What do you mean triangulating on their locations?"

"Liz invoked the privacy protocol, so I wasn't able to ask ADI, but I could ask about some other things. Based on some deduction, I determined that they must be in Liz's cabin."

"ADI couldn't just tell you?"

"No, I could not," ADI said. "I respect everyone's privacy."

"So how did you figure it out?"

"Liz ordered room service."

"So?"

"Breakfast for two."

"Oh."

"That and the fact that Miguel didn't eat in the restaurant at his hotel those days. *Ipso Facto*, they must have been together."

"Well, he was pretty hot."

"I'm happy for her. She hasn't been with anyone since Logan."

"You can't count that; he was spying on her."

"But he was romancing her. She had fun."

"Well when we get back, you can go in and get Dr. Metra to do a makeover so you'll be able to get around as Alex or whoever. Then you and Yvette can go shopping for men."

Board Meeting – Oct 3rd

"Good day, everyone. This should be a quick meeting," Marc announced once his Comm showed that everyone was logged in. "Fred any business issues we need to deal with?"

"Not anything that can't wait or isn't in the monthly report. It seems we have more important things to spend our time on."

"You would think, but the galaxy keeps spinning. Last week, I had to deal with a colonist who decided he would help us out by picking the choicest piece of land and moving out of his condo and onto it."

Everyone laughed at the thought of Marc dealing with such minutia, much less the audacity of the colonist.

"Dr. Metra?"

"It's in my weekly report, but our process for growing and delivering organs for transplants is up and running. We're meeting twenty percent of the world-wide demand now and should be able to ramp up to seventy percent by the end of the year. We've had a dozen emergency requests, where we needed to ship one of the pregrown organs. So far, they've all been a success. We'll have to see whether the patients decide to have an operation to replace them with one grown from their own DNA, or just go on with the pregrown organ."

"That's excellent news. I'm sure we're all very proud of the accomplishment. Now, Kal, anything to report?"

"Most of my Marines have deployed to Onisiwo, so things are quiet here. Chief Nawal has everything under control and the Prime Minister seems to be happy."

"Good. Then let's turn our attention to what's on all of our minds, Onisiwo. Blake, what's the status?"

"We're still playing cat and mouse with the Fazullans. They send a probe through, we destroy it. The probe we sent into their system is continuing to send data back, but we haven't found a key vulnerability yet. But we'll keep looking."

"Have you contacted the Onisiwoens yet?" Samantha asked.

"We're waiting until the probe gets closer. Don't want to have too much delay. Hopefully, we'll awe them with our technology."

"I think the fact that you're in their system should be enough to awe them," Kal said.

"One would think." Marc laughed a bit. "Now Catie and Samantha, how goes it with our reluctant allies, the Paraxeans?"

"They're pretty much committed," Samantha said. "We have a few more issues to iron out, but I'm sure we'll get there this week."

"Good. So Admiral Michaels, what about Earth?"

"I think we'll get there. They still don't get the idea of a United Earth, but fear that the Paraxeans will come out as the dominant race in the galaxy should be a big enough stick to get their attention."

"Anything we can do?"

"Get the Onisiwoens and Paraxeans on board, but give me a few days' lead time. Earth is going to want to be first. That's my ace in the hole."

"Okay, anyone else? . . . No, then get back to it."

◆ ◆ ◆

"Cer Catie, the captain is preparing to make the first communication with the Onisiwoens," ADI informed Catie.

"Tell Charlie to meet me in my office in twenty minutes."

"Done."

Catie got up, it was 0500 ship time. She hurried through her morning routine and then got dressed. A message from Samantha told her to wear her dress uniform.

Charlie arrived wearing a version of an Onisiwoen uniform that they'd had made for him.

"You're finally going to contact my people?" Charlie asked.

"Yes. Please be seated and we'll join the conference."

Catie turned on the main display. Blake was wearing his admiral's uniform, her father was wearing the fancy uniform they had designed for him as governor of Artemis, and Samantha was wearing a uniform similar to Catie's.

"We're preparing to open the channel," Marc said.

"Daddy," Catie said, "you know that as soon as you make contact, the relay cat will be out of the bag."

"Yes, I assume Charlie has already deduced that we have faster-than-light Comms, so unless you're going to keep him on the Roebuck, I think that ship has sailed."

"Okay," Catie said, glancing at Charlie who was giving her a stare. "I thought we might be able to fool you."

Charlie snorted.

"This is President Marc McCormack, with whom am I speaking?"

"This is General Zeemar and Ambassador Tuleian. Can you explain who you are and what this dire emergency is?"

"We will. Would you like to join via video link?" Marc asked.

"Of course we would," the general said. It took a couple of minutes before the general and the ambassador's images showed up on the monitor. At that point, Marc ordered ADI to add the video link to their transmission.

"Who are you?" General Zeemar demanded as he realized that he was not looking at Onisiwoens.

"I'm hoping you can recognize Charlie," Marc said.

Charlie leaned forward. "General, I am Charmaxiam Margakava; I was the leader of the mission to Ditubria. I believe we've met."

"You do look like Charmaxiam Margakava, but that mission was lost over five years ago."

"We were captured by an alien starship and taken prisoner. These people rescued us."

"I don't believe you. This must be a hoax. With a little makeup, it would be easy to make someone look like your friends there."

"General, we are communicating via a satellite which is trailing your planet. We are now going to push that satellite into orbit around your planet. It will enter here. Please do not try to destroy it," Marc said.

As the satellite moved into orbit, Charlie shared details of his mission and the parameters the crew had been given. The general continued to be doubtful of the situation.

"General, the satellite is now entering orbit; your space station should be able to see it now. Here are the coordinates," Marc said.

"Why isn't your ship entering orbit?" the general asked.

"General, this is Admiral Blake McCormack. Our ships are at the fringe of your solar system preparing to defend it against the aliens that attacked Charlie and his crew. We cannot afford to spend the time and resources to send a crewed vessel to your planet."

"McCormack, are all of you people named McCormack?"

"General, let me finish the introductions," Marc said. "With me is my wife and our interstellar ambassador, Samantha Newman; you've met my brother, the admiral; and with Charlie is my daughter, Captain Princess Catherine McCormack. She was leading the mission to return Charlie and his crew to your world when we detected the enemy vessels preparing to invade your solar system. Admiral Blake McCormack was called to bring a fleet to help defend your system."

An aide entered the room where the General was and handed him a note.

"Okay, we can see your satellite, but if you're out at the fringe, how come we don't have a delay?"

"We are able to have instant communication with the satellite, which is why we only have a thirty-second delay with you."

"Ah, quantum coupling?"

"Yes."

"Okay, so what do you want us to do? We cannot send anything out that far," the General said.

"We thought it only right that we communicate with you before we started a small war on the fringe of your system."

"What makes you think these aliens are invading us?"

Samantha leaned forward, signaling she would take over the discussion. "General, we had expected that the Fazullans, who are the alien race we're talking about, would just attempt to raid your system for resources. But when Princess Catherine arrived in your system, we detected an entire fleet preparing to enter your system. It is our belief that they intend to colonize your planet and remove or enslave your population."

"Why would they do that?"

"Our best guess is that something has happened to their system to make yours far more desirable. We assume you'd prefer not to be conquered."

"Yes, of course not. But . . ."

"General," Catie interrupted. "Do you know what a wormhole is?"

"Some scientific mumbo jumbo about space-time."

"Well, they are real," Catie said. "We have developed a drive that allows us to form a wormhole. We are not aware of any other race capable of doing so. We first met the Fazullans at our colony of Artemis. After investigation, we determined that their home system was next to a natural wormhole that moves between three different systems as the stars around it move."

"This is insane!"

"General, please," the Onisiwoen ambassador said. "Princess Catherine, please continue."

"Apparently about ten years ago, the wormhole made a significant shift. After that, it started to connect with your system. We would guess that this is the first habitable system it has connected with, and of course, you are inhabiting it."

"So where are these Fazullans?" the ambassador asked.

"They are currently on their side of the wormhole," Blake said. "They are still trying to ascertain whether the wormhole is connected with your system."

"I don't understand," the general said.

"They left a satellite in your system that they can connect with by sending a small probe through the wormhole. Since the wormhole moves around, they have been waiting for it to move to your system. We have disabled their satellite."

"So does that mean we're safe?" the ambassador asked.

"No. They launched a large probe, essentially another satellite a few days ago. We destroyed it. But they will keep trying."

"Can't you just keep destroying it?"

"Possibly; however, the wormhole jumps around inside your system, so it is likely that it will jump to a location out of range of our weapons," Blake explained. "At that point, they'll know what is in this system."

"Won't your fleet discourage them, make them go home?"

"We don't think they can go home," Blake said. "They have the ability to put their people into stasis, so they can survive for years while they wait. The wormhole will be in your system for . . ."

"Three to four months," Catie added.

"Thank you. And unfortunately, their fleet is much larger than our fleet," Blake said.

"Then how do you plan to help us?" the ambassador asked.

"We are asking for help from other civilizations," Samantha said. "We have gotten the commitment for another space carrier from one of our allies and we are negotiating for more from their homeworld."

"Is there anything we can do to help?"

"What we all want, and what will help, is trade," Samantha said.

"But interstellar trade, how can that work?"

"Well, it just so happens that Princess Catherine has a company that does just that. It is capable of making a trip between two worlds in just six weeks. Its cargo capacity probably exceeds the capacity of your largest ocean cargo ship."

"This is giving me a headache. It is so much to comprehend," the ambassador said.

"I would like to propose that we set up a meeting between you, your trade ministers, and myself. We can let these military types go back to figuring out how to win this war, and we can figure out how to win the peace," Samantha said.

"Ambassador Newman expects to sign an agreement tonight," Admiral Michaels announced. "She has already gotten a tentative agreement with the Onisiwoens."

"Has she maintained alignment with us?" the Chinese ambassador asked.

"She has maintained alignment with the principles we set out, but she has not attempted to incorporate all this drivel that you people keep coming up with."

"How dare you!"

The American ambassador leaned in and took the floor. "Look, if we want this treaty to have Earth as its core, we need to make some decisions. President Novak is adamant that she intends to sign an agreement with Delphi so that America is a primary signatory, so unless you want to have every country making its own decision you need to quit this quibbling and come to an agreement."

"Yes, and my president also intends to do the same," the Russian ambassador said.

"What are we calling this thing we're trying to create?" the French ambassador asked.

"The League of Planets," Admiral Michaels said, wondering how someone could have attended two weeks of negotiation and not already know that.

"We should find a way to stamp Earth on the name," the French ambassador said.

"I don't think any of the other worlds are going to be interested in joining the Earth League of Planets," the German ambassador said.

"But can't we add some modifier that is uniquely from Earth? What about United Federation of Planets?"

"Unfortunately, the Paraxeans are well familiar with Star Trek. They'll spot that right away," Admiral Michaels said.

"What about the Delphi League of Planets?" the British ambassador asked. "It's uniquely from Earth and Delphi has started all this. Who wouldn't want to acknowledge the people who invented the jumpdrive and made all this possible?"

"Can we focus on the treaty and worry about the name later?" Admiral Michaels pleaded.

As soon as Catie finished her final meeting with the Paraxean president, she hurried to the Lynx and headed back to the Roebuck.

"Set course for the fringe, ten-G profile," Catie ordered as soon as she entered the bridge. She would have ordered them to break orbit earlier, but nobody could walk around when under a ten-G profile acceleration.

"Aye-aye, Captain. Ten-G profile."

The ship's speakers blared out, "Prepare for high G acceleration, acceleration in five minutes."

"Breaking orbit now," the pilot announced. "Course plotted."

"Very well," Catie replied.

"The Fazullans launched a second probe. Strategy meeting in five," Blake announced.

"Did you destroy it?" Catie asked.

"Meeting in five!"

Once everyone logged into the meeting, Blake provided an update.

"The Fazullans launched a second probe. They did this right after the wormhole transitioned to a new location, so we had to use a laser to destroy the probe."

"How long did it take?" Admiral Michaels asked.

"Thirty seconds to get a targeting solution," Blake answered. "We decided we couldn't afford to wait until we reached the range of the plasma cannons."

"So what's that going to tell them?" Admiral Michaels asked.

"Do you think any of the wreckage transitioned back?"

"Likely."

"Then they'll know something destroyed it. They haven't sent another one through yet?" Catie asked.

"No."

"Hmm, I wonder why not."

"I'm guessing they realized that someone is here and destroyed it. So they're trying to figure out how to get better information," Blake said.

"I recommend you expect a series of probes next time," Admiral Michaels said. "They're going to want to get more data."

"Any reason not to use the lasers now?"

"I recommend we continue to use plasma cannons for now. We want to reduce the probability of wreckage transitioning back through the wormhole. We don't know for sure that any wreckage made it back. It's best if we can keep them guessing."

◆ ◆ ◆

"What happened to our probe?" demanded the Fazullan admiral.

"It appears to have been destroyed. Some minor wreckage transitioned back through the wormhole, indicating that it exploded."

"Why?"

"Because it would have taken the force of an explosion to create enough reverse . . ."

"Not that, you idiot; why did the probe explode?"

"Either it hit something, or a starship is sitting by the wormhole and destroyed it."

"Who? The Onisiwoens were barely exploring past their second gas giant. There is no way they would have developed the technology to reach the fringe yet."

"I cannot explain it."

"Then what good are you?! I want you to send another probe through, but wait until the wormhole wanders again!"

"It will take us two days to get a probe into place again."

"Why?!"

"We have to move it up to the wormhole. We only sent one probe to the wormhole and it has been destroyed."

"Idiots! Why didn't we position more probes?"

"We didn't expect to need them."

"Move at least four up there. I want to be prepared."

"Captain, do you want to start deceleration?" the navigator asked Catie.

"No, we'll deal with our velocity when we get to Onisiwo," Catie replied. "I want to get into the system as fast as we can, but cut acceleration so we can move around."

"Aye, cut acceleration."

"How will we manage two jumps?" First Officer Suzuki asked. Since they did not have jump probes in place between Paraxea and Onisiwo, they were going to have to jump to Earth and then jump to Onisiwo.

"We'll let Earth power the jump to them, then we'll power the jump to Onisiwo. That will make things easier since they won't have to adjust for our velocity and vector when we do the second jump."

"I see, thank you for the explanation, Captain."

"The wormhole just moved," the Sakira's sensor operator announced.

"Where to? Who's closest?" Blake demanded.

"It's two million kilometers from the Enterprise."

"We've got it," Captain Clements announced. "Moving to new location at max acceleration."

"A probe just transitioned."

"Use your lasers," Blake ordered.

"A second probe has transitioned."

"We've got targeting solutions on them."

"First probe is destroyed. ... Second probe destroyed."

"Well, what will they think of that?" Blake wondered aloud.

"What happened?!" demanded the Fazullan admiral.

"We don't know, Admiral. Neither probe has returned."

"Any wreckage?"

"Not this time."

"This cannot be happening. I've planned this mission for five years, we cannot fail."

The bridge crew remained silent. Nobody wanted the admiral to turn his frustration onto them.

"Wait until it moves again. Send a probe and a relay probe. Maybe we can get the relay probe back with some data."

"Yes, sir."

"Have alfa squadron move up to the wormhole."

"We have detected movement in the Fazullan fleet," the Sakira's sensor operator announced.

"What kind of movement?"

"It looks like they're moving twenty ships forward to the wormhole."

"How long for them to get there?"

"Two days, maybe a bit longer, they don't seem to be in a hurry."

"Keep us posted."

"Yes sir."

17 Delphi League

"We are jumping," Catie informed Blake.

"Good. Where to?"

"We'll enter the system thirty degrees counter orbit on the ecliptic plane."

"We promise not to shoot you."

"We'll be cutting a chord through the system to decelerate, we're at point one C."

"Hmm, should you save some of that velocity?"

"We could," Catie answered. "We can keep doing microjumps around the edge, but I would recommend we decrease to point zero five C."

"I agree."

"What are you planning to do with that velocity?" the captain of the Galileo asked.

"I'm not sure, but only the Sakira and the Roebuck can hold that kind of velocity by using microjumps to stay in orbit. It might come in handy. It's always good to have options," Blake explained.

"Strategy meeting in five," Catie's Comm informed her. They had just completed their first microjump after transiting a chord across the fringe orbit.

"First Officer, you have the bridge." Catie stood up from the command chair and headed toward her office. "Kasper, join me."

"Strategy meeting?"

Catie just nodded as she left and walked into her office.

Suzuki frowned, she would have liked to attend the strategy meeting, but she knew that they needed to have a senior officer on the bridge. *"Maybe I could review the recording."*

Catie took a seat at her conference table so that she and Kasper could sit side by side. She brought up the feed for the meeting and notified Blake that they were in.

"We're all here," Blake said. "Marc, do you want to lead?"

"No, you've got it. I'll jump in if I need to," Marc replied.

"Okay. Undoubtedly, the Fazullans are suspecting that there must be at least one starship sitting by the wormhole. We've seen them wait for it to wander before sending a probe through. They're moving about half of their fleet up to the wormhole, so we can expect that they will become more aggressive about getting information from this side. Given all that, what should we do?"

"Is it time to open negotiations?" Samantha asked.

"Why?"

"We might be able to persuade them to accept a truce where we provide them with an alternate system and they promise to wait."

"How would we talk with them?" Captain Clements asked.

"We have a satellite probe in their system," Samantha said.

"But if we use it to communicate, they'll know where it is and be able to destroy it."

Kasper made a line on the table where the Fazullan fleet was displayed. It went from the wormhole up at ninety degrees from the Fazullan fleet. Catie nodded at him.

"Sir," Kasper said.

"Yes," Blake answered, giving him permission to talk.

"We could send another probe through. They do not have anything within weapons range of the wormhole yet, and based on our knowledge their probes are not armed."

"Wouldn't they just shoot a missile at it?" Captain Clements suggested.

"If we flew it at ninety degrees from their fleet, it wouldn't be much of a threat. And we could have it outpace a missile given the distance to the closest ship," Kasper explained.

Catie drew a circle around the Fazullan fleet.

"We could even have it orbit their fleet at high velocity. They would have to waste a lot of resources to try to destroy it. And if we were using it to communicate, wouldn't they hold off? At least until they had a chance to learn what they could get out of us," Kasper added.

"That would work," Blake said. "But we would have to do it within the next four hours before they're too close."

"Prepare a probe," Marc said. "We can always decide not to send it."

"Agreed!" Blake nodded to Captain Desjardins to have it taken care of. "Our problem is that we cannot stop them from transitioning several ships through the wormhole right after it wanders."

"Sir, we could rig up a few missiles with plasma cannons and shoot them at the wormhole when it settles. They can be programmed to fire on anything that transitions," Catie suggested.

"But a missile like that wouldn't stop a ship from transitioning. And its plasma cannon wouldn't be strong enough to destroy the ship even if it could reach it in time."

"But it would be able to get close enough to fire its plasma cannon right after the ship transitions. If it does, the ship would likely send back a probe to warn the fleet that it was under attack," Catie explained.

"I like that idea; confusion to the enemy," Blake said. "Captain Clements, can you have your weapons officer work on that?"

"Yes, sir, he's on it now."

"Do our Paraxean captains have any suggestions?" Blake asked, referring to the captains of the two Paraxean space carriers that Paraxea had sent. The Galileo was under command of a Delphinean.

"This is beyond our experience. We have never had to actually engage an enemy fleet."

"Don't be afraid to offer a suggestion if you see something that might help," Blake said. "Now, what about negotiations? When would we start, how would we start?"

"It depends on the posture we want to take," Samantha said. "The first Fazullan captain we encountered was very aggressive; however, Captain Lantaq has shown himself to be more thoughtful."

"Well he was planning to surrender, so he might not be the best reference," Captain Desjardins argued.

"But he was second in command, so he cannot be that unusual," Samantha countered. "Of course, we don't want to appear weak."

"So do we act aggressive or determined?" Marc asked.

"I always prefer determined," Samantha said.

"If we're determined, then we would start negotiations as soon as our satellite establishes its position. Aggressive, I would think we would let them wonder what's going on for a while," Blake said.

"How is that aggressive?" Catie asked.

"It shows we're going for an advantage. Holding our cards close versus laying some of them on the table," Blake explained. "An assertive and wily type of aggression, kind of like you."

"Oh, I see."

"As much as I admire Catie's strategies, I suggest we opt for determined," Marc said.

Blake got nods from the majority of captains.

"Then I suggest we launch the probe when it's ready," Blake said. "We'll meet again when it is in place."

"Admiral, a probe has transitioned the wormhole!" the Fazullan sensor operator announced.

"Destroy it!"

"Missile away. But the probe is accelerating away at ninety degrees, the missile may not reach it."

"How can that probe accelerate? I don't see an exhaust plume."

"Gravity drive?" the sensor operator suggested.

"That small? Impossible!"

"It is the only thing that I can think of."

"Our satellite is in place; we'll start communication in five," Blake announced.

Catie and Kasper returned to her office and joined the conference. Catie looked around at the others. All the captains were there, as well as the Onisiwoen ambassador. Next to Marc, there was a big, kind of ugly dude wearing a fancy uniform. Catie didn't recognize him.

"Strange, why add someone new now?" she thought. Then she noticed that Samantha was missing. *"Hi, Sam. I like your new look,"* Catie messaged.

The ugly guy tapped Marc on the arm.

"Ambassador Newman will be handling the negotiations. But since the Fazullans are so harsh and chauvinistic, she's decided to use an avatar."

Most of the captains laughed as Samantha gave everyone a salute.

"Blake, you open the discussion," Marc instructed.

"I knew I should have had a drink," Blake said. "Alright everyone will be on mute to the Fazullans. We'll be able to talk to each other, but keep your comments to a minimum so you don't distract our negotiator.

"Open the channel," Blake ordered.

"Channel is open. Outgoing is hooked only to your Comm and Ambassador Newman's Comm."

"This is Admiral McCormack; I wish to speak to the leader of the Fazullan fleet that is gathering at the wormhole."

"Admiral, we're getting a transmission from the probe that is orbiting us," the Fazullan communication officer reported.

The admiral let out a weary sigh. "Replay it." He adjusted his seat in the command chair as he turned to the display. The video feed came up showing a collection of several people. He recognized two as Paraxeans and one looked like the people from Onisiwo. The others all looked like they were the same race, but he didn't recognize it.

"This is Admiral McCormack; I wish to speak to the leader of the Fazullan fleet that is gathering at the wormhole," the big man in the fancy uniform said.

"How can they expect me to have a conversation with a satellite?" the admiral hissed.

"Sir, I expect that they have some way of relaying communications through the wormhole via the satellite," the first officer said.

"How?"

"Possibly they have a way to transmit energy through the wormhole."

"Then why put a satellite here?"

"To observe us. Possibly their method of communicating through the wormhole must be relayed into a communication channel that we can receive."

The admiral nodded to the communication officer. "This is Admiral Martaka."

"Good, it works," Blake said. "Now we can talk."

"What do you have to say?"

"The system you are trying to enter is part of the Delphi League of Planets. I have a fleet of starships here to defend it. We cannot allow you to enter this system."

"Then you had better have a big fleet," Admiral Martaka said.

"Admiral, this is Ambassador Newman of the League. Possibly we can find another option," Samantha said.

"Ambassador, isn't that a fancy word for beggar?"

"I have been known to beg. But generally, I explore options to find one that is suitable for both parties."

"What would be suitable for us, is for you to leave. You're welcome to take anything you can with you."

"That is not an acceptable option for us. Perhaps you could be more specific about your needs."

"We need that solar system!"

"Why this solar system?"

"Because it suits me!"

"Perhaps we could offer up another solar system."

"I think not. We like that one."

"And you're prepared to risk your entire fleet to take it?"

"I think we're willing to risk *your* entire fleet to take it."

"You're worse than Captain Shakaban, and he was an arrogant fool."

"That — bastard!" the admiral spewed a long rant.

"That's a lot of words for saying bastard," Catie messaged ADI.

"Their language can be quite inefficient," ADI replied.

"You're here because of him. That makes twice that his selfish, idiotic actions have harmed this mission. First, he dares to capture a vessel when he was supposed to only be gathering intelligence, and instead of killing him, they reward him with a second mission. Now what did he do? Wait, how could you be here if you've met him? He must have been two hundred light-years from here."

"This is not the only wormhole in existence," Samantha said. "His ship was similar to the ones you're commanding. We didn't have any trouble defeating it."

"You wouldn't with that fool in command. But I will check with the emperor and see if he has a beggar he wants to have talk with you." The admiral motioned to the communication officer to cut the channel.

"Channel is closed, Admiral."

"I want that probe!"

"Yes, sir," the first officer replied.

"Sir, that probe has disappeared."

◆ ◆ ◆

"That channel is closed."

"Thank you. Put the probe in stealth mode and move it farther out from their fleet," Blake ordered.

"Yes sir."

"Sam, what do you think?"

"We'll have to see. I certainly don't trust him. Based on his comments, it looks like they've been planning to take over the Onisiwo system from the beginning."

"It does."

"Hmm, that's funny," the sensor operator mused over his Comm channel with Blake.

"What's funny?"

"A gravimetric wave. It has hit both of our probes, and the timing indicates it came from the Fazullan fleet."

"That would act like sonar!" Catie shouted.

"Move our probes again," Blake ordered.

"Yes sir."

"Won't they just keep pinging?" Captain Clements asked.

"Yes, so we'll have to keep moving them."

"If we put the probes out another one million kilometers, we'll be able to generate a counter wave, and the interference pattern at its fringe won't reach the Fazullan fleet," Catie said.

"Are you sure?"

"It's simple geometry."

"Do it," Blake ordered, wondering how anyone would call spherical geometry simple.

"Have you captured that probe yet?" the admiral demanded.

"No, sir. We only got one echo from it, then it disappeared. Everything else we've found has turned out to be an asteroid. We did get another echo that disappeared after the first ping just like the one from the probe."

"How can a probe disappear?!"

"They must be making themselves invisible. If they have gravity drives, possibly they're able to cancel our ping."

"Don't blame your failures on some magical powers that they possess. Nobody can control a gravity drive like that, much less create one that is so small. It must be a problem with your technique. Keep trying."

"Yes sir."

"The Fazullans have pinged us," Blake announced.

"Should we open the channel?" Marc asked.

"They'll use it to try to capture the probe."

"Our probes are two million kilometers away from their nearest ship. They can't travel that fast. If they try to close in on one, we can just have it go dark again," Catie said.

"Okay, then is everyone ready?" Blake asked.

"We have a delay on our end, Ambassador Newman is indisposed," Marc said. "We need thirty minutes."

"What's she doing, feeding Allie?" Blake asked.

"That's my guess. We'll ring when she's ready."

The navigator let out a groan.

"Young man, I'll remember that groan the next time you ask to be relieved from your duty station to go to the head," Captain Vislosky said.

One of the pilots giggled, thinking, *"it would serve him right if he had to take a dump in his suit while on duty."*

◆ ◆ ◆

"We're all set," Marc said.

"Open the channel. Admiral McCormack here. Do you wish to talk again?"

"Yes, the emperor has sent one of his ambassadors to talk. This is Ambassador Sharlitz," the admiral said introducing the Fazullan next to him.

"Ambassador Sharlitz, Ambassador Newman," Blake said nodding at Samantha.

"Hello, Ambassador," Samantha said via her burly avatar.

"Ambassador. Our emperor has graciously offered to allow you one year to move your people out of the system."

Samantha snorted. "I think you overestimate your position. We are willing to discuss helping to relocate your people to another star system, but we have no intention of uprooting the Onisiwoens."

"No, it is you that overestimate your position. The emperor has not given the order to attack because he would like to minimize the cost of taking the system. But we intend to take it."

"I appreciate your desire to minimize the losses," Samantha said. "We find it annoying to have to repair a starship after a battle; it is such a waste of resources. But we usually make up for the cost with the starships we capture."

Catie could see the admiral's eyes widen at Samantha's remark.

The ambassador frowned, then gave a feral smile. "Then I will enjoy having you work in my garden. Admiral!" The ambassador rose from his chair and turned his back, walking away from the camera.

"Ah, I love a negotiation that ends in war," the admiral said.

"Not much of a negotiator," Catie said.

"Nope," Samantha agreed. "So now what?"

"We prepare for them to send ships through the wormhole," Blake said. "Sensors, what's the status of their fleet?"

"They're still moving toward the wormhole. They haven't increased speed. But they did just launch fighters toward our probe."

"Take it dark and move it," Blake ordered.

"Already doing it, sir."

"We're reaching the fringe," the navigator announced.

"Prepare for a microjump," Catie ordered.

"Captain, won't we be putting ourselves farther away? How will we get back to the engagement area if we keep doing microjumps around the system?" First Officer Suzuki asked.

"We'll reverse the polarity of the wormhole," Catie said. "That will have us jumping in but heading back toward the engagement area, not away from it."

"I didn't realize you could do that."

"We have to, that's how the Roebuck opens a wormhole for another ship to use; we reverse the polarity so we're behind the wormhole . . ." Catie's eyes went wide. "That means . . . Get me Admiral Blake!" she ordered as she rushed to her office.

"What's up, squirt?" Blake asked.

"Uncle Blake!"

"Hey, just trying to lighten the moment. What do you have?"

"I just realized something we can do to the Fazullans when they come through the wormhole."

"What?"

"We need to test it, but I believe the Roebuck can create a zero-point strong enough to move the wormhole."

"Okay, even so, how would that help us?"

"You know that any ship that goes through the wormhole picks up any velocity that the end of the wormhole has."

"Right, otherwise you might be sucked back into it."

"Yes. So if the Roebuck is at 0.05 C, then when we move the wormhole, the Fazullan ship would pick up that velocity."

"That doesn't sound like a good thing, it just gets them into the system faster."

"Not if we set the polarity of the wormhole so it points out of the system."

"Oh, . . . then the Fazullans would be flying out of the gravity well even farther. And they're barely able to use their gravity drives at this distance."

"I doubt their ships will have enough reaction mass to stop themselves, much less turn around and come back into the system," Catie continued.

"How do we test your theory?"

"We're preparing to jump. We'll jump right back and see if we can power up a zero point with enough strength to move the wormhole."

"Do it."

◆ ◆ ◆

"It works," Catie reported.

"Good, is there any reason the Sakira can't do the same thing?"

"Her grav drives aren't as powerful or as efficient as the Roebuck's, but she probably can. I'll send the parameters over and you can test it. I wouldn't bother accelerating until you know it will work."

"Admiral, we have the parameters. I've loaded them," the navigation officer reported.

"Then execute."

"The wormhole has transitioned to us," the sensor operator reported.

"Okay, it works, so we should each maintain the velocity profile, timed so that when you have to jump, we're just finishing our jump."

"So what tells us to grab the wormhole?" Catie asked.

"They should send a probe through before they send a ship. If we see a probe, we grab the wormhole when the probe retreats; if it's a ship, we grab it immediately. That should leave the fleet with the maximum of one starship to deal with."

"Okay, if we head out-system for two million kilometers, then we can do a microjump back into the system. We can hold the wormhole for the two hours we're heading out-system. If we alternate, then we can cut a chord through the edge of the system for the two-hour recharge before we head out again," Catie explained.

"I think I have it. Send the plot map to my navigator and we'll review it."

"Yes sir."

"While we're doing that, why don't you call your father and explain it to him. Then we'll have a strategy meeting."

"On it."

◆ ◆ ◆

"Waa!"

"Your turn," Samantha said as she rolled over and tried to go back to sleep.

Marc got out of bed and picked Allie up. They left the room so Samantha could sleep. Marc checked to see if Allie was hungry or needed a change. It was a little of both. Since the diaper was like the shipsuits and did an exceptional job of taking care of moisture, he opted to feed her first. Hopefully, that would settle her down before she woke Samantha up again.

Marc grabbed a bottle from the preheater and started feeding Allie. ZMS had designed the preheater for Samantha. It UV-sterilized the bottle, and then on a timer, filled it with breast milk from the refrigerator, and heated it. That way Samantha wouldn't have to deal with a fussy baby while waiting for the bottle to warm up. The timer setting was based on Allie's feeding cycle with built-in margin; keeping it warm for an hour didn't hurt the milk. The whole thing was really for Marc and their nanny since Samantha would just put the baby on a breast if she was too fussy. She breastfed whenever possible, only using the bottle when her schedule wouldn't allow it, or she wanted to sleep, like now.

"Come on, Allie," Marc cooed. "You know if you could just hold out for another hour, I would wake up naturally and come feed you." Marc never needed much sleep, but having to wake up on a semi-random schedule based on Allie's rate of digestion was not the same as waking at his usual time in the morning after working late.

"Come on, sweetie, we can come up with a deal. You sleep for at least three hours and Daddy will buy you whatever you want, a pony even."

Marc switched Allie to the other arm so she would stay used to alternating sides and kept walking her around his office. He had his HUD up and was reviewing the data Catie and Blake had sent him last night while he cooed to Allie.

"Welcome, Captains. Thanks to Captain McCormack, we have a potential new strategy we would like to review," Blake said. "Captain, you have the floor."

"While discussing our jump plan with my first officer, I realized that we had a control point with the wormhole that we were not exploiting. Most of you have only transitioned a wormhole using our jump ships and jump probes, so you might not even be aware of it. The fact is that when we open a wormhole, we have the option of reversing its polarity. Essentially that means that the wormhole will be pointing away from the star instead of toward the star. By reversing the polarity we can have what is transitioning through the wormhole actually head away from the sun at the same velocity of the ship anchoring the wormhole, plus its own velocity. This means that the Sakira or the Roebuck can be heading away from the sun at high velocity while maintaining the wormhole with reverse polarity, so a ship emerging from it would be heading away from the system at the same velocity."

Catie paused while the captains absorbed that information.

"But if you're out-system won't you eventually get too far away to jump back?" Captain Clements asked.

"That is correct. So we would first do a microjump back to the system once we reach two million kilometers. We would be at 0.04 C, so it would take us four hours to reach that point. At that point in time, the other ship would be just heading out-system and be ready to take over."

"But will the Fazullans come through the wormhole if it's moving like that, and if they did, wouldn't they just go back?"

"That's two questions; so first, we would not grab the wormhole until they had sent a probe through and back, or a ship comes through. Second, while we're traveling away from the fringe, we will need to maintain a one G acceleration orthogonal to our direction so that they would not be able to re-enter the wormhole. That has the added benefit of scattering their ships even more."

"How will you be able to be back at the fringe when you jump back if you're carrying so much velocity, oh, never mind, you'll just do another microjump and reorient your vector," Captain Vislosky said.

"Correct."

"Any more questions, . . . suggestions?" Blake asked.

"So let me say it in simple terms," Captain Vislosky, the Sakira's captain, said. "The Sakira or the Roebuck will always be positioned to grab the wormhole in such a way as to vector anything coming through it at 0.04C to 0.05C away from the Onisiwoen sun. If things work as planned, we should have at max one Fazullan starship to deal with in-system, while the rest will be struggling to kill off the velocity that's sending them into deep space."

"Correct."

"What do you do when they quit sending ships through? Release the wormhole and start the process over?"

"Correct."

"I like the plan."

"Couldn't we use the jump probe we have here to hold the wormhole in place?" Captain Vislosky asked. "It would be nice to be set up for anything that comes through it."

"I don't think so. The Fazullans are most likely to only send something through it when the wormhole moves," Catie said. "And if you have something there waiting, they'll detect it and the probe will return with a warning, or the ship will launch a probe to warn them."

"Okay, just thinking."

"I like your thoughts. Keep them coming, we may find something that we've missed or that enhances the plan," Blake said.

"What about missiles?"

"I worry about that, too," Blake said. "I assume we'll follow the same procedure if a missile comes through."

"I think so. The wormhole will be projected in front of our ship; that will mask our ship from any sensors the Fazullans have active. The biggest risk is when we have to release the wormhole. If ships are still coming through, they will be able to see us, but with a delta-V of 0.05C, it seems manageable," Catie said.

"We're at the end, we need to jump back into the system," Catie reported.

"We're ready to jump," Blake said. "See you on the flip side," he added as he nodded to his pilot to grab the wormhole.

An hour later the sensor operator yelled, "A probe just transited the wormhole!"

"Admiral Blake, are you guys ready?" Catie asked.

"We are; let us know when the probe retreats."

"Probe is retreating."

"Now!" Catie said.

"The Sakira has the wormhole," the Roebuck sensor operator reported. "Fazullan ships are transiting."

Over the next four hours, six Fazullan starships transited the wormhole. After another hour the Roebuck had done its microjump back to the engagement area and was heading out-system. It was prepared to grab the wormhole if necessary, and then the Sakira released the wormhole as it started cutting the chord through the Onisiwoen system.

"What now?" Blake asked once everyone was back on the strategy conference.

"Should we call the Fazullan admiral and tell him we've taken care of his ships?" Samantha asked.

"No. Our spy probe shows them moving another fourteen ships to the wormhole. I think he's hoping these will occupy us, and he plans to transition the rest of his ships when the wormhole moves again."

"How long do we have before those ships are too far away to rescue?" Samantha asked.

"Why should we rescue them?" Catie asked.

"Not everyone on those ships is guilty," Samantha said. "Besides they might have slaves on them as well."

"Oh! Well, right now, they're dumping all their reaction mass trying to slow down. It might take a couple of microjumps to reach them, but they'll always be in range. We can power the wormhole from the jump ships here at the fringe, so we'll be able to jump them back," Catie said, feeling a little foolish for her insensitive comment.

"Okay, then let them panic for a while," Blake said. "We need to be prepared to deal with the next attempt."

Eight hours later, the Roebuck had just jumped out when the wormhole wandered again. A probe was immediately detected transitioning the wormhole. When it left the system, the Roebuck grabbed the wormhole.

"A ship is preparing to transition!" First Officer Suzuki reported. She was watching the feed from the spy probe on the Fazullan side of the wormhole. "They're accelerating hard to the wormhole."

"Excellent," Catie said.

It only took two hours before all fourteen ships had transited the wormhole. Catie had the Roebuck hold the wormhole for another hour before they released it and jumped back to the fringe.

"Should we call the admiral now?" Catie asked.

"I wonder if he is on one of those ships?" Samantha asked.

"I would expect so. He would want to be able to control the battle," Blake said. "But I think we should give them a few hours to waste their reaction mass. Then we'll see if they would like to talk."

"Admiral Martaka, would you like to reopen negotiations?" Blake said over the communication channel to the Fazullans.

"You — arrogant fool. My people will realize that I was unsuccessful and adapt. We will defeat you."

"More inefficiency in their language?" Catie asked ADI.

"Yes."

"Hmm, maybe we should have Captain Lantaq talk to him," Samantha suggested.

"Okay. Security, bring him up here," Blake ordered.

It only took a few minutes to bring Captain Lantaq to the bridge. Blake ordered the channel to the Fazullans opened again.

"Admiral Martaka, we have someone we think you might wish to chat with. He can give you a better appraisal of the situation," Blake said.

Admiral Martaka came back online. He took one look at Captain Lantaq and spit on the deck. "I should have known you would be involved. I should have had you cashiered out of the military years ago. Admiral Blake, I have no interest in whatever this man has to say!"

With that, he cut the channel.

"He doesn't like you very much," Blake said.

"He never liked the way I treated my women," Captain Lantaq said.

"Your women?"

"You might say, wives." Captain Lantaq smiled. "Perhaps if you would give me an open channel on a different frequency, I will be able to help," he said.

Blake turned away from Captain Lantaq. "Any reason not to give it to him?"

"We can cut it off if he says something we don't want him to," Marc said.

"Very well, communications, put a two-second delay in the channel," Blake said before he turned back to Captain Lantaq. "Which channel do you want?"

"This one," Captain Lantaq said, reciting the frequency he wanted. "And it would be best if the message went to the entire Fazullan fleet."

"Make it so," Blake said, nodding at the communication officer.

"Channel is open."

"Omega has risen," Captain Lantaq said. He smiled and turned away from the display.

"What does that mean?"

"Just my last words," Captain Lantaq said.

"Would you care to explain?"

"I think not. But I would be happy to provide you a short history of Fazulla while we wait for an answer. That is, if you would like it?"

"I'd be interested in hearing that," Samantha said.

"Very well, we'll convene in five minutes," Blake said as he led Captain Lantaq to his cabin.

◆ ◆ ◆

"You have our attention," Blake said once everyone was on the comm channel.

"Thank you," Captain Lantaq said. "As you know we are from another planet. The colony ship that founded Proxima Fazulla reached it over two hundred years ago. As the years passed we dropped the Proxima label and just called our new home system Fazulla.

"We have been told that some problem occurred with the colony ship which forced it to select Proxima Fazulla for our new home. No one knows if that is true, or if our ancestors just didn't want to admit that they had chosen such an unsuitable star system. They were too far from any other system to attempt to relocate, so they settled there.

"It was a harsh planet, but we made it our home. The population started out at fifty thousand, and after fifty years, it had only climbed to one hundred fifty thousand. At that time, Fazullans tended to only have two children at the most, and after fifty years the population was plateauing, which is not necessarily a good thing for a new colony.

"Then we discovered the wormhole. Over the next four years, we learned two critical things. One: the wormhole did not lead to an acceptable alternative to Proxima Fazulla, and two: we were not alone. One of the expeditions through the wormhole detected radio traffic that indicated there was another race out among the stars.

"This created a great upheaval in our society. There was a lot of debate among our leaders about what to do with this information, as well as unrest in the general population. Eventually, it led to a military coup. The most militaristic members of our society took over. They appointed the first emperor. One of the first things he did was pass a law that said every Fazullan woman must bear five children."

"That is absurd," Catie said.

"I agree," Captain Lantaq said. "There were protests, riots; eventually, the military quelled them. And because of the riots, the emperor stripped Fazullan women of most of their rights. They became little more than household slaves. They were given the responsibility of maintaining the household and educating the children. That at least allowed them to be educated.

"Then as with all things considered valuable, the rich and powerful decided they deserved more than the rest of the people. The laws were changed allowing a man to have more than one wife. I have five, the emperor has one hundred. I believe Admiral Martaka has twenty. Any more, and it would draw the attention of the emperor.

"Then we detected the Paraxean colony fleet coming toward one of the wormhole's exit points. The military immediately made plans to seize it. Analysis showed that it would be difficult to grab control over all the ships, so they focused on what they determined was the cargo ship. As you know we seized it.

"Then we had to decide what to do with the Paraxeans. It was decided that they would be slaves, used to do the tasks that Fazullans didn't care for. A breeding program was instituted to increase their number. We captured two thousand and we now have over one hundred seventy thousand."

"This is sick," Catie said.

"I agree," Samantha said. "Did no one in your population object to this treatment of a sentient race, much less of your own women?"

"Of course people objected, but it didn't take long to learn to keep those objections to themselves. The emperor dealt harshly with any critics."

"So what do those people do?"

"They pray for an end to the empire."

18 Omega Has Risen

"Omega has risen!" Chazqita said to herself. *"I thought I'd never live to see the day."*

Chazqita was Admiral Martaka's favorite wife at this time, so she was with him on his ship. Usually, Fazullan women were not allowed on the ships, but since this was a mission to move the colony and it would last for years, they had made exceptions. The men hated to do the necessary cleaning on the ships, and they trusted their women more than they did the slaves. Two of his other wives were in stasis on the ship in case he got bored with her. Chazqita went to the hold where the stasis chambers were. She was wearing a cleaning outfit, so the men automatically assumed she was just there to clean. As cleaners, the women had access to most of the ship.

Chazqita nodded to the woman who was in the bay where the stasis chambers were located. The man who was there monitoring the stasis chambers ignored Chazqita, she was beneath his notice, even though she was the admiral's wife.

Chazqita motioned for the other woman to distract the man. The woman nodded back to her, then moved in front of the man and bent over to clean an area of the floor. Of course, the man was immediately distracted as he looked at the woman's bottom showing through her thin skirt. He was thinking about what he would do with her if she was his wife when Chazqita cut his throat.

"Omega has risen," Chazqita told the other woman.

"Oh my, we must hurry," the woman said. She immediately went to the controls of the stasis chambers. With Chazqita's help, she started the process to bring all the women out of stasis. They also selected twenty men to bring out of stasis.

"Go, I'll take care of them."

Chazqita took the sidearm from the dead attendant and hid it under the folds of her skirt. She exited the bay and headed to the crew quarters. When she arrived, she was met by four men.

"We got the signal," one of the men said.

"Yes. We must take over engineering. Go there and tell them you have been ordered to relieve them so they can rest up for the next phase of the battle."

"Your will!"

The four men left hurriedly, racing toward engineering as fast as they could. Chazqita continued into the crew section, pausing at the door to her cabin. Looking around quickly, she entered the cabin.

"We are ready," said one of the six women who had gathered in the cabin.

"Good," Chazqita said. She moved to the far section of the cabin and removed a panel. Behind it were several weapons the admiral kept secreted in their quarters in case of a mutiny, and she quickly distributed them to the women. "You know the priorities. Only kill if you must. I'll go to the bridge now and take care of our admiral."

"Your will."

Chazqita left the women to take care of the off-duty crew and hurried to the bridge. She paused to catch her breath and relax before entering.

"I have been ordered to clean the bridge," she said as she entered.

"Then do it, we don't need to hear from you," Admiral Martaka said.

Chazqita made a show of cleaning the area around the pilot station. Then she moved to the communication station and dusted around the officer there. She nodded to him and whispered, *"Omega has risen."* Then she made her way behind the admiral's chair. She bumped the chair as she bent over to wipe the back of it down.

"Must you be so clumsy?!" the admiral snapped.

"I'm sorry."

"Just be careful," the admiral said as he turned back to the main viewer.

Chazqita slipped the stiletto she had gotten from the arms cache into her hand. She whispered something to the admiral. He laughed, then she pushed the stiletto into his skull. She pulled out the hand weapon and fired at the First Officer who was standing next to the sensor operator.

The navigator pulled his weapon and shot the security guard who was standing at the bridge entry. "Nobody else needs to die!" he said loudly.

The weapons officer reached for his weapon. Chazqita shot him before he got it out of its holster. The rest of the crew on the bridge put their hands up.

The navigator moved to the communication console. "Engineering, status report!"

"Omega has risen," came the reply.

"Madam, we have the ship," the navigator reported.

"Very good. Put everyone we don't trust into stasis," Chazqita ordered.

"Your will!"

"Admiral, we're getting a message from the Fazullans. It's from the other side of the wormhole."

"Put it on," Blake ordered. He quickly Commed the rest of the strategy team.

When the feed came up a female Fazullan was sitting in what appeared to be the captain's chair of one of their starships.

"Admiral McCormack, I believe," she said. "I'm Empress Cyrianisa. I would appreciate your help in getting the status of my fleet that is on your side of the wormhole. Captain Lantaq will explain."

"Give me a minute," Blake said. The security guard was already on his way to retrieve Lantaq. "I'll continue this in my office."

The empress just sat there smiling while they waited for Captain Lantaq. When he entered, upon seeing the empress he immediately saluted. "Empress, your will!"

"I need to know how we have fared on your side of the wormhole," the empress said.

Captain Lantaq turned to Blake. "We have been planning a takeover of the empire for years. This situation provided the perfect opportunity."

Blake opened the Comm channel to the rest of his team. "Thoughts?"

"I say we let him call in," Samantha said.

"Very well. What do you need?" Blake asked.

"Open the same channel," Lantaq said.

"It's open."

"Omega has risen," Lantaq said.

"Captain Lantaq, it is good to see you," Chazqita said as she came on the channel.

"I have the empress on another communication channel. She is asking for an update."

"I am Chazqita, the late admiral's wife. Is it possible to combine the channels?"

"Of course," Blake said. "Sakira, please combine the channels."

"Done."

"Chazqita, it is good to see you. Can you tell me the status of your squadron?" the empress asked.

"We have control over fifteen ships. We are still fighting for control over the other five."

"Admiral Blake is it possible for you to provide assistance before more of our people are killed?" the empress asked. "We could also use some help on this side of the wormhole as well; we have seven ships that we are still fighting for control over. They're immobilized, but that could change quickly."

"Captain Clements, can you take the Enterprise and Victory to assist the empress? I'll use the Sakira and Roebuck to take care of the problems here."

"Yes sir," Captain Clements said. "We are one hour from the wormhole. We should have enough momentum to reach the Fazullan fleet in three hours."

"Can your people hold out that long?" Blake asked.

"We will have to. I'll send you the identifiers of the ships we need help with. Chazqita will send the same for her problem ships."

"Captain McCormack, you need to pick up Marines from the Galileo," Blake said. They had to use the Roebuck and the Sakira to deal with the Fazullan ships since it would take a microjump to get close to them.

"We are under max deceleration now. We should match velocity with her in two hours," Catie reported.

"Very well. We will be ready to jump in two hours as well. We'll take the three ships in the second wave. You take the other two."

"Yes sir."

"Do not allow the Roebuck to get close enough that they can capture you."

"Yes sir. We will send our Marines over in the Lynxes with Foxes as cover."

"I still say we should put Takurō in another Lynx and send it to the other side of the ship!"

"Very funny," Takurō said. "Now mount up!"

"Yes, Sergeant."

The platoon boarded the Lynx wearing full space armor. Takurō nodded to Ensign Racine as she boarded the second Lynx. Her team would provide backup until Takurō's team entered the Fazullan ship, then they would go and take the second ship.

"We're ready," Takurō reported.

"On our way," the pilot replied.

The Lynx left the Roebuck's flight bay, followed by two Foxes. Ensign Racine's Lynx then followed with two Foxes on her tail.

"The blue team reports that they have control of the airlock," Kasper told them. They'd designated the empress's Fazullans as the blue team, and they were all wearing blue armbands.

"We'll be ready to board in one minute," Takurō reported.

"You're clear to engage," Ensign Racine said. "Good luck."

"Thank you, ma'am. Check your suits," Takurō ordered his team. "Make sure you're airtight, we're decompressing this bay in thirty seconds!"

The airlock of the Fazullan starship was opened and a blue flag was attached to the door. A Fazullan with a blue armband was standing in the doorway.

"We're off," Takurō announced as he and four other Marines launched toward the airlock. Once they reached it, they quickly cycled into the ship to allow the second group of five Marines to launch.

"Status?" Takurō asked the Fazullan on the other side of the airlock.

"We have the bridge and crew section, we were unable to take engineering," she reported.

"Good, that's what we were told. We're here to remedy that. Please lead the way."

The bad guys were holed up in engineering and environmental. They had about one-third of the ship and, unfortunately, they controlled the power and the air. They hadn't opted to escalate the situation since the blue team had control of the weapons, so it was a standoff. Neither side could afford to force the issue without risking their own destruction.

The second team of Marines went directly to the main entrance to engineering, while Takurō's team went to the back door.

"Our schematics show that there is an access tube here," Takurō said.

"There is, but it doesn't go to engineering."

"We know, but it passes right by this air duct between environmental and engineering. Our plan is to cut through the air duct and access engineering that way."

"Won't they notice the loss of airflow?"

"We're going to create an airlock. That way we can get in with minimum disruption."

"What do you need from us?"

"We brought all the toys we need. It might help if you could create a distraction, maybe start negotiations again."

"We will do that," the woman said as she Commed the bridge.

"Jackson, you're on," Takurō said.

"Okay, Diaz, you're with me. You bring that blow-up chamber and I'll carry the tools."

They crawled into the access tube and worked their way up and over to the air duct. Jackson quickly cut a hole in the access tube, allowing them out into the open space between the decks. There were lots of vertical bulkheads put in place to prevent just what he was planning to do, go from one compartment to the next.

Jackson assembled the bubble against the air duct sealing it into place, then he inflated it and used ties to attach it to the various struts and bulkheads so it would stay in place. He entered the bubble, sealing it behind him. Pulling out a sharp knife, he prepared to jam it into the air duct.

"I could use a little noise right now."

Takurō nodded to the two Fazullans who were waiting for his signal. They started a fight, shouting at each other. Then one threw the other into the bulkhead. It was a pretty good feat to accomplish in microgravity, but the two seemed to have done it before. Jackson counted to three, then hit the knife with his hammer just as the second Fazullan was thrown into the opposite bulkhead, the one adjoining engineering.

With the incision made, Jackson took out his shears and cut a large opening into the air duct. Then he put tape on the edges to avoid anyone snagging it.

"Your portal is ready."

Takurō's team climbed through the access tube and made their way to the bubble. One at a time they entered the bubble, sealed it behind themselves, then climbed into the air duct, sealing it behind themselves as well. Thirty minutes later, all five members of the team were in the air duct. The Fazullans had wanted to join them, but Takurō had told them that his crew had trained as a team, and adding someone else into the mix would upset the chemistry.

The team edged their way to the various outflow registers and prepared to make their entry into the engineering compartment. They released six hornet-sized drones into the room. They allowed the Roebuck to control the drones, placing them in the optimal position to give the team a full view of the enemy positions inside the engineering section.

Four Fazullans were lying on the deck, apparently dead. A fifth was tied up and wedged between two pieces of equipment. The remaining four Fazullans were spread around the engineering space, all of them were armed. And unfortunately, they were wearing battle armor, so it wouldn't be easy to take them out.

"Positions, everyone," Takurō ordered.

"We're in position."

"Arm the charges." Each air register had a set of charges placed on it that would blow the register into the engineering compartment allowing the Marines to dive into the room.

"On three. One . . . two . . . three!"

On two, the fight in the corridor escalated with two other Fazullans joining in. On three the registers blew and the Marines pushed off soaring into the room right at their assigned Fazullan. Each had a blade in their hands; it was easier to drive a blade into the joints of the Fazullan armor than to shoot and try to get something through it.

Takurō hit his man dead center; he grabbed his helmet and used his knife to slide under the edge and hit the carotid artery. He pushed the Fazullan away from him and turned to see if anyone needed assistance.

CRACK!

One of the Fazullans fired a shot as he was falling to the ground. The frangible projectile hit one of the modules of the gravity drive, shattering into pieces and ricocheting into Takurō's right hip. Two small pieces managed to catch the seam and tore into his thigh.

"Damn it!"

"Hey, what did I say? It never fails, same leg too."

"Lance Corporal, if you want to keep those stripes, then I suggest you save your comments for when you and your mates are having a drink. Because right now I have no sense of humor!" Takurō shouted.

"Yes, Sergeant," the lance corporal said. She turned to one of her mates, "Just saying."

"I can still hear you!"

Takurō stood up and drifted over to the main hatch.

"Engineering secured," he announced as he opened the hatch, thankful that he was in microgravity and didn't need to support his weight on his injured leg.

The team waiting outside the hatch entered engineering and looked around. "Do you want us to take environmental?" the team leader asked.

"I'd appreciate it," Takurō said. "I'm not sure I can stand getting shot in my leg again."

"You're not serious?"

"As a rip in your spacesuit."

◆ ◆ ◆

"We've secured the ship," Takurō reported.

"We've secured ours as well," Ensign Racine reported. "Should we return to the Roebuck?"

"Yes," Catie said. "We'll leave the Fazullans to clean up." She switched to a private channel. "Uncle Blake, how are you guys doing?"

"We're done here," Blake said. "We're waiting on Clements' team to finish up. They've got one more ship to take care of. I'll call a meeting in thirty minutes."

"Okay."

"Hey, Sweetie," Marc said as he broke into the channel. "So things went well?"

"Ensign Racine is a real badass. Only casualty on our side was Takurō getting shot in the leg again. Just a flesh wound this time. The Marines killed all of their bad guys. Racine says dead men don't shoot you in the ass."

"I guess I'd have to agree with her. See you at the meeting," Marc said before he signed off.

"Empress, Madam Chazqita, are you ready to discuss the situation?" Blake asked.

"We are. I see you have Ambassador Newman there. Will he be leading the negotiations?" the empress asked.

Samantha's avatar smiled, then dissolved, leaving Samantha's image on the screen. "Yes Empress, I will be leading the negotiations."

"Ah, I see you really have a balanced society," the empress said.

"Not balanced, but we're getting there," Samantha said. "Delphi Nation works hard to support people as individuals, ignoring things like sex, race, or other preference. But we all bring our biases to the table."

"We understand. Let's begin. I recall that you offered to help us find another suitable solar system. Can we start there?" the empress asked.

"We did make that offer, and it still stands," Samantha stated. "However, we do have conditions."

"We expected that, what are they?"

"You must release all of your slaves, any non-Fazullan has to be turned over to us."

"We would be more than happy to do that. We want them to be taken care of, and it would be taxing on us to do so. They are a shameful reminder of the barbaric nature of our former rulers. Unfortunately, we're talking about over two hundred thousand people."

"Oh, my. I assume most of them are Paraxeans."

"Correct. There are 173,324 Paraxeans, 28,722 Aperanjens, and 20 Onisiwoens. Quite a few are children."

"We had expected their numbers to be biased toward children, but the total numbers are higher than we had originally anticipated, but we will still be able to deal with them."

The empress looked visibly relieved at Samantha's pronouncement that they would be able to handle all of the slaves.

"Your other terms?"

"We will deal with the slaves first. As we remove them from your ships, we will move your ships into another isolated system. We will eventually need to take a few of your ships to hold the slaves. We will take your advice on which ships we should use. They will be returned to you. You will wait in the other system until we find a planet for you."

"I understand. How long do you expect this search for a planet to take?" the empress asked with obvious skepticism. She was clearly feeling uncomfortable with this turn in the negotiations.

"We are already searching for habitable planets. We have been ignoring those that have gravity over 1.3 times our standard gravity. You seem to like gravity at 1.5 times standard. Those worlds have been logged, so we can send an expedition back to them to determine if they are suitable. We would be happy to have a few of your people accompany us. But you must understand the Aperanjens will get first choice."

"A time frame?"

"One to two years," Catie said. "That includes actually visiting the world to verify its suitability."

"That sounds acceptable. Other terms?"

"Given that you have been oppressed and were not directly responsible for the problem, we believe that covers the main issues. We will need to spend time working through the details, but that will mostly be around logistics," Samantha said.

The empress visibly blew a sigh of relief. "I don't see any problem with your terms. How do you wish to proceed?"

"We will start with the Onisiwoens since that will be easiest. Can you identify which ships they are on?"

"That will be easy. They are all on the same ship; I've sent its designation to you. The other aliens are mostly segregated on different ships, but we do have two ships with partial populations of each."

"We'll try to handle the Paraxeans next. I need to spend time with their governments to decide how to best handle that large a population, but getting the ships identified will be a good start. Do you have any specific requests?" Samantha asked.

"We only ask that you allow us to rotate through stasis based on our own schedule," the empress said.

"I don't see a problem with that."

"Okay, 173,324 Paraxeans, and most of them children. How are we going to deal with all of them?" Samantha asked.

"I'm not sure that Mangkatar can take all of them. Especially when there is such a high ratio of children," Marc said.

"We should ask the other Paraxean colonies and Paraxea," Catie suggested.

"Why Paraxea? We know the colonists didn't want to go back to Paraxea. They felt that they'd be too out of touch," Samantha said.

"But Paraxea should feel a responsibility for them. They might be willing to help relocate them and provide resources so it would be easier for the colonies to absorb them."

"We'll need to ask. And we have to put a priority on finding a planet for the Aperanjens," Samantha said.

"I've already directed two probes to go back to the best candidates," Catie said. "There are five other likely candidates, and they will check all of them out once they've done the survey of the best two."

"Only two probes?" Blake asked.

"Weird statistics, but the best candidates were all in either sector five or sector eight," Catie said. "I've changed the search parameters on the other probes, so they might find a good candidate going forward."

"We can only work with what we have," Marc said. "Sam, do you want any help talking to the Paraxeans?"

"Not yet. I'll yell if I do."

19   The End Game

"Captain McCormack, please rendezvous with this ship and pick up the Onisiwoens. I think it's time they all went home," Blake ordered.

"Yes sir. Navigator, please put us next to the ship."

"Yes ma'am."

Everyone was relieved that the fighting had ended without too much actual fighting. Getting back to the primary mission of taking the Onisiwoens home was just what the doctor ordered, and to be able to bring the other members of the crew as well was just icing on the cake.

"Jump is programmed," the navigator reported.

"Engage."

"I need five minutes to maneuver into position. Are you going to send a Lynx to pick them up?" the pilot asked.

"I think that would be prudent," Catie said. "Kasper, can you have Charlie and Dr. Juxtor added to the crew of the Lynxes? One on each, I'm sure the people we're picking up would appreciate a familiar face."

"Yes ma'am," Kasper said. "Lynxes will be ready to launch as soon as we're in position."

"Captain Margakava, it's so good to see you," the Onisiwoen woman said as Charlie met her at the airlock. She was almost as tall as Charlie and had hair that was even bluer than his. She was also very pregnant and was carrying a small child and had another child in tow.

"Magaxia, I thought we'd never meet again," Charlie said. "I'm so sorry for what has happened to you."

"We weren't abused, apparently we're too fragile for them," Magaxia said. "And I do finally have a family; I've always wanted children."

"I see," Charlie said as he knelt down so he was even with the three-year-old. "Welcome to Onisiwo," he said. "Do you want to go home and see your grandparents?"

The child just nodded, obviously confused and uncomfortable in the microgravity. Charlie picked up the two-year-old and moved into the

Lynx. "Let's get you aboard. We'll be able to take twelve on this ship, the others will be put on the next ship. Then we'll be headed home. Captain McCormack assures us that once we head out, she'll keep us in gravity until we land."

"Oh, that will be nice. Some of the children are not handling the microgravity well."

"Don't worry. The accommodations on the Roebuck are exceptional. We'll have everyone settled in a couple of hours and be on our way."

Catie met the first Lynx in the flight bay. As soon as it was pressurized, she had rushed out to meet the released prisoners.

"Magaxia, this is Captain Catherine McCormack," Charlie said, introducing the first woman to Catie. Two other women quickly appeared at the Lynx's hatch cautiously making their way down the stairs, each was pregnant and carrying a young child. Marines followed them carrying their other children.

"I'm happy to meet all of you. We were so happy to learn that you all had survived," Catie said. "Please follow me and we'll get you settled into your accommodations."

Charlie grabbed Magaxia's oldest child, a girl. He whispered in her ear, "She's a princess."

The child's eyes went wide in wonder. "Really?"

"Yes, just wait, you'll see," Charlie whispered.

Catie led them to the cabins that were right next to the flight bay. They had rearranged things so the twelve cabins closest to the flight bay were available for their new guests. Everyone wanted to ease their transition.

"Magaxia, thank you for agreeing to this interview," Catie said as Magaxia joined her in her office.

"Call me Maggie, Charlie suggested it would be easier on both our ears," Maggie said.

"And call me Catie," Catie said. "Has everyone settled in?"

"Yes, we're doing well. Thank you and your crew for taking such good care of us."

"You're welcome. I would like to explain a few things, and answer any questions you may have before we begin the interview, or debrief might be a better word for it. First, how are you handling the translations, is your earwig comfortable?"

"Yes, it seems fine."

"Some people like to use two when they're engaged in long conversations, it helps to limit the volume of the foreign language, so they only hear the translator."

"No, I like hearing your voice," Maggie said.

"Okay. As you know, I'm Catherine McCormack, the captain of the Roebuck, the ship we are on. We were bringing Charlie and the part of the crew we rescued with him here to Onisiwo when we realized that the Fazullans were about to invade, which is how I came to be captain of the Roebuck instead of a more experienced military captain," Catie said.

"I see, you do seem to be quite young."

"I am. Our world is still fractured into many nations. Delphi, my nation, controls our space fleet. Actually, it's controlled by a corporation that is controlled by a very small group of people. My father uses that core group for certain missions, our way of keeping some of our technology and plans secret."

"I see."

"Let me introduce you to our DI, ADI. She is a sentient digital intelligence, much more than an AI that you are probably used to."

"Hello, Maggie," ADI said. "I'm pleased to meet you."

"She's sentient?"

"Yes. She is our only sentient DI now," Catie said. "The Paraxeans have a few, but they're rare. We also have several AIs, and the ship's AI is called Roebuck, or ship. Say hello, Roebuck."

"Hello, Maggie. I am pleased to make your acquaintance."

"Both of them have female voices."

"Yes. The history of the culture I grew up in, tends to give ships a female gender. We've adopted it. We might change to using both genders; it seems funny to call the Galileo 'she' since the person she was named after was male. Now, ADI has been keyed to your Comm, so any time you want to talk to her she will answer. The same for Roebuck. The rest of your crew will have access to Roebuck. And all of your Comms are very powerful computers. Your Comm is handling the translation."

"Oh, interesting."

"As I said, they're powerful. But we're still learning the subtleties of your language, so if something sounds odd, or even improper, I hope you will first assume it is a bad translation."

"Of course."

"We're still eighteen days away from your homeworld, so be sure to ask us for anything you need to be comfortable."

"Eighteen days? How is that possible?" Maggie asked.

"We're under constant acceleration," Catie said.

"Oh, so that's why there's gravity."

"Correct. We are actually accelerating at 1.4 times standard gravity, but it cycles to make it easier on your heart."

"I see. So that would mean your standard gravity is similar to ours."

"Yes, Onisiwo is .95 standard gravity," Catie explained. "Another thing, I would like to express my sympathy for the horrible experience you had to endure. Right now, our doctors do not have enough experience with your physiology to help much, but Dr. Moreau is going to stay on Onisiwo and work with your doctors to adapt the Paraxean and Terran medical technology to your species. Eventually, they should be able to help."

"How would they help?"

"They have the ability to dull memories. I've had it done to deal with a bad experience I had four years ago. My best friend, Liz, had it done to deal with an experience she had before then. Liz is the strongest, most confident woman I've ever met. She's like a sister to me. But even she had nightmares. I'm telling you so you can talk to your crew, let them know there's hope for anyone who is suffering. Liz told me that you and your crew are probably the toughest of the Onisiwoen women, having been selected to be astronauts, but like I said, Liz is the toughest woman I know."

"Did you make this offer to the men?"

"We have, but they spent most of their time in stasis, so I don't think they were as traumatized as the women. Their nightmare ended right after you were captured, while yours just began."

"Thank you, I'll let everyone know about the option. Some of the women are struggling with being forced to become mothers and being treated like slaves. I'm sure knowing that those memories can be dulled away will help. But some may not wish to have it done. They wouldn't want to lose the memory of their children's first years."

"The procedure is far more selective than that. I remember everything that happened around my incident with clarity. Only the feeling of being trapped has been dulled."

Maggie nodded her head. "That sounds better. I'll make sure everyone understands."

"Now, if you don't have any more questions, I'd like to start the debrief," Catie said.

"I'm sure I'll have questions, but I'm okay with starting."

"For the debrief, we'll be joined by that core group I mentioned. They will only be listening in. They might send me questions that they want asked, but you shouldn't notice them."

"No, I would prefer to see them if you don't mind," Maggie said.

"Okay, let me register your Comm to the conference. . . . There you go. Now, this is my father, Marc McCormack. He is the CEO of MacKenzie Discoveries and the Monarch of Delphi, which just means he's the big boss. Next to him is my uncle, Admiral Blake McCormack, he's the head of our space fleet. They're not actually in the same location. On the other side of my father is his wife, Samantha Newman, she's our interstellar ambassador. Beside Admiral Blake, is Commander Elizabeth Farmer, she's a close friend as well as an experienced wing commander. And beside her is General Kalani

Kealoha, he's the head of our Marines. They represent the inner circle of MacKenzie Discoveries and Delphi's Security Council."

"I'm honored to meet you."

"We're all honored to meet you as well," Marc said. "We'll try to let Catie run the debrief, but feel free to direct questions to any of us."

"Are you all related?" Maggie asked.

"No, just the three McCormacks," Samantha said. "I married Marc last year. But we all behave like one big family."

"Thank you, that helps put things into context."

"Now, could you tell us what you can remember of what happened?" Catie asked.

"I'll try. You already know about the capture of our ship. Once we were captured, the ship was towed back to their base. I now realize that means to the fringe of our system and through the wormhole. It took about four weeks. During that time there was a physical exam, and a lot of follow-up exams. We didn't speak each other's language so there wasn't any sharing of information.

"At their base, the women were offloaded from their ship, and then I believe that ship departed, I guess to go to Artemis. We women were placed into a section where we had beds for sleeping and food. It didn't take us long to realize we were all pregnant."

"What base?" Blake messaged Catie.

"You keep mentioning a base, can you explain what it was?" Catie asked.

"It was a space station," Maggie said. "It must be right next to the wormhole. I didn't feel any high acceleration, just about 1.5 Gs, so it couldn't have been far if we got there from our second gas giant in just four weeks."

"A space station, not a ship?"

"Yes, I'm very confident it was a space station," Maggie said.

"I'm not doubting you," Catie said. "I'm just wondering what happened to it. There isn't a space station there now. ADI?"

"Cer Catie."

"On the common channel," Catie ordered.

"Cer Catie. One of the ships the Fazullans are flying looks like it could have been the hub of a space station. Eight other ships have sections that might have been part of the ring," ADI said.

"That makes sense. They were putting everything they could into space to move their population. Using the space station that way would increase their carrying capacity."

"Yes, I estimate an additional fifty thousand Fazullans could have been accommodated by the sections from the space station."

"Sorry, Maggie. Please go on."

"We were on the space station for four years. I've had two children in that time as did most of the women. Based on their features, we believe they all had different fathers."

"Maximizing the diversity of the population," Catie whispered.

"Yes, that was our thought as well. We were forced to clean the space station. There were only a few Fazullan women on the station, so since the men refuse to do anything menial if there is a woman to do it instead, we were kept busy.

"After the first year, there was a flurry of activity. The Fazullans seemed to be very distraught. Then things settled down, but there was a sense that something major had changed. Our lives were mostly the same. Then after four years we were all herded into another ship and put into stasis."

"I suspect the first event was when they decided they were going to take Onisiwo for themselves. The timing of when you were put into stasis would probably have been when the first of their fleet reached the wormhole and they started to wait for it to cycle to Onisiwo so they could invade," Catie explained.

"How were you treated?" Samantha asked.

"There was some physical abuse, but not much. I think the Fazullan women did things to protect us, but I'm not sure."

"That is consistent with what we've been told," Samantha said.

"Was there anything else of significance that you can remember?" Catie asked.

"Not really, except there did seem to be three classes of Fazullan men on the station. The first was treated just a little better than the women. They seemed to be like a lower caste, or common people. The other two classes were treated like aristocracy. But within it there seemed to be two classes; the head of the station and others like him were the most cruel. They seemed to actually enjoy tormenting their women and the first class I mentioned. The second class seemed to be less cruel, almost like they were pretending to be cruel. The cruel ones seemed to think the second group wasn't cruel enough, as if that were a requirement to reach the elite class."

"I suspect that those were the men who were planning the revolution with the women. Apparently, the history of their culture wasn't based on cruelty," Samantha explained. "We're still learning as we go."

"Now, Maggie," Marc interjected. "We have a final question for you today."

"What is it?"

"What do you want to have happen to you and your crew? We're returning you to Onisiwo because we think that's what you would want. But you may prefer something else."

"What else can we do?" Maggie asked.

"You could delay your return to Onisiwo. You could stay on the Roebuck, or go to Artemis or even Earth," Marc said. "We don't understand your culture well enough to know the impact your return will have on you and your children."

"I'll talk to my crew," Maggie said. "This is a lot to absorb."

"Don't hesitate to ask me questions," Catie said. "Or ADI. We'll do everything we can to help."

"Liz, Kal, thank you for sitting in. If you have any thoughts or questions, please let everyone know," Marc said once Maggie had left Catie's office.

"*Okay*, I guess we'll talk later," Liz said, wondering why they were being kicked out of the conference.

"*Daddy*, what's up?" Catie asked, clearly wondering why Kal and Liz had been dismissed.

"We need to talk," Marc said.

"Well, should I be worried?"

"No!" Samantha said. "But there are some big decisions that we have to make."

"Okay, what?"

"It is going to take months to get the Fazullans and the Paraxeans separated, not to mention the Aperanjens."

"I realize that," Catie said wearily.

"I would like you to stay at Onisiwo and run the resettlement efforts," Marc said.

"That's going to be a long time."

"I know, but I think it needs to be one of us. I could come there and do it, but I'd rather not uproot Allie, and I think Artemis still needs me here," Marc said.

"And Uncle Blake has to run Delphi," Catie said.

"Right, so that leaves you."

"I guess I can do it. Are you sure Captain Clements or Captain Vislosky couldn't do it?"

"I think it has to be a McCormack."

"But we need to keep at least one or two carriers here until we've resettled the Fazullans."

"You're correct, that brings up the second issue."

"What would that be?" Catie asked, struggling to see where this was going.

"In order for you to be in charge of the mission, you have to be Princess Catherine, not Captain McCormack," Marc said.

"I still don't understand."

"You can't be captain of the Roebuck."

"Now I really don't understand!"

"Catie," Blake said. "The captain of the Roebuck cannot give orders to Captain Clements, but Princess Catherine can."

"Plus, it would make things easier with the Onisiwoens," Samantha added. "It would mean we had a state presence there to negotiate the transition and help them adjust to being part of the league."

"Just think," Blake said, "it would kind of make you my boss."

Catie laughed at that.

Afterword

Thanks for reading **Delphi League!**

I hope you've enjoyed the tenth book in the Delphi in Space series. The story continues in Delphi Embassy. If you would like to join my newsletter group go to ⬚https://tinyurl.com/tiny-delphi. The newsletter provides interesting Science facts for SciFi fans, book recommendation based on books I truly loved reading, deals on books I think you'll like, and notification of when the next book in my series is available.

As a self-published author, the one thing you can do that will help the most is to leave a review on Goodreads and Amazon.

Acknowledgments

It is impossible to say how much I am indebted to my beta readers and copy editors. Without them, you would not be able to read my books due to all the grammar and spelling errors. I have always subscribed to Andrew Jackson's opinion that "It is a damn poor mind that can think of only one way to spell a word."

So special thanks to:

My copy editor, Ann Clark, who also happens to be my wife.

My beta reader and editor, Theresa Holmes.

My beta reader and cheerleader, Roger Blanton, who happens to be my brother.

Also important to a book author is the cover art for their book. I'm am especially thankful to Momir Borocki for the exceptional covers he has produced for my books. It is amazing what he can do with the strange PowerPoint drawings I give him; and how he makes sense of my suggestions, I'll never know.

If you need a cover, he can be reached at momir.borocki@gmail.com.

Also by Bob Blanton

Delphi in Space

Starship Sakira

Delphi City

Delphi Station

Delphi Nation

Delphi Alliance

Delphi Federation

Delphi Exploration

Delphi Colony

Delphi Challenge

Delphi League

Stone Series

Matthew and the Stone

Stone Ranger

Stone Undercover

Stone Investigations

Made in the USA
Las Vegas, NV
13 November 2022

59333092R00144